ALMOST SURE

A SWEET SMALL TOWN BILLIONAIRE ROMANCE

CLAIRE CAIN

Cover design by Emma Robinson

E-Book: 978-1-954005-27-3

Print: 978-1-954005-28-0

CHAPTER ONE

Quinn

I stared at the phone clutched in my hand. It nearly cut into my palm from my tight grip as ice-cold fury pumped through me and pooled at my feet like lead. I'd never hated someone, like, *really* hated them, and yet lately, the bodies were piling up.

He'd continued speaking and I'd stopped listening, so I shoved the phone back to my ear and grit my teeth so hard, I knew I'd hear about it from my dentist. Danielle was super nice, but she wouldn't stop badgering about my teeth grinding habit.

"...you'll see I've changed. But you're too stubborn and selfish. You refuse to give on anything. You're determined to think the worst of me because you can't stand the idea of me being the good guy, that I've grown as a person."

Rage crawled up my throat, and I wanted nothing more than the satisfaction of destroying this man with my words.

How had I ever found him attractive and charming? *How* had I fallen so freaking fast and gotten myself tangled up with him?

Actually, I knew exactly how. He was gorgeous, I was twenty-one, and he spent all night telling me how much he loved my voice. We slept together, and he offered me an insane amount of money to essentially be his mistress, but he didn't want a relationship. I turned him down, then realized I'd gotten knocked up and let him know. At which point, he offered me that same amount of cash to get rid of the baby, which I refused, so he bailed completely. All of that would've been a regretful memory, but it turned out to be the greatest mistake-that-worked of my life because it gave me the best person on earth, my daughter, Cara.

"I'll say this again, Chuck. I can't have you blazing in here trying to become a dad because you finally decided to feel guilty. It doesn't work like that."

How was that *not* clear?

"I get that I've been an idiot—far worse than an idiot. But I want to try now. Shouldn't you let her decide? She's old enough."

Oh, this man was just asking for trouble, wasn't he?

"Hmm, and let's remember why she's old enough to make this choice. Oh, that's right, because you essentially didn't exist for the last fourteen years. Which means you don't have rights. You even signed those away. If that happened in a cocaine-induced stupor, I can't help you."

A string of expletives trailed through the speaker, so I held the phone away and let my eyes wander from the conversation.

My shift here at work started soon, and I did not have time for this. "Listen, as creative as your swearing is, I've got to go. You can have your lawyers contact mine, but please don't call again."

And thank goodness my lawyer was actually my friend John Wallace, who wouldn't charge me for taking my call.

Chuck hung up—after another lovely line or two about where I could go and what I could kiss, et cetera. I slammed my phone facedown on the counter and slumped over it, an elbow on either side of its unbreakable black case, and held my head in my hands. I had approximately seven minutes to get my crap together and gear up for a Friday night at the lounge, which meant I needed to lock all this rage and disappointment and horrifyingly, heartbreak, down.

Not heartbreak for *me*, or my heart, but for my daughter's. Her biological father was an utter idiot, and I hated it. That said, she was wonderful. As much as I disliked him, I wouldn't have her without that small part he'd played, so I couldn't hate him completely.

"Ms. Darling, are you unwell?"

I exhaled slowly, willing my last shred of self-control to do its job in the face of this new complication. That voice. I knew the low, clear tenor of it well by now, and it could fairly be categorized as belonging to another person on my as-close-to-hate-as-I-get list.

With a deep, calming inhale, I straightened, a customer service smile pasted on my lips. "No. Everything's fine."

"You don't seem fine."

I didn't meet his eye in order to respond. Instead, I did my usual blurring out of his face, looking vaguely in his direction. He was too hawkishly good-looking, and I couldn't stand the way my stomach dipped when I saw him, like it was tipping a cap to the physical gloriousness of this man. Light brown eyes, salt-and-pepper hair always immaculate, that curated stubble on his face, and a suit so sharp it could slice you open, in either coal black or slate gray.

"I assure you, I am." I'd gritted the words out, but who could blame me?

That man? Julian Grenier. Billionaire. Part-time Silverton resident since a few years back, when he and Jamie Morris, one of my best friends, began developing land east of the city. Sincerely odd duck.

Oh, and bane of my existence.

"If you're unwell, you should call a replacement."

How could a voice be devoid of tone? Of any inflection, really. Not even a hint of an accent. So unnerving. And those actual words...

Lord, help me not murder this presumptuous know-it-all.

I stepped around the corner of the bar and flipped on the tap, pumping soap into my hands as I spoke. "Due respect, Mr. Grenier, I—"

"Julian."

"Mr. Grenier. I am perfectly fine. Thank you for your concern." *Although,* no *thank you, because you can just butt out.*

When no response came, I heaved a silent sigh and looked up. *Guh.* Just like always, the very sight of him sent a flash of awareness through me. Awareness of *what,* I had no interest in pinning down. The fact that he looked like the cover model of a billionaire romance novel? Awareness of myself as a woman who hadn't been touched or kissed by a man in way too long?

Or was it awareness of the fact that he'd ruined my master plan but didn't know I knew it was him? Could it be that little fact stuck like a splinter in my thumb?

His gaze, with its piercing intensity, felt like he could eventually peel my layers and get to my core if he stood there long enough. How it unnerved me, yet also at the same time sent a sizzle up my spine. My body and mind had gone to war over their opinion of him.

My body crooned "Hey, boy!" while my mind yelled, "You are the actual worst." This left me functioning on an uneven keel, walking around like the boat had been tipped on its side, but I still had to walk from one end to the other.

"You are upset."

No change of expression. No pinched brow. Also no clear explanation as to why he'd gotten stuck on this subject when normally, he had very little time for anything or anyone beyond whatever he needed them for.

I didn't try to hide my exasperation. "Mr. Grenier, I—"

"Please. Julian."

Over my dead body. "Mr. Grenier. I took a personal phone call before my shift began, but as you can see, there's still one minute until my time on the clock begins. So please, if you don't mind, would you allow me to finish my prep?"

Hands behind his back, he offered only a curt nod. "Of course."

But he went nowhere.

And because I couldn't exactly shoo the man away, I focused on my job, washing a strainer of limes, eager to get the fruit and veg prep done. Brandon, my co-bartender for tonight, would typically be here already, but he had an appointment that ran late or something like that. I was on my own for prep and the first forty-five minutes tonight.

Grenier's eyes still lasered in on me. I could feel his gaze, piercing again, and shifted from foot to foot as I sliced the first lime. I wouldn't be the one to speak next— I'd said all I had to say to him. If I sounded like a petulant kindergartner, so sue me. The man had bought my building out from under me, and I couldn't soon forget that.

The knife slipped and thunked against the cutting board, making me wince.

"Did you cut yourself?"

"No."

"Those knives need to be sharpened."

Yes. Thank you, Captain Obvious. "They don't sharpen any more than this. They're the cheap set we had when we first opened."

Theo, the sous chef at the restaurant across the lobby of the hotel, popped his head in the entrance. "Quinney, you need dinner tonight?"

"I'd love it. Thanks." I smiled and winked at him, and he returned the gesture.

"Oh, hi, Mr. Grenier."

Grenier only nodded, then glanced at the phone in his hand. Theo's eyes widened at me, then he slipped out the door again.

At least I had that going for me. Cara was with my mom and grandparents—one of her favorite places in the world. I got to sing later, a definite bright spot to the day. I had lunch plans with friends tomorrow.

And at some point, Grenier would have to unglue his foot from the floor directly in front of my station and leave me in peace.

In fact, why was he still here? From my understanding, he had about eight thousand projects and businesses going on. He moved from one thing to the next in a straight line— no greetings, nothing to distract or delay him. Why would he stand here when he could sit literally anywhere in this bar—*his* bar—and do whatever it was he had going on?

"Did you need anything else?" I asked, not even

attempting to mask the irritation in my voice at this point. Seriously, did he have zero social awareness?

He blinked up at me, as though he'd entirely forgotten I was there in the sixty seconds he'd had his head in his phone.

"No. I'm fine." And he went back to his device, fingers flying in precise little taps.

"*Super*," I said, more than ready to be left alone.

"Oh, but I did have one issue I need to bring to your attention." He continued typing, not looking up to say this.

"Okay. Shoot."

Tap, tap, tap. The next moment dragged out so long, I thought I might scream, but finally, *several* limes later, he tucked his phone into his inside breast pocket and spoke.

"I'm raising rent in your building when leases renew in the next few months. I believe your store's lease is up end of October. I'll have my assistant set up a meeting to discuss the way forward."

Somewhere, a clock tick-ticked as his words tipped into place and registered.

Crap. And also, *seriously?*

Oh, so he wasn't ever going to directly acknowledge he'd bought the building I'd been trying to get loans to buy? He was just going to barrel in here and tell me he might be elbowing me out altogether. I loved Jamie, but the fact that he'd brought this pushy, greedy man into the town I loved made me want to strangle my old friend. Grenier had his hands in everything, and it made my skin crawl just waiting for the other shoe to drop. That familiar simmering rage hit the boiling point, the pot containing all that bursting black energy tipping right on over. My throat burned as the words rose to my tongue.

"Listen, Grenier. I don't know who you think you are

coming into this town, buying up all the property, and getting rid of every good thing we have going here, but I'm done with it. Tell your assistant she can shove your meeting up her—"

"That wouldn't be particularly wise, as you'll need—"

"*Honestly*, can you just leave me alone? Let me do my prep in peace and you go do… whatever it is rude billionaires do on a Friday night. Plot the demise of a small country? Buy up some local businesses and bulldoze them down before the owners find out? Shop at a Restoration Hardware?"

His only reaction was to slow blink before saying, "My assistant will contact you."

And then, he walked out and left me to cut the last limes with a dull knife and stew over how infuriating he was. Oh, and worry over how on earth I was going to make ends meet for everything on my plate *and* pay for Cara's winter formal dress *and* face a rent hike.

CHAPTER TWO

Julian

The jet landed in a bumpy swoop onto the small runway. I'd accepted that the pilot could do nothing about the turbulence when landing this high in the mountains. And while I loathed the uncontrolled ruckus of every approach and finalization of a flight into Silverton, it hadn't yet stopped me from coming back.

Despite the inelegance of the landing, we were precisely on time. A little push of adrenaline knocked through me as I confirmed the fact on my wristwatch. *Yes. Good. Still on track for the day.*

Smith quickly moved through the process of opening the doors, and the ground crew assisted in lowering the small stairway. I tucked my tablet under my arm and shot off a handful of texts that'd been dependent on landing on time here. As soon as my shoes hit the pavement with a satisfying *pat*, Kelly launched into her usual updates.

"Your conference call is waiting. I told them ten minutes—"

"Why are they waiting? The meeting isn't for another twenty." Irritation slithered up my spine. Why did people insist on wasting their time waiting on other people? Did they have no self-respect?

"They are overeager, sir." Her eyes widened before she ever saw my face. "Sorry, er, Julian."

Kelly was new, and so far, had done an excellent job, save for her tendency to treat me like lord and master rather than boss. I'd made very clear she wasn't to call me *sir*. I had no desire to treat my staff, who made my plans possible, like they were beneath me. We were a team, each person valuable.

"What saccharine, do-gooder posturing."

I shook my mother's voice away, even as unease tapped at me. Normally, I was far better at keeping her and all other distractions at bay.

Normally. Small distortion of the truth, wasn't it? Because lately, I'd been highly distractable. Especially when here in Silverton. And when I was away from the small town I'd come to think of as home. But all of that thinking proved to be even more of a distraction, so I pushed it into a deposit box, mentally locked it, and slid it into place among the myriad other things I compartmentalized at any given moment in order to be as productive as I was.

"I got confirmation of signatures from the legal team on the Southwark project. The Haitian donations arrived safely in country and the organizational leadership has obtained them." She listed three or four more updates by the time we reached my car.

"Are you sure you don't need Scott? He said he'd be very happy for a week in the mountains during the leaf change." Kelly clutched her portfolio to her chest, talking through the driver's side window.

"I know I'm an uptight jerk sometimes, but I really do love driving here. But if Scott needs a week in the woods, fly him out." I pressed the button to start the car.

She nodded. "Sounds good. And should I bring up Thanksgiving plans? Do you want me to RSVP to your mother?"

"No. Thank you. I'll take care of it." It'd be the last visit of the year with her, and I'd do my best to avoid being set up with any of her vulturelike friends' daughters. Plus, she'd complain about my bad manners if I had Kelly RSVP instead of doing it myself.

"All right then. See you Monday."

She made a soft salute, one that any decent soldier would be mildly embarrassed by, but she meant well.

And fortunately, she performed well. Because I could not abide people who meant well but couldn't execute their given tasks. Intentions are well and good, but depending on the situation, good intentions and bad execution can get people killed. I'd seen it in my factory, I'd seen it in design work, and I'd even seen it as we'd developed the neighborhood here with different contracting crews.

As I pulled onto the scenic little road leading from the Silverton airport into town, I breathed in the fresh air tunneling through my open window. I'd allotted eight minutes for this ten-minute drive. Eight minutes to relish the changing leaves crunching under my tires, the last slow dribbles of the waterfall that slipped between rocks where the road curved past the canyon, and the general splendor of Silver Ridge Peak and her sisters.

This was why I came back. I'd failed to notice my surroundings on too many occasions. When Jamie Morris, world-renowned rock star and Silverton native, had approached me about the project to develop a high-end neighborhood up here, I'd initially scoffed. On the map, the town was a blip in the middle of a difficult-to-navigate mountain range, too far from the airport to become the next luxury destination.

Or was it? Upon arrival, after a harrowing trip through the Salt Lake City Airport and what felt like a year of my life spent in the car, I'd seen what drew him here. Why he wanted to make something lasting in this little town that had more charm than most places in LA ever dreamed of. But it needed infrastructure—airport, more roads, pressure on the state's department of transportation to review the closure of a strategic route that would cut the commute here in half.

Now, it had all of those things, and my house had been finished for over two years. I spent every third week of the month here, sometimes more, depending on my other travel obligations. And while I wouldn't say I belonged here, really, people had become used to me. Not so much that they felt comfortable coming to beg for sponsorships or donations, but enough that they didn't stare at me like I'd gotten lost on the way to the resort.

Pulling into my driveway, I smiled at the mountain home. I'd started building it more than three years ago, but it'd taken time to furnish it. My LA home was largely clean lines and sleek grays. I'd wanted something more rustic here and, though I rarely used the word in speech or thought, something cozy.

"Nice to have you back, Julian."

Donald, my butler if one needed to call him something, greeted me by opening my door, accepting the key fob, and trailing me into the house. He peppered in small updates on the goings-on of the house, though he knew I trusted him with everything.

He followed as I padded through the hallway, up the main staircase, and stopped at my bedroom door. "Carol has the call to patch through when you're ready."

With a small thanks, I entered my room. On the far side, huge windows showcased an unbeatable view of the mountain and the changing foliage. I took a moment to freshen up, drank eight ounces of water, and straightened my tie again. Normally, this was when adrenaline would hit, a little nudge toward the success that would come from this call. But something about arriving here made that sluggish to activate.

Maybe it was the deal itself—a kind of business I had no interest in anymore. Or maybe it was that most of these things didn't capture my full mind the way they used to. Before Silverton. Before I'd had a glimpse of something else.

Yet, here I stood, shooting off a text to Carol that I was ready to start the meeting, nineteen minutes from landing at the airport. And though I didn't look forward to the call now lighting up my phone, I highly anticipated what came after.

It was Friday. And on Fridays, I allotted two hours for one very specific activity I only did here in Silverton. And I never double-booked.

Quinn Darling sang like it might be her last song. Every time.

I wasn't someone who was awed by things. The natural beauty of Silverton couldn't be denied, but it wasn't what had drawn me in about the place. The investment had, and the opportunity to partner with Jamie Morris, as I found him one of the more agreeable people I'd met, and a loyal one at that. But music turned my head. It was how I'd come to know Jamie, and what'd started our friendship.

Quinn Darling most certainly turned my head. The first time I'd heard her, it'd felt like the part of my brain that held all sense of urgency had melted. I'd become transfixed by her voice, the inflection of her phrasing, and the way I could hear her smile in certain words without looking at her. The way her lips formed words, and even how skillfully she used the microphone.

That was when she sang.

Any other time?

The woman was needlessly stubborn. To date, Kelly had contacted her in three different formats—phone, e-mail, and a visit to her place of business—not the bar, but her daytime workplace, Pluck. When Kelly approached her at her store, Quinn had reportedly reluctantly agreed to meet with me next week.

As I sat in a high-backed leather club chair in the far corner of the bar where she sang each weekend night, pleasure simmered in my gut. I'd have her undivided attention in the meeting, which would likely prove challenging since her presence was notably charismatic and appealing. I had a hard time keeping my eyes from taking their fill, which was rarely a problem for me.

But tonight? Tonight, I'd sit here with my scotch and I'd watch her sing. I'd feel my heart swell when her voice did. I'd experience every manner of emotion when she imbued the music with raw, untamed feeling I instinctually knew she'd felt in real life. I'd revel in her, and I'd envy her.

Then tomorrow, I'd show up and do it all over again.

CHAPTER THREE

Quinn

Grenier had returned yet again. I'd noticed him last night during sets but had pointedly ignored him. No eye contact. No chin nod to acknowledge his existence.

But tonight, my gaze had wandered over to him during a song, and I'd almost lost the phrase. My voice had caught, I'd added an extra breath, and I'd had to immediately look away. Because the man was devastating.

He sat in one of the fancy chairs that filled the whole bar. Normally, his posture was pin-straight, but tonight, he'd slumped in his seat just enough to look relaxed. His long legs were spread, his arms resting on either side of him, a glass of something dark in his glass—scotch, if I had to guess, because that was usually what billionaire supervillains drank, right?

And maybe that wouldn't have given me pause, though

he made a downright pretty picture there, but his hair... Normally perfectly coiffed and controlled, tonight, his dark salt-and-pepper locks looked like he'd run his hands through them. Not something I could imagine him doing—touching his hair.

Until that moment, it wasn't something *I'd* ever imagined doing, but faced with the evidence that it could be done, I wanted to be the one to do it. And that's how I knew I shouldn't have had the beer before my set.

It was the only explanation for my body's response to him. Yes, he was an irritatingly attractive man, but on every other front, he was purely irritating. And his assistant, Kelly, had done her best to seem kind, but she'd hunted me down and nailed me to the wall so I couldn't escape setting a meeting with him.

Not that I thought I could avoid the discussion, but I didn't want to do it *right now*. I had a hundred other things to worry about—most importantly, paying for material for Cara's dress, making sure my mom wasn't too burnt out, and confirming Chuck understood that no matter how many times he texted or called, he wasn't going to bully me into letting him break my daughter's heart.

Sometimes, I wondered how we'd gotten into this mess with my grandparents and me working my butt off in my midthirties to make ends meet for all of us. But that's the thing about medical debt—it usually comes after an unforeseen disaster. And ours sure had. Grandpa had a heart episode—not officially an attack, but because of a snowstorm, the canyon had been impassible and they'd lifeflighted him to the hospital. The procedures, including an open-heart surgery and rehab care, piled up fast. That would've been enough to create a challenge, but then Grandma got sick, and almost the same thing happened except sub the helicopter for an ambulance and a different malady that knocked her on her butt for months.

My mom quit her job to care for them because it was legitimately a full-time job, and we couldn't afford a home health nurse. They'd saved for retirement but had some issues along the way with their investments and ended up with very little to pad things. Amidst it all, the only break came through me. And I was not about to let my family struggle so I could have my weekends off or some other BS.

The stress overwhelmed me often enough, but we were making it. We *would* make it. And for two nights a week, I had this small, bright outlet to help me cope.

The final notes of the last song played. I thanked the remaining guests, likely all people staying at the hotel, and clicked the microphone back into its stand. Without actually looking, I could tell Grenier had stood. *Good riddance, grumpy weirdo.*

I helped Chase, the guitarist and my long-time friend, and our percussionist, Angel, tidy up the stage. At the bar, Brandon handed me my purse. I thanked him, and he snuck a peck to my cheek. *This kid.*

"Thanks. Good night?" I asked.

He shot me a sly look and nodded, evidently pleased with his tips. "Did you see the little bachelorette group? Only four of them, but yeah, they liked me."

The kid was adorable, but he was just that—a twenty-three-year-old kid. And don't get me wrong, I was all for people dating who they wanted, but I was not about to date a man closer in age to my daughter than me.

I patted his shoulder. "Good for you. See you soon."

Thank God I wouldn't be back here again until next weekend.

"Ms. Darling."

I jumped at Grenier's voice behind me as I exited the bar. "What the hell, man! You don't sneak up on a woman at eleven o'clock at night. Are you kidding me?"

He held out a hand. "I didn't realize I was sneaking by standing here in a well-lit hallway."

Not cute. Not funny. "What did you need?"

"I only wanted to tell you that your musicality is astounding. Your voice is magnificent, and hearing you sing is the highlight of any week I manage to do it."

My mouth dropped open.

What?

Of all the things to come out of his mouth, something like that... *What?*

I recovered quickly though, uninterested in him seeing how shocked his compliment made me. "Oh. Thanks."

He nodded. "See you Tuesday."

Then he walked off, that purposeful gait so upright that it looked like he carried a stack of invisible books on his head.

And I went home with an odd flutter in my chest, and a warring sense of anticipation and dread for Tuesday.

"Cara, honey, are you ready? If you want me to drive you, I need to go *now*."

My beloved daughter usually walked to school, but she planned to wear new shoes and didn't want to get them dirty, plus it looked like we might get rain. I had no problem dropping her at school, but she needed to kick it into gear or the girl would get left.

The first time I'd left her—exactly like I'd warned her no fewer than seven times leading up to my departure, mind you—she'd stomped into Pluck in a fit. I'd had to take her to school, sign her in with a tardy, and we'd both learned our lesson. She wouldn't call my bluff... and I wouldn't call hers.

It was a delicate détente, as were most things having to do with fourteen-year-old girls.

A minute later, she came run-stomping down the stairs. "You don't have to yell. I know how to tell time."

Oh. Good. One of those mornings.

I'd started my period, which meant she probably had, too. If I'd thought I hated my menstrual cycle as a teen girl, I had no idea how much I'd hate my daughter's. Mostly because she went from occasionally moody and emotional girl-child to an edgy, frequently snarling beast of a person for several days each month. And because it hit at the time when I felt most calm, collected, and full of grace, our interactions during these days were naturally those I wanted captured by a documentary film crew and sent forth to the *Mom of the Year Awards* committee.

"You do know how to tell time. I affirm that." See me not pointing out that if she can tell time so well, she needed to be downstairs five minutes ago? *I'd like to thank my morning coffee...*

She shuffled to get her backpack, and I sucked in a breath. *Calm. Calming thoughts. This is not a problem. She is in the worst years of her life as a ninth grader.*

"Did you get the stuff for my dress yet?"

I dumped the dregs of my coffee into the sink and flicked on the tap to rinse it down. "It should be arriving this week. We'll measure you this weekend and—what the hell?"

Water dribbled out from under the sink and dripped

onto my shoe. I turned off the water and dropped to peek into the cabinet and *yep*. Of course.

"What? What's wrong?" Cara bent down next to me. "Oh, that's not good."

Because I was an idiot, apparently, I turned the water back on and bent to watch to see where the leak originated and got shot in the face with a spray that wet the entire front of my shirt.

"Mom!"

I smacked the lever of the faucet and straightened, panic rising steadily. I did not have time for this. I didn't know what Grenier would do if I missed this meeting, but I couldn't risk finding out. The man had a notoriously militant approach to timeliness, and I didn't want to be at any more of a disadvantage than I already was.

Cara handed me a towel. "This is bad."

I dabbed my face, inhaling slowly. "Yeah. It's bad. But I have to go to this meeting. So load up, and I'm going to grab another shirt and be right there."

She hesitated, like she wanted to argue, but then turned and made for the garage. I sprinted to the laundry room, thankful I'd finally done a load last night. Darks were in the dryer, so I could pull on the long-sleeved black T-shirt I owned. It wouldn't look particularly professional or stylish, but it wasn't sopping.

I pulled open the dryer door, and instead of a dry tumble of clothes, I found a wet little jumble.

"No. Come on, you jerk." I'd spent three hours trying to DIY a fix on this thing weeks ago, and it'd held. It'd been working! "Why now, you wretched beast?"

No help for it, I ran up the stairs two at a time and yanked open my closet door. The options were slim pickings. I stripped off my wet shirt, then grabbed for the nearest and only remaining non-sweater shirt option—a plain white T-shirt. Not ideal, but again, better than soaking wet

I snatched the cardigan I liked to wear around the house at night—because I was an old lady like that—from the bed and shrugged into it on my way back down the stairs. I grabbed my purse, keys, blessed travel mug full of coffee, and ran for the door.

Twenty minutes later, I'd dropped off Cara, poured steaming hot coffee down my shirt to my stomach, and realized the shirt I'd grabbed was a half-shirt thing I'd worn as part of a costume and didn't cover my navel. *Neat.*

I was all for fashion and trends, and I could admit I had the stomach to show off because I worked damn hard for it—those FitCross-style workouts three times a week with Warrick yelling at us destroyed me every time—but would I ever walk into a meeting with a man I considered as close to an enemy as I had on this earth looking like that? No. I'd like my skin fully covered, thanks.

Moody daughter. Burst pipe. Broken dryer. Weird shirt. Coffee stain. Lunch forgotten on the counter. None of this would faze me on a normal day. I'd grown used to feeling like a walking three-ring circus most days, and I had long since made peace with the fact that Murphy—yes, him of the "If it can go wrong, it will go wrong" law—had come to live with me.

What I wasn't sure I could handle was everything else stacked atop my already teetering pile. The bigger problems that didn't just irritate—they dragged at me, cuffs at my ankles and wrists, because I had no way to solve them.

Pulling into the Silver Ridge Resort's parking lot, I

ground my teeth. I'd planned to park in town by my shop and walk up here so I could take a minute to enjoy the glorious fall morning and calm my nerves. But the ten-car pile-up making up my morning meant I had no time for a stroll and therefore had to drive here and park. I found a spot in employee parking because I damn well could.

I entered the lodge through the west employee entrance closest to the bar—figured familiar territory would help me feel a little less off-balance. I liked working at the fancy hotel, and I enjoyed most of the clientele. But I never forgot about the disparities between us. I was there to sling drinks and entertain. They were there to enjoy a luxury mountain experience with their high-end lifestyle.

I had plenty of wealthy friends. Somehow, I'd recently collected two more fancy friends—Calla Rice, who was just as famous as Jamie, if not more so, and Sadie Miller. Her status was more unobtrusive, but she came from one of the wealthiest families in the state, and she was dating a former NFL player. The fact that I'd known said NFL player my whole life and called him my friend too mattered not.

Because the man I was about to go head-to-head with over my measly rent payments put all of those people to shame. He could take all their money, lose it, and be no more affected than if he'd lost pocket change in a couch cushion.

In the last few weeks, whenever I thought about him, anger, righteous indignation, and a determination to fight for myself rose in me. But just now? After this morning? I felt shaky and weak. I didn't feel like conquering, name-taking Quinn. I felt like small, unsure, barely-holding-it-together Quinn.

Crap, did I hate feeling like that little snot.

"Hi, Ms. Darling. Go right ahead in."

Kelly, the woman who'd ceaselessly tracked me until I gave in to this meeting, waved me through giant polished wood doors to what was presumably Grenier's office. He didn't own the hotel outright—from what I'd heard, he and Jonas Bauer had both invested in the project. But for all I knew, and based on what I'd noticed in the last few years, he'd probably bought it out from under Jonas to have for himself.

Behind a large desk at the far end of the large room sat Grenier, head bowed over a tablet. I stood just inside the doors, both hands holding the straps of my purse in front of me, both because I suddenly felt the need to shrink and be even smaller in this giant room, and to cover the gap in my cardigan that showed my bare stomach. Curse the thing for not having buttons or zippers or *something* to hold the edges together.

After about a minute without being acknowledged, irritation surged past the nerves. "Are you ready to meet, or should I come back another time?"

His head jerked up like I'd truly startled him. He shot to his feet and leveled me with that serious, focused look that sent my stomach to my toes. "You're two minutes early, but I am ready."

Rounding the desk, he buttoned the top button on one of his probably-costs-more-than-my-car suits and held out a hand to a leather chair situated in front of a low coffee table. An identical chair sat just a foot or two away, next to it a couch and a fireplace that currently had nothing burning in it.

Paired with the rich carpeting, the wall of windows, and a chilly winter's day, this would be the perfect place to curl up with a book and just be.

Lucky jerk.

"Would you care for some coffee? Water?"

Hmm. Did not expect that. Somehow, I'd imagined walking into his office, plunking down in a seat across from an even-larger-than-his-real-one desk, and having him doom me to doubled rent before I got a word out.

But starting with coffee was smooth, I had to give it to him.

"Yes, please. Both, if you don't mind." I'd left my water bottle sitting right next to my lunch, so might as well.

He tapped out a message on his phone—presumably to request the beverages—then seated himself in the chair next to mine. It put us at odd angles—we weren't directly opposing each other; we weren't on different sides of a table or desk. The lack of separation made me restless because I hadn't anticipated this comfortable, almost warm approach to a meeting I'd been dreading.

He looked at me, eyes narrowing the barest bit like he'd noticed something.

"What? Lipstick on my teeth?" I said this because I knew for a fact I didn't have lipstick on my teeth since I'd forgotten to put any on. One more thing to make me feel naked in front of him.

"You look tired."

A small, disbelieving laugh jumped out. "W-what?"

"I said, you look tired. Are you all right?"

Oh no. No no no no no. This was not what I'd been expecting, and I felt those words pierce through my hard shell right into my gooey, very-close-to-breaking-down middle. *Crap.*

"Me? Sure. I'm fine."

"That sounds like an evasion."

"How so?"

He shook his head, as if disappointed. With me?

Himself? *With how weird this damn conversation is going, because what is happening right now?!*

"Fine is always covering something else up."

I grit my teeth, and mercifully, Kelly arrived with a tray.

Oh, hello. A tray with a coffee service, small plates, fresh grapes, several kinds of cheese, and what looked like scones.

When I glanced at Grenier, he simply nodded as if to say *help yourself.* So I did. Because food would help stave off this verge-of-tears zone I'd been skirting since waking up twenty-three minutes late this morning.

"While you eat, let me tell you about the impending changes."

Half a scone stuffed into my mouth prevented me from speaking, so I simply nodded. And he launched into the new lease, the new guidelines for tenants he'd be enacting, and set a new rental contract in front of me on the table.

"I'm sure you'll want your lawyer to review this. Take your time. When you're ready, simply return it and we'll proceed."

I glanced from him to the printed and neatly stapled packet of papers. John would do me a solid and review it just in case Grenier was trying to pull one over on me, but I had to know. After a swig of coffee, I flipped to the final page and found the new monthly rent fee.

My heart sank. Three hundred dollars more than it had been. And really, in my gut, I'd been expecting a lot more. With the way Silverton had grown and all the wealthy new residents, he very well could've increased rent by far more than that. I'd feared it'd be a thousand more a month, especially after Kelly had mentioned replacing windows and a few other improvement projects that would be taking place in the next few months.

But three hundred might as well have been a thousand

for me right now. I already worked six days a week at the shop and Friday and Saturday nights at the hotel. I'd cut back on seeing friends so I didn't spend money eating out. I ate peanut butter and jelly sandwiches most lunches and sometimes dinner, too. My only luxury expense was Warrick's gym, Grit, because without it, I'd lose my ever-loving mind, and I was fairly sure he'd already given me a discount, though I hadn't wanted to know for sure.

I felt it coming. I sniffed, scratched next to my eye, shifted in my seat. I crushed my teeth together and clenched my stomach muscles. But no luck. Because there they were—tears.

Why did he need another three hundred dollars a month from each tenant? What on earth would that do for someone whose net worth sat in the actual billions according to article after article that popped up when I searched his name online? And how dare he ply me with coffee and scones to make it more palatable?

"Are you crying?"

Grenier's curt, almost sharp voice cut through my little mental spiral and the tears popped out and tracked down my cheeks.

I steeled myself. "For the record, I am not crying because I'm sad or trying for pity. I'm crying because I'm angry and this is just the liquid overflow of rage."

Something flickered across his face that I might've taken as surprise or even a little humor, but that couldn't be right because this soulless, humorless, impenetrable man wouldn't have that kind of reaction to me crying, would he?

No. He wouldn't.

He didn't. In fact, his reaction threw me far more than I ever would've imagined. In my wildest dreams, I wouldn't have guessed what he said next.

He leaned forward, that serious brow furrowed with what looked like concern. His brown eyes tracked back and forth between mine, and then he said, "How can I help?"

CHAPTER FOUR

Julian

Quinn's shock showed like every other emotion on her face—fine and clear as a line drawing down white paper in felt tip black pen.

Her mouth dropped open, then shut and she clenched it tight. Her big red-rimmed green eyes blinked down at the coffee table, and her brow wrinkled.

I hadn't meant to confuse her. I'd meant to offer assistance, however unusual she might assume that was for me. Apparently, my ability to communicate with her was even worse than usual.

Maybe she hadn't heard me? I tried again. "I asked how—"

"I heard you," she snapped, her eyes blazing.

I dipped my chin, effectively chastised. Evidently, she would've preferred I wait for her to respond. My question had made her uncomfortable, that much was clear.

She opened her mouth to speak more than once but each time stopped herself as she battled internally for well over a minute—an interminable amount of time to wait for someone to respond after crying. And though Quinn's ability to convey emotion with her songs lured in me in like a moth to flame, I found sitting next to her in this state excruciating. If pressed to describe the feeling, I might've said it felt like my skeleton was trying to exit my body by pressing through the layers of muscle and sinew and skin in slow motion—a kind of exodus of everything that kept me upright. *Awful.*

Not sure why. Perhaps the tears? I couldn't say for certain, but I didn't recall anyone crying in my office in memory.

She cleared her throat, bringing my attention back to her.

"Forgive me. That was unprofessional. Between waking up late, a broken clothes dryer, and a busted pipe in my kitchen that sprayed all over my shirt resulting in me showing up like this, I'm not handling this well."

She gestured to her torso. I did not follow the sweep of her arm, as I'd noticed the bare skin of her stomach the moment she'd walked in and knew it would be fatal to me to indulge in acknowledging it. Quinn was a beautiful woman —I couldn't ignore that.

She continued. "But worse is that my grandparents need to move, and my mother has been caring for them and —you know what? Why the hell am I telling you this? You don't really want to know. You're—"

"I do want to know," I cut in, compelled. Something about her words... They gripped me. I not only wanted to know, but suddenly *needed* to. Someone in need—I could rarely resist that.

She shot to her feet. "I don't understand you or any of this. You're raising my rent, and I get that it's nothing to someone like you, but it's not that easy for me. A few hundred bucks a month is the difference between me and— whatever. Again. I'll deal with it." She glared at me for a minute, then reached over and grabbed the scone remaining on her plate. "I'm taking this."

She rounded the chair, so I hopped up and met her at the door. She couldn't just leave after dropping all this at my feet. "I asked what I could do. Tell me."

Her eyes were so full of blazing passion when she leveled me with her gaze, my stomach tightened into a fist. *This woman.*

She lifted her chin. "Don't raise my rent. How about that, Daddy Warbucks? Don't try to make an extra couple thousand dollars a year off me or anyone else in that build- ing, especially since I should've gotten the building in the first place. If my loan had been approved—"

"There was no competition when I placed my bid to buy it outright."

I'd never seen anger sprout wings and carry someone away, but it seemed like today might be the day. Her face reddened like every part of her was holding back from yelling.

"Well. Good for you." She crossed her arms tightly over her chest, bits of the scone crumbling to the ground when it bumped against her sweater.

Perhaps the reminder that I'd bought the building out from under her with an all-cash offer hadn't been wise. But it was true. No owner would want to sell to someone with a loan when he could have cash in hand within hours of sealing a deal. This should've been obvious to her. Based on observation, Quinn was exceptionally smart, so the fact that she hadn't made the connection didn't make sense. Additionally, the whole thing required upgrading and then sustained upkeep—a loan would cover only so much.

But I would refrain from pointing any of that out in this moment. Instead, I set a hand on the office door to make it clear I would open it for her, and she let her hands drop to her sides. Her shoulders deflated, and everything in her being said *get me out of here.* I could tell that much, at least.

I opened the door and stood to the side. She stepped past me and got a few steps into the lobby before I spoke again. "Ms. Darling."

She turned and narrowed her eyes. "What?"

"I'll have my lawyers draw up a new lease. No rent increase."

Her brow furrowed deeper, like this wasn't what she'd just asked of me. "Why?"

I blinked back at her and shrugged, though she was unlikely to see it. The answer was obvious, wasn't it? "Because you asked."

CHAPTER FIVE

Quinn

Because today was *today*, the day Julian Grenier broke my brain, work went especially slowly. And by slowly, I mean two people had come into the shop by three in the afternoon. I really had to get my arms around some marketing or I'd end up losing the store altogether.

I had a few key customers that kept me in business. Namely, Jamie Morris—real family name Morrison, of the local clan—and now Calla Rice. They both bought their instruments from me, and even used me to special-order crazy expensive stuff—Jamie's way of supporting me without just handing me money like he'd tried to more than once over the years, the fool.

The bell chimed over the door, and speak of the devil. "What are you doing in town? I thought you were on tour?"

"Can't I stop in to visit my favorite local instrument merchant once in a while?"

He flashed his lady-killer smile, and I just rolled my eyes.

"Sure you can, but you giving me your look-how-charming-I-am smile tells me you're up to something." I eyed him, wondering what he had up his sleeve. Usually, when Jamie popped up out of absolutely nowhere instead of texting to set up lunch or invite me to dinner with Bel and the kids, he had an agenda.

"I'm not sure what you mean." He leaned a hip against the glass counter I stood behind and glanced around the store. "Looks good in here."

"Thanks," I said, partly annoyed he'd noticed, partly proud.

I'd been organizing, trying to weed out some of what I used to think of as the old charm of the place, but which I'd realized came across as more of a hindrance to customers—almost every inch of the store was covered in instruments and sheet music and had been since I was a kid. I'd taken over managing the place after Cara started school, and when Mr. Corrigan wanted to retire, I begged him to let me take it over. Since the shop was one of about eight in the building, he'd sold the building, taken the profit, and I'd rented from the next owner. I'd been working toward buying the building myself.

And then, we know how that turned out.

"So..." He leaned down on the glass countertop and looked up through those ridiculous dark lashes with his stupid-blue Morrison eyes.

"You need to stop. This is just getting weird."

He barked out a laugh. "Bel's going to die when I tell her my moves have failed me."

"First, why are you using moves on me when I am

almost as close to you as your sister? Second, what are you trying to get, and why will you not just use your words?"

I was prickly today but couldn't hide the smile at seeing him. He and his wife, Bel, had been in town a lot more often the last year, but he'd been doing a smattering of tour dates in the US and had taken his entire little posse with him—wife, two kids, two cats. A veritable Morris zoo.

He beamed at me. "I missed you, ya grump."

I came around the counter and wrapped my arms around him for a quick squeeze. "Missed you too."

He ducked his head, those eyes surveying me. "So, how are you really?"

He knew a bit about the issues with my grandparents. He also knew he couldn't just pay for them to move into Silverton Springs, though he'd offered once years ago, before we'd gotten into the tight spot we were in with the medical bills, and he'd faced my wrath for it.

"I've had a crap day. My pipe burst, I have a busted appliance haunting me, Cara is in full-on moody teen mode, and Grenier—" I cut myself off, suddenly remembering who I was talking to.

Jamie and Grenier were friends. Pretty good friends, actually. I'd met him through Jamie before I'd known him as the inimitable and peculiar billionaire. I'd heard about his philanthropy and what he'd done for Jamie—solving a security problem, and several other small but meaningful things.

Jamie didn't miss the name or the odd tone I'd used when I'd said it. "Julian *what?* What happened?"

"Why do you say that like you expect something to happen? Is he a creep and you've never told me?"

He reared back. "What? No. But he can be brusque, and if you've interacted with him much, you know he comes off as a bit of an ass. He's got every minute of his day planned out, and once he's done, he's off to the next thing. It takes some getting used to, and if he was rude, I'm sorry."

I frowned. "You don't need to apologize for him. And he was... I honestly don't know. I'm still processing."

"What happened?"

"Well, you know he owns the building. My lease is up this month, so he scheduled a meeting. He's raising the rent three hundred bucks a month."

He swore. "Sorry. I could talk to him and—"

I held up a hand. "That's the thing. I kind of lost it on him—like I said, it's been a crap day. And he asked me what he could do."

Jamie's mouth tilted up into a small smile like that didn't surprise him at all. "Sounds like Julian."

I crossed my arms over my chest like it'd protect me from the confusion that'd clouded me since this morning's meeting. "Not the version of him I've ever witnessed."

"Then what'd you do?" he urged.

"I apologized for crying and told him what he could do was not raise the rent. And then he opened the door and I walked out, and before I was out of sight, he said the rent wouldn't be raised and he'd send over a new version of the lease to reflect the change." It still made me feel dizzy with relief and irritation and dread and hope.

I didn't understand it. I didn't understand *him*, and I hated that feeling. I was generally good with people. I was straightforward, told people what I thought of them and could take it when they did the same. But Julian Grenier had this maddening secrecy to him—both in terms of why the hell he would do something like change his master plan, not to mention what he'd expect from me in return.

That brought a fresh wave of dread. He hadn't said anything about it, but he was a powerful man used to getting his way. What would the price for not having raised rent be?

"What's that face? Isn't him not raising it good?"

I sighed and slumped down on my stool behind the counter again. "In theory. But... what does it mean? Why would he do that, and what is he going to want in exchange?"

Jamie leaned a hand on the display and gave me a look I feared was pitying, so I studied the harmonicas inside the case between us instead.

"Honestly, I don't know. I'd like to say nothing, but he may have something in mind. Nothing sketchy, but he doesn't do much without thinking every angle through. My guess is you'll figure it out pretty soon because he'll make it clear."

Not the answer I'd been hoping for, but I was done talking about this. "Enough of that. Why are *you* here?"

"I've been sent to request you and your daughter come to dinner this weekend. We're leaving Monday, but Bel wants to catch up, and the small ones want to see Cara."

My chest warmed. I loved Jamie's family and always enjoyed time with them. Lately, seeing them so happy and settled made me ache, but I wouldn't let that keep me away. "I can come any night before my shifts at the bar start."

We chatted a while longer before he left, and soon enough, five o'clock rolled around and I closed up. Cara would be at soccer practice a little while longer, so the time had come to face the pipe and the dryer and see if I could figure out a fix for both before she made it home and needed to wash her uniform.

When I pulled up, Chip Macallan sat on my front

stoop, his large form hunched over his phone. It looked like he'd been there a while.

"Hey, Chip. What are you doing here?" I said, greeting Silverton's handyman in chief.

He perked up, then pushed off the step with a groan. "Got a call about a broken kitchen pipe."

Jamie! Overstepper overstepping yet again!

"I think I may be able to fix it myself. I'm sorry you were waiting a while, but—"

"No problem, Quinn. My time's already paid. I'm supposed to look at your dryer too." He leaned down and grabbed his large toolbox.

I pushed the frustration out with an exhale. Not Chip's fault Jamie had gone around my back and arranged this. And if he was getting paid, I supposed it wasn't a terrible idea to let him come in and give everything a look. It'd be wasteful, otherwise.

"All right. Come on in."

He followed me in and got to work on the pipe first while I changed into a T-shirt that I usually slept in but I figured would be more comfortable for both of us. I piddled around the house, staying out of his way, until he'd diagnosed the problem with the pipe and fixed it, and then sadly identified the issue with the dryer and broke the news that he didn't think it was fixable today. He planned to order a part and hopefully come back on Thursday.

Crap.

I thanked him, tried to tip him, but he refused and said it was already taken care of, and waved as he drove away in his big truck.

It wasn't until after Cara had gotten home and we'd eaten, after I'd washed her soccer clothes and hung them to dry, and after I'd snuggled into bed in hopes of a better day tomorrow, that I realized something.

I'd never told Jamie which pipe had burst, but Chip knew exactly which one. I'd never told Jamie it was my dryer that had broken, yet Chip also knew that detail.

And the only other person I'd told was Julian Grenier.

CHAPTER SIX

Julian

Like something out of an old Western, Quinn Darling stormed into my office three days later. Kelly had gone home hours ago, and I'd done what I always did when in Silverton on a Friday night—work myself to distraction until my alarm sounded and I could go watch Quinn sing.

But to my pleasant surprise, here she was, black dress hugging her curves in a slightly shiny material that looked dangerously appealing. Black heels with a patent leather shine look to them tipped her another few inches in the air, and she'd pulled her hair back from her face in some way I couldn't see from this angle. She'd never been anything but exquisite, though having her in my space brought a reality to her that unsettled me.

I checked my watch just as she stomped across the room to stand opposite me, hands on hips, fuming. In my professional life, I didn't shy away from pushing people. Strong reactions to my methods weren't unheard of. And yet, the writhing intensity of her caused a physical reaction I hadn't experienced. My heart thudded increasingly faster, a little shot of adrenaline pushing into my veins at her arrival, her nearness, and though it made me a bastard, her fury.

"May I help y—"

"How *dare* you."

She gritted this out between teeth clenched so hard, I suspected her jaw would disintegrate in minutes if she didn't desist.

"Elaborate, please."

She huffed invisible fire. "How dare you pay Chip to fix my pipe and dryer?"

Ah, that. I'd given only brief pause to the possibility she might react like this. Not that I hadn't expected it, but that I'd embraced it as an outcome I found wholly acceptable. "You mentioned the situation at our meeting. I thought it would be helpful."

"It was helpful. It was *too* helpful. It's not appropriate. I don't know you. You're a stranger! You're—"

"I'm hardly a stranger, Quinn."

She double-blinked, and I realized my thoughts had escaped via my mouth and rushed to fix it. "Ms. Darling, excuse me. But I'm hardly a stranger. We've lived in the same small town for several years now. One of your best friends is, in fact, one of mine as well."

She tossed up her index finger. "One, I live in this small town and you live in... I don't know. A billionaire mansion in the sky? Wherever you fly off to in your fancy jet every week. You don't actually *live* here. And two, Jamie and I have been friends since we were in grade school. I admit you seem to be a very good friend to him, but our mutual friend in common does not mean *we* are friends. It most definitely doesn't mean you can pay for a handyman and *then a new dryer when said handyman can't fix the dryer.*"

Her shoulders rose and fell, her cheeks and neck flushed, and her voice had escalated to an intensity I recognized as quite close to yelling. She was breathing through her nose, evidently trying to calm herself.

I didn't typically relish sending a beautiful woman, or anyone for that matter, into an apoplectic rage. And yet, Quinn Darling in a rage proved to be utterly captivating. She was an undiscovered masterpiece by a renowned artist, a rare stretch of verdant grass in a sea of desert earth.

It hit me then. Her singing entranced—her voice could do wonderful things and the sound wrought pure pleasure. But it all came from her dedication to the songs, her interpretation and artistry, the attention she gave every note, every lyric.

Right now, she was giving *me* that full attention.

After a protracted moment, I slowly stood. I would've the moment she'd entered, except I'd been held in place by her energy and intent. Also, I had no desire for her to see me as a threat or a danger any more than she already did.

"You're not going to say *anything?*" Her voice shook and she pressed her crimson lips together so forcefully, they almost disappeared.

For a moment, words had indeed eluded me. "I simply wanted to give you a moment to get it all out."

She grew an inch. "Are you joking?"

"No."

Her lashes, which looked particularly long in the makeup she wore tonight, fluttered in disbelief. "You're unbelievable."

"What I am, Ms. Darling, is someone who likes to solve problems. You came for the lease meeting and admitted to having some. I had the means and motivation to fix at least a few of them, and so I did. If you find that so mortally offensive, you can feel free to call up Chip MacCallum, pay the bill for his two days of services, and contact the hardware store to set up a retrieval of the new appliance. If you prefer I handle all that, I'll have Kelly get right on it on Monday."

She sucked in a breath and let it out audibly. "I can't afford to pay Chip right now. I wouldn't have called him."

"What would you have done, then?"

She crossed her arms. "Why do you care?"

"I'm curious. I want to understand why my actions are so offensive, and perhaps knowing your alternate course of action will do just that."

Her eyes would raze a city. Thankfully, I was immune to such glares.

"Ultimately, it doesn't matter what I would've done. You were presumptuous at best and completely sketchy at worst. *We*"—she gestured between us, talking slowly—"do not have a relationship. You are my landlord. For my business. You have no business in my home and no right to do anything like what you did. It was high-handed and gross and made me feel—"

She looked away, inhaling sharply, then swallowed, cleared her throat. When her gaze settled back on me, I saw she was visibly shuddering with emotion. Not tears this time, but what had to be anger, when placed in the context of this conversation.

"It was inappropriate, and you can't do that again. I don't understand why you did it to begin with, but I'm telling you now, I'm not going to owe you anything."

I raised a brow. "*Owe* me?"

"You know. Whatever it is you're expecting me to do to pay you back. I've made it clear I don't have money. I don't know what you want from me, but I'm not going to be beholden to you for something I didn't even ask for."

I rounded the desk, stopping short when she stepped back. Was she actually scared of me? I couldn't imagine Quinn Darling being afraid of much at all, so the thought unsettled me. "I don't want anything from you."

Not entirely true. Maybe I could *want something.* An idea had indeed started taking shape. But for the purpose of this conversation? Fairly true. *Mostly* true.

She raised her chin. "I don't buy it."

"What is so hard to believe?"

Her arms flew out and gesticulated wildly. "People don't do this crap! You can't just—just—do this. You make no sense. If you don't want something from me, why would you spend what amounts to at least a thousand dollars on me? I don't get it and I don't like it and you—you're infuriating."

My pulse pounded as I stepped another foot closer, and this time, she didn't retreat. She stood her ground, and flames lit in my chest—yet another unexpected response to her tempestuous reactions. As if fire were calling to fellow flame. "You know I'm extremely wealthy."

She scoffed.

"Then you know I have money at my disposal. And though I am a businessman, I do also occasionally help people. Is it so incomprehensible that I might help you?"

She closed her eyes and inhaled. "Yes. Yes, it is. Because people don't do this."

I leveled her with a look I hoped conveyed my veracity. She didn't know me or how often I did this kind of thing. She had no knowledge of what I'd done for Kelly's mother months ago or Scott's brother. She might not even know how I'd helped Jamie years ago. Her suspicion made sense, and I wouldn't trot out my list of good deeds to appease her. Rather, I could do what I'd done so many times before and take her off guard. "Fine. I do want something from you."

She swallowed. "Say it."

A twinge of nervousness edged in but I banished it. "I'd like to be your friend."

The idea had hit home soon after she'd left the other day. I'd made as much progress with Silverton itself as I could. Making friends with the locals—the ones who actually lived here instead of just parachuting in from time to time like Jamie did these days—might prove to be the next phase of approach to ultimately cementing my position here as one of *them*. Quinn had handed me an opportunity on a silver platter. Everyone knew the first rule of networking was to befriend one of the people from inside the circle and then follow that path to find a footing into said circle. Enter Quinn Darling, Silverton original and one of its most beloved residents.

She reared back and her face became a mask of bewilderment. "Uh. What?"

"It's simple. I'd like to be your friend. In my experience, friends help each other. I saw an opportunity to help you, so I did. If my methods were pushy or overstepping, please accept my apology and let me know a day when the dryer can be removed from your home. Otherwise, accept my help as a gesture of goodwill and nothing more."

Her mouth opened like she planned to speak, then snapped shut. Opened again, just as an alarm blared from her pocket. She whipped out her phone, silenced the alarm, and slipped it back into her pocket. "I have to go."

Without another word, she turned on her high heel and beelined for the door. Since it'd been left open when she stormed in, she'd made her escape very quickly and without even a pause to grapple with the door.

I tugged at my tie and tossed it onto my desk, shucked my jacket and hung it on the coat hanger in the corner, and rolled up my sleeves. It'd gotten warm in here, despite the cooling autumn night outside the large-paned windows covering the east wall. Perhaps all that fire and flame? Ludicrous notion, so I shook it away and focused on the view. In a few weeks, the mountains would get their first snow, and soon enough, the whole plaza outside would be covered in families here for their ski trips.

People would mill about, calling to friends. Laughing together. Carving into the snow and then ending the day with a beer at the tap room or maybe even at the bar watching Quinn sing.

It all seemed so trivial at times, and yet something made my stomach clutch at the thought of seeing it this year. Some aching part of me *needed* to be here more, and that was exactly why I'd leave for my second to last trip to LA this year in eight short hours.

But first, I'd watch Quinn sing. Maybe her voice could help me comb through these incessant thoughts that felt foreign to me even now. Maybe she'd choose a song that would calm me, center me again.

A fleeting thought burst across my mind—perhaps it was the woman herself who could do that?

Another inane sentiment. It was her song that called to me.

Not her.

CHAPTER SEVEN

Quinn

Usually, singing settled me.

Cliché as it might sound, I made sense of things through song. It was one reason—despite my lack of desire for fame and a career as a singer, even though in theory I had all the right connections to pursue such a thing—why I persisted in performing.

"You should really send a demo to a record company or something. You're just so good." A girl who'd been over-served by dear Brandon grabbed my arm and shook it.

I'd done a thirty-minute set and was taking my first of two breaks at the end of the bar when she'd come up and, well, here we were. Me gently prying her fingers from my arm, and her slumping her head to the side as she tried to figure out what was wrong with me.

People did this. They heard my voice, saw the decent-looking package I presented, and wondered what'd gone wrong. If anyone told them I became a mom at twenty-one, they'd shake their heads in pity and probably silently wonder if I resented my child.

I didn't. From the minute I knew she was growing in me, every plan I'd ever had for my life had changed. Yes, I'd dreamed of doing exactly what Jamie had done. But when he asked me to go out there with him—not romantically, but as a friend who was established enough to get me the attention I'd need to have my own start—I'd just found out about Cara. And I'd known it would change my trajectory, and even early on, I'd been okay with that.

Yes, there'd been times I wished I could play on a stage of forty thousand people while they sang along to a song that I wrote. Usually, those moments came in bittersweet pleasure-pain when I went to one of Jamie's big shows in Salt Lake when he toured the US. But mostly?

Mostly, I loved my life. I loved living in Silverton and owning Pluck. I loved giving Cara the stability of living in the same town her grandmother and great-grandparents did. I even loved that she attended the same seventies-built high school I did.

But I did need the outlet of singing, and I'd always taken any I could get that didn't take away from my life with Cara. Gigs around the valley, playing local festivals, and in the last year or so, singing here at the lounge on Fridays and Saturdays.

Ever since Calla, aka Miss Mayhem, had debuted her self-penned songs here months ago, the bar's traffic, even in the off-season, had picked up. And people were inspecting me for signs of stardom on the rise.

I hated to break it to them, but the only thing rising over here was my blood pressure as the girl kept gushing. I loved a good compliment, make no mistake. But she was on the verge of tears, begging me to do something to get my voice "out there" like she knew what that meant, what it cost, or whether I wanted it.

"Where's Jose? Isn't he security tonight?" Grenier's voice cut in before he bent to the now-crying woman. "Ma'am, may I direct you back to your seat? I'll send a complimentary charcuterie board to your party. Please, enjoy." He ushered her away back in the general direction of the people watching the whole thing wide-eyed.

I steeled myself, wholly unprepared to deal with him again. I'd shut him out when I walked out of his office, decided I didn't need to spend the night obsessing about all the peculiar, confusing things he'd said. But of course he was here, up in my face, making himself impossible to ignore.

Also, he'd done the thing. The thing men who wore suits to work did that drove me a little crazy. He had his top button open and his sleeves cuffed just below the elbow. As someone who used her hands for playing instruments, I liked a man with good hands and forearms.

Of course that jerk had them. Really good ones. His hair might've even been a bit disheveled again, like walking into the bar was the place he unwrapped and unraveled a little, and it sent my stomach to my toes to see him stalking back in my direction.

Watching him approach felt like looking down a long hallway that stretched out longer the more steps he took. His intensity gave me tunnel vision in a confusingly plea-surable way.

"Are you all right? Did she hurt you?" He dipped his chin so he looked directly into my eyes.

"Fine. She was just being nice."

He scowled. "Touching someone without asking isn't

nice. It's harassment. You could sue her, or at the very least have Jose throw her out."

"I don't need to do either of those things. She'll stay over there now that you escorted her back. And I'm sure the food will help, too." It'd been a surprisingly nice gesture.

He glanced over his shoulder, then whipped his head back to me when he saw half the bar was watching him. An odd expression flashed across his face before he leaned in and said, "I just don't want to see her pawing at you."

"Because you'd like to be the one pawing at me?" I quipped, immediately regretting my big stupid mouth. "I shouldn't have said that. I didn't mean that."

Too late. His face had shut down to that severe, impenetrable mask. I wouldn't have been able to detect anything beyond the usual resting jerk face, but then he spoke.

"I wouldn't ever touch you without your consent. Ever."

Ugh, stupid big mouth. "I shouldn't have said—I didn't think you would."

He nodded but didn't move. A beat passed, and in any other conversation, the other person would've left me to feel like a jerk for spewing idiotic things. They'd sense my discomfort and let me drown in a bit of self-loathing while also still being irritated with him for generally provoking my stupid trigger tongue and confusing me with basically everything he did.

But not him.

"You shouldn't tolerate it from anyone."

Something about his tone made it sound like he thought I had to deal with crowds mauling me all the time. "I don't. And honestly, it's not that much of an issue. I'm not exactly turning away offers. More like, I'd have to issue an invitation."

And why did this veer off into a weird, masked version

of me explaining my unsuccessful love life to him? Why did he, more than anyone else in my life right now, make me say strangely honest things?

He ducked his chin again. "I'm certain should you ever decide to offer an invitation, anyone here would be prepared to accept."

Gazes locked, the moment hung between us for one, two, three seconds before he turned. My eyes followed his movement back to the chair where he always sat at the far end of the bar, noting how he whipped out his phone and began typing immediately upon sitting.

What. Is. Happening?

My eyes registered what I was seeing, yes, but my brain couldn't comprehend. The last few hours had too much to parse out. I'd effectively avoided a mental breakdown after the meeting with him earlier when he said he wanted to be my friend in exchange for his kindness—like that was a thing. Like spending that kind of money on someone was a *friend* thing. And then this?

This... this... *suggestion?* Was that the word for it? *Should you ever decide to offer an invitation, anyone here would be prepared to accept.* Had he meant an invitation to touch me? He couldn't have meant that, could he?

But what else would it be, in the context? I'd just made the crack about him pawing at me, he'd said the extremely intense and somehow very appealing thing about consent, and then... then I'd veered off into my weird comments about not having many offers because I apparently tended to lose my mind in the face of his gorgeous intensity.

Then *that*. The suggestion that if I offered an invitation —to touch me? Date me? Be with me? The type of invitation was unclear, but something personal and significant, I knew that much—*anyone here* would accept.

Anyone?

As in, anyone in the bar right now, to also include him?

And why, after all of my outrage in the wake of his completely inappropriate gift and help, was I feeling a mix of anticipation and gut-level pleasure at the thought that he did mean him?

CHAPTER EIGHT

Quinn

The bar ended up packed out during my second and third sets. I stayed and took a few requests, and by midnight, my voice threatened to revolt. I'd stopped singing long ago, but I'd jumped in to lend a hand with the bar. Sometimes, I'd take off after my last set if things were quiet, but October could be hit or miss with crowds, and tonight was most definitely a hit.

Grenier had left ten minutes ago—my desire to leave had walked out right behind him. Yet another little stick added to the pile of nonsense I'd cleverly titled "Things Julian Grenier has me thinking and or feeling that make absolutely no sense."

Okay, so any writing prowess I had was reserved exclusively for songwriting. Pithy labels for tangled emotions and confusing thoughts, not so great.

Earlier tonight, I'd been shaking a martini that some guy

had ordered "extra shaken," which I supposed meant he wanted it really cold, though it also ultimately served to slightly decrease the strength of the drink so maybe he wanted it to have a lighter touch, and out of the corner of my eye, I saw Grenier stand.

Some percentage of my brain had tracked him every minute of the night. Even before that weird exchange earlier with the handsy girl, I'd been aware the minute he walked in, and now it was like someone had flipped on a light. Not one of the beautiful blown-glass fixtures like the bar sported. More like a closet light that you could only see under the closed door. Lurking in the corner, visible but also mostly unseen.

He stood and I pivoted a bit as I shook, shook, shook the Boston shaker, and my lungs tripped and skidded to a halt when his darkened gaze met mine. I nodded, and he... well, he didn't. Or if he did, it'd been so minute I hadn't actually seen it. But the way he looked at me was like a nod itself, though I fully realized that didn't make a lick of sense.

Next, he'd left. Abandoning me to the land of *what the heck is going on with me?* Not long after, I'd dragged off home and poured myself into bed, shutting out all thoughts of Grenier or touching or invitations or stupid gifts.

By Saturday at four, when I knocked on Jamie's door, Cara and I had successfully enjoyed an extremely lazy day, minus the time I'd been in the shop. For the first time in a while, she'd come with me, deciding to keep me company and practice her piano on the dinky upright I kept in one corner rather than the far nicer one Jamie had given her for her tenth birthday.

Yeah. A piano. And when I'd told him it was too much, he'd said, "Tough luck, your mom said I could," and that was that.

Secretly, in this one instance of spoiling, I'd been pleased. Because I didn't have cash to get her a piano, and definitely not one that nice. He'd probably considered getting her a concert grand, and I bet I had Bel to thank for reeling him in.

Cara had always loved to play at the shop, until she turned eleven and became aware of how good she was and how much attention it got her. She shriveled up and asked to just read or stay home, and I couldn't force her.

I'd successfully avoided forcing music on her. She'd come to it naturally, and right on the heels of her astounding ability came the reality that I couldn't teach her. We both got frustrated, and though I'd felt it was a failure for about the first ten years of her childhood, I'd finally embraced that other teachers could offer her more than I could anyway. Especially considering I worked my butt off to pay the bills, and having her in lessons with someone other than me helped me do that.

"Come in, come in! We've missed you!" Bel waved us in, her golden-brown hair and green eyes just as lovely as ever, but the warm, bright smile the most beautiful part of it all. Well, that and the dark-haired, blue-eyed Jamie look-alike on her hip.

Bel had been sad. For a long time. And though Jamie's little sister, Leo, had been a good friend to her, she'd struggled for a lot of years. I'd always felt like I couldn't do much for her as a good friend of Jamie's since things between them had been so bad for so long. I never stopped feeling that sense of relief and joy at seeing them together, happy, settled.

"Cara, come see." Jamie's three-year-old grabbed Cara's hand and they were off.

Ally loved Cara, and the inverse was also true. Cara

hadn't done much paid babysitting, but I figured in the next year or two, she could if she wanted. It'd help her with spending money, but if she wanted to focus on homework and practicing her instruments, I didn't want to make her work. She'd have a lifetime of that, and I wanted to give her as much time as I could before it became a necessity.

"Well, they'll be busy until dinner, so fill us in," Bel said, walking me into the gorgeous open living room and kitchen. A fire blazed in the stonework fireplace, and Jamie covered a pot on the stove before he came and took the loaf of bread I'd brought.

Thank God for Sadie, I thought as both Jamie and Bel beamed at the loaf.

"Figured the least I could do was supply your bread habit," I said, knowing they both loved and missed the Rise and Shine bread. I'd gotten a loaf of the month subscription gifted to me by someone, and though it rankled me not to know from whom, I'd never been happier to have a loaf to pick up, already paid for, this afternoon. It was the first month, and as much as I would've loved to sit down and devour the entire loaf, it felt far better to share it with friends.

Slipping into a seat at the bar, Bel tipped her head to one side in question. The little bundle resting against her seemed fairly content, so I hated to disturb him, but yes. I wanted to cuddle a baby I could give back—a thousand times yes. I reached for him, a hum of pleasure in my throat as I snuggled the tiny one to my chest.

"I always forget how sweet they can be since mine was a demon spawn at this age." Little Jamie, as he was affectionately known, was nine months and sleepy. His Morrison-blue eyes were blinking up at me, and my heart clutched.

Something about the simplicity of holding him—this

baby who would grow up to be a man—made me feel like I'd tip over if I stood. But one thought penetrated the odd mix of nostalgia and sadness and joy. *No one will ever trust me like this again.* Cara had long since discovered I could let her down. Nothing major, but in all those human ways a mother failed her child. I snapped at her when I was hungry, misunderstood her, forgot to sign a paper or buy oranges at the store. Again, nothing life changing or therapy inducing, I hoped, but she knew I wasn't perfect.

Little Jamie had no idea that Bel and Jamie weren't perfect. That they wouldn't provide for his every need indefinitely and completely. And something about that made me so happy, but for some stupid reason, incredibly sad.

What is wrong with you!?

"He can be a challenge, but he is a super sweet baby. I think after seeing Mia with *two* at once, I realize any issues I have are small." Bel chuckled softly and smiled at little J.

Jamie ground pepper over a pot of what had to be chili based on the smell. "I've always liked Mia, you know? Always thought she was a great mom, and Kai is evidence for that. But seeing them add to the family cemented it. And honestly, seeing Danny carrying around two babies at once is the weirdest thing ever."

"Don't say that," Bel said, defending her old friend and Jamie's brother. "He's an incredibly natural father. Arguably more of a natural than you."

Jamie turned and lifted a hand. "I'm not saying that. It's just sometimes, I have these flashbacks of times where he wouldn't show interest in anything other than skiing and hanging with buddies. I'm glad he figured himself out. And I think he's in for a treat when the season kicks in and he's running patrol and a father of *four*." His brows raised like four was an incomprehensible number of children.

Honestly, it was. I couldn't imagine more than Cara. Granted, that was probably thanks to the fact that it'd been me and her for so long that I didn't know how to think about myself in a way other than her mom. I'd been Cara's mom first and foremost these last fourteen years—I couldn't really wrap my head around the fact that I only had four years left with her before college.

Anxiety coiled in my belly. *Four years.* I only had four years to get my crap together and make some more money so I could pay whatever astronomical bill Juilliard was going to exact when they accepted her. And they would accept her, because she was remarkable. If they didn't, it'd be another music conservatory, and I'd need a crap-ton of money in either situation.

"I think we'll stick with our two," Bel said, bringing me back to the moment.

I petted a hand over the baby's soft, dark hair. "I support you two cranking out as many babies as you like. I'll be here to hold them whenever you're in town."

Little Jamie burbled and swooped his arm out for Bel's hair and managed to grab a handful.

"Oh, guess he's ready to go back." I shifted him to Bel, and she received him with one hand while gently prying his fist open to save her hair.

The doorbell rang and Bel hopped off the stool next to me, little J on her hip. "That must be Julian."

I froze, then my eyes cut to Jamie—the big one—a shot of panic bolting through me.

He held up two hands. "Chill."

Clearly, he read the death threat in my glare. I couldn't see Grenier right now. Not with my guard down. Now when I had absolutely no idea how to handle him. Not with my daughter here, with Jamie and Bel watching.

"Chill? *Chill?* What about this situation is okay? I don't—"

He rushed toward me. "Bel invited him when we ran into him this morning. She worries about him, wants to check in on him. So getting him here under the guise of a group thing was the way to go. I don't think he knew you'd be here either. Just—" He swiped his hand sharply to one side like that would tell me first, how to behave when I came face-to-face with a man I had a Mount Everest-sized pile of confused feelings about, and second, keep me from responding.

I raised my chin and gave him a shark-eyed stare. "You're dead to me."

He made an unimpressed face, then started gathering bowls and spoons and carting them to the giant wood table. Bel's nearing voice and a baby squawk had me hustling over to help him to avoid sitting there with nothing to occupy me when Grenier entered the room.

I didn't need to be looking to know he'd walked in. I felt him—call me crazy, but I swore I could. I plunked down a bowl a little too aggressively and caught Jamie's expression. Yes, he thought I was losing it, and yes, maybe I was a little.

Because really, *really,* I wanted to say, "You tell me how to act when a man who has control of my livelihood and bought me a dryer and is confusingly cold and businesslike but somehow also generous and almost warm and makes my brain short-circuit with his stupid handsome face walks in and I found out one of my best friends ambushed me."

I didn't say that, but I hoped my continued glare would communicate it.

"Julian, you know Quinn Darling?" Bel said, sweetly oblivious to my turmoil.

Though not. I didn't buy it. Jamie was a little schoolgirl with his wife and he told her everything, so she had to know about the whole landlord thing, and probably the dryer thing—I'd texted him yesterday before I stormed into Julian's office to ream him for overstepping.

All told, this felt like a big fat setup, and I hoped with every fiber of my being that Grenier didn't think I had any hand in it. Just that thought made my nerves crawl into my throat.

"Yes. Hello."

A laugh made my stomach flip as I looked at him for the first time. *Gut punch.* Oh, crap, this man was handsome and it did not help my jumbled feelings. Instead of his usual perfect suit, tonight he wore jeans and a thin charcoal long-sleeved shirt that, if I wasn't seeing things, had a hood. Not quite a hoodie—the more stylish, designer version, no doubt, but oh, boy, did it look good on him. My eyes threatened to gobble up this dressed-down sight of him, but I pulled my face away.

Why couldn't he be horrible-looking? Or even just... medium. Like, if he was just an average-looking guy? No problem. High five, glad to see ya, no big deal. But all other things being equal, he'd been making my stomach drop since the first time I met him years ago. Granted, in the intervening years, I'd grown to loathe him. Except now... I wasn't sure I did. I mean, *I did.* He'd snatched the building out from under me, and I hated that. But maybe some part of me knew it would've been too much right now, so I didn't actually hate him. Not after he'd said he'd keep the rent the same—assuming he followed through on that.

And the dryer thing. And the compliments. And the

saying he only wanted to be friends in payment for the whole hiring-Chip-and-dryer thing. *Ughghghg.* Why couldn't he crawl back into the little box I'd assigned him, the one with "evil greedy billionaire genius" scrawled on the front and left in a corner of my mind?

"Hello," I responded, because responses were things functioning humans did. Ones who weren't having internal meltdowns precipitated by nothing more than another person walking into the room.

That said, I couldn't stick around. I wasn't going to bail completely, but I had to steal a second to gain some perspective and sanity, and I couldn't do it with Grenier in the room and Jamie and Bel pulling out popcorn and snacking on the show. "I just remembered Cara made cookies, and I think we left them in the car. Be right back."

I slipped around Grenier and Bel and basically high-tailed it to the door, narrowly missing stepping on the tail of the more social cat, Squish. Seconds later, I closed myself inside the back seat of my ancient Jeep and sucked in a breath.

This was fine. We'd sit down, eat chili, and I'd leave. Cara would want to get back home to talk to friends and do homework, and I clearly needed more sleep. Plus, oh! Yes! Plus I had to work tonight. Of course! That's why we were here so early anyway, though Bel and Jamie never minded since their little kids ate early too. But I *did* have an excuse. I had a hard out, and I could use it and not feel a bit bad because I had to get to work.

A sharp knock on the window made me jump out of my skin. Seriously, I wouldn't have been surprised to see my skeleton open the door and walk back inside. One look to my left showed me the very man I'd been semihiding from waiting with hands clasped behind his back, face tilted down.

He was all sharp, masculine angles. His hair stuck up a bit in front, which made my stomach dip in a predictable, maddening way. And I knew I couldn't stay here in the car, hiding behind a pane of glass. Plus, I wasn't a wuss. I was a strong, independent, fully-functioning woman, and I wasn't going to hide from him anymore.

I shoved open the door and he stepped back. I sucked in a breath and let it out, deciding not to care if he heard me since he clearly knew I'd come outside to escape him or he wouldn't have bothered to follow me.

"Would you like me to leave?" he asked without looking up.

"W-why would I want that?" *Curse you, nerves! Curse you!*

He raised his head and hit me with his eyes. Our gazes locked and my heart kicked once, twice, then sprinted.

The side of his mouth pulled up into the closest thing to a half smile as I could imagine for this man. He had a glint of *something* in his eye I couldn't quite pin down.

"You're out here hiding. I thought I'd offer to leave so you didn't have to anymore."

The steel in my spine went rigid. "I was getting cookies." I held up a Tupperware and congratulated myself on the foresight to say something true when I left.

"You were hiding."

Irritation sizzled in my chest—it didn't matter that he was right. He didn't know he was right, and his assumption that I was hiding really lit my fuse. Again, that he was absolutely correct had nothing to do with it.

With my teeth clenched, I said, "I. Was. Getting. Cookies."

His eyes ticked back and forth between mine like a metronome for a beat longer than would be comfortable for anyone. Then finally, he gave one of those slight nods, turned on his heel, and said over one shoulder, "If you insist."

And because I'd discombobulated enough to lose my filter, plus I tended to say stupid things to him whenever we interacted, I yelled, "I do insist!" just as he slipped inside. Then I gave myself another five minutes to get myself together and face this man, who clearly had my number and wasn't afraid to use it.

CHAPTER NINE

Quinn

I made an error in judgment.

Really, no surprise there. The theme of my life set into a sentence would likely be *I made an error in judgment.* Sometimes, like with Cara, it worked out beautifully.

Other times, like tonight at Jamie and Bel's dinner table, it backfired fantastically.

Because here's the thing I'd never considered when plunking myself down in a seat across from Grenier, the only seat left by the time I'd recovered my sanity and forced myself to return to the dinner.

He was good at eating.

Okay, I know, this sounded insane. How could one be good at eating? Especially when the meal was soup and bread? But trust me, he could, and he was. Of course. Because he was probably good at everything. Well, except talking to people.

Maybe it was because I'd never really seen him eat—if I had, I certainly couldn't recall when. I'd seen him sip his drinks at the bar, and even then, only from afar. At his office earlier this week—*crap. Had that really been just days ago?*—I'd piled my plate high while he'd not even taken a sip of water.

Subconsciously, I think I'd assumed he consumed his calories via pill or injection—something sterile and expedient. Eating seemed so human and personal and almost passionate. The act of eating had suddenly become intimate, and seeing him do it for the first time tonight all the more so.

Sitting across from him and watching him take a bite of the hearty chili Jamie had made sent me into a weird internal conniption. He had such a sharp jaw dusted in a little more stubble tonight, making him look kind of rugged instead of his usual polished precision. When he bit down, his jaw flexed and then his throat worked to swallow, and all of it seemed unbearably... well, honestly, it was just...

It was sexy, okay?

What is wrong with me? True, I hadn't even attempted dating in years, and before that, it always ended the same way—me getting home to the babysitter and the guy telling me to have a nice life. Maybe not in so many words, but I didn't date people I already knew in town—it was just too small here. Cara was old enough to hear rumors or notice if something went wrong with someone in the community, and I'd never wanted to mess with her equilibrium like that. Point was, maybe I was just starved for attraction, and Grenier, for some utterly insane reason, was on the receiving end of it tonight.

"Juju, you look tired," Ally said in her tiny, adorable three-year-old voice.

Bel gasped. "Honey, that's not—"

"Good observation, Ally. I am tired. I haven't been getting much sleep." Then his eyes flashed to mine, and away.

Whut.

Was that comment directed at me? Also, I'd never imagined Grenier talking to the kids. Or... or doing anything with the kids. I imagined him as a kind of antiseptic in the room—useful for a purpose, but only in certain instances, and otherwise, left completely alone. But just thinking that made guilt slip through me, and I wondered yet again why I judged him so harshly.

Because he took your building, and he's a pushy, entitled butt.

Well. Good to see we're keeping it above board.

Jamie, meanwhile, was practically cackling. He'd discovered one of his favorite things about parenthood was Ally's directness, even when it lacked manners. I couldn't say I blamed him—it was absolutely adorable.

"Juju?" I couldn't help asking, because another thing I'd never imagined was Grenier having a nickname.

His gaze met mine, but Jamie cut in to explain before he spoke. "Ally couldn't say Julian when she was little, but she loved him. I think Danny and Liam were jealous, because *Juju* was her favorite. She'd follow him around, and if he picked her up, she wouldn't let him put her down. There was a good six months where she sat on his lap for dinner if he came over."

My mouth dropped open. I straight up could not imagine that man holding baby Ally, let alone having her sitting on his lap. I couldn't imagine him interacting with a toddler, period. I also wondered if I'd ever witnessed it and just not been as affected, but no. I would've noticed. I'd always noticed Grenier, even before the mess with the building.

"That's so... sweet." It was a hundred things, sweet being one of them. My cheeks heated after saying it aloud, so I focused on my chili and bread, and mercifully, Bel asked Cara how her practicing was going.

Not long after the subject change, I felt Grenier's eyes on me. Sitting back in my chair, I met his gaze and experienced a jolt of awareness. I'd dressed for work since I really did have to leave in about thirty minutes and didn't want to spend the time changing at home. The black wrap dress had a vee created by the crisscross of the material over my chest, then tied around my waist. Flattering, but fairly nondescript. Not my favorite of my little black dresses I wore to the bar, but it did the job, and I tried to rotate through my selection so it didn't seem like I wore the same thing every night if people came back, which they often did.

It felt like he was looking at *me* instead of making eye contact. Like somehow, through that gaze, he saw the twisted bra strap at my left shoulder blade, or the thin strip of my right leg I'd missed when shaving this morning. Like he could see the way my heart accelerated under his attention.

His eyes stayed on mine, steady and unflinching, until Jamie broke the moment.

"You played at the hotel last year, didn't you?" he asked Cara.

"I did some of the Christmas playing last year, and I play at Silverton Springs every few weeks too."

My heart warmed as I watched heat climb to Cara's cheeks. Sometimes, it felt like she was nothing like me. I'd always been a little brash and pushy, but I'd had that too— that shy confidence about my ability and determination.

"You played at the hotel?" Grenier asked her.

The hotel's lobby featured, among its many charms, an absolutely stunning grand piano. They invited locals to sign up for slots to play through the holidays. I absolutely loved that they did this, and Cara had relished the chance to play the instrument last year.

"Just twice after school."

"I must've missed you. Will you sign up again this year?"

"I hope so, if I'm able to get a spot this year. The list was almost full by the time I had a chance to look at it last time."

She'd been thrilled to find two afternoon spots. Low-traffic times, so limited audience, but that'd worked well for last year. I wondered how she'd do with more people milling around, though if her formal recitals and performances at school were any indication, she wouldn't be fazed. Something about the dinky piano in my shop made her clam up, but a stage with a hundred people in the audience? No problem.

"I'll make sure there is. Have your mother let me know your preferred times, and I'll set them aside."

She blinked. "Okay. Yeah. Thank you."

He nodded. "And if you want to play before Christmas, we're always happy to have live music in the lobby. Again, just have your mother let me know when you want to play, and we'll arrange it."

She tilted her head. "You don't even know if I'm good."

"I suspect you're very good indeed if you are your mother's daughter. Beyond that, I've heard people speak of your talent, and Jamie and Bel have mentioned it more than once. I trust their judgment, so I needn't see for myself to know it would be satisfying for listeners."

For once, his eyes didn't flicker to mine, but I wished

they would. I wished I had a key to read his expression so I could figure him out.

Here he was yet again *giving* to me. Of course, he didn't know that being nice to my kid was a level-ten-thousand upgrade from being nice to me in the *How to Charm Quinn Darling* playbook. He couldn't know that, and yet here he was doing it so thoroughly that I feared I might've been coming down with something.

"Bel, did I tell you that Mrs. Wallace assigned us that crazy yellow wallpaper story? Remember telling me about that?" Cara launched into a story about her English teacher, who'd also been my English teacher, and possibly Bel's as well. I couldn't recall since she'd been a few years younger, but Jamie had been with Mr. Holiday.

Everyone listened to Cara expound on the horrors of "The Yellow Wallpaper," and laughed long and loud at her fury with the main character's husband, John.

"Seriously, Jamie, if you'd tried to lock Bel away after she had these two, Mom and I would've stormed in and saved her. And if you put her in some creepy room with crazy wallpaper? Just... no. No."

"I think Bel would've murdered me for isolating her any more than she already was," he said, then grabbed his wife's hand and squeezed it.

Ugh. Such a hurt-so-good feeling when I saw them be sweet—like it was so precious, it made me want to fold up the moment and tuck it away to look at later. To remember that out of darkness and genuinely years of despair, they'd come to this—a full home, two beautiful kids, and restored family relationships.

"And hey, it's a good thing there was no one to do that for you when I was born, right, Mom? Grandpa wouldn't have dared." She nudged me with her elbow.

I snapped back into the moment. "Absolutely. Grandpa would've punched ol' John in the face."

I hoped none of them could hear the raw edge to my voice. I didn't regret not having a husband, and I damn sure didn't regret not having Chuck around when Cara had been born. My mom and grandparents had—like they always had—provided everything I'd needed.

But with motherhood came a kind of isolation I don't think any mother is ready for. And when she's in it, life can be rather lonely and limited. Nights are unending, feeding a baby at all hours in a body that feels only vaguely familiar.

What. Is wrong. With me? Gosh, I was a mess of emotions today, and it was not a good look. I straightened my spine and took the last bite of chili. My phone buzzed, providing a nice distraction. Two texts from Chuck telling me he'd contacted my lawyer—*neat*—and my blessed alarm signaling my five-minute warning before it was time to leave.

About time, too. I was off-kilter in a major way, and it'd serve me well to go bury my head in singing for a few hours until I worked through this miry mess of emotion.

"You have to go?" Cara asked, noticing my phone.

"Yep, time to go."

"Can I stay?" she asked, hope in her eyes.

Ugh. I didn't want to impose on Jamie and Bel, but I didn't want to deny her. It was good for her to be around someone like Jamie—affectionate and loving to his kids, and to her. He'd known her all her life, since weeks after she was born when he'd made it back to see me, and he'd always been an attentive pseudo uncle.

"I'll drive her home, if you're okay with it," Jamie offered.

"If you're sure," I said, discomfort twisting in my gut

even though I told it not to. Him driving Cara home was not some huge debt I'd owe him and was entirely acceptable. It was great, even. They were only here one more day before they headed back to LA until Thanksgiving.

"I'm sure. Have a good time," he said, a look on his face telling me he knew I was off my game tonight.

No surprise. Everyone at the table could probably sense my weirdness, but since I didn't know my deal, none of them were likely to figure it out either.

I said my goodbyes and slipped out the front door, relief hitting me as soon as the crisp fall evening air did.

Slipping into my car, then buckling, I didn't see him come out the door. I didn't notice until he was right next to the car, startling me just like he had earlier.

Why on earth had he followed me?

CHAPTER TEN

Julian

Quinn looked at me like I was a murderer. Like instead of simply standing outside her car waiting for her to turn enough that I could catch her attention, I'd purposefully set a trap and had been lying in wait for her to see me and scare herself into an early grave.

She cranked the car on and rolled down the window. "Yes?"

The irritation shone through her words, blazing at me. As usual, she did nothing in half measures.

"I thought I'd see if you'd decided about the dryer."

Lamest of all excuses to speak with her, but she'd seemed agitated all night, and I hadn't been able to let her leave without... checking in. That impulse she incited in me couldn't be ignored, even if it didn't make sense.

She clearly hadn't appreciated me approaching her at the bar. Maybe it was weird for her to talk with me since I owned the place, but I hoped that wasn't actually a problem. And technically, I wasn't the only owner or even technically her employer.

She sucked in the world's longest breath, then let it out slowly. "I haven't had a chance. Now, if you'll kindly step back from the car, I need to go."

As often happened, I didn't have any way to respond to that, at least not one that would've tripped off my tongue easily. So I nodded and stepped back, hands still in my pocket. She rolled up the window and eased her way around the circle of the driveway before slipping down the street.

After admiring the mature trees flanking Jamie's property and the explosion of fall mums bursting from pots at the entrance, I let myself back inside. Quinn wouldn't be singing for another hour, but I imagined she got good tips, even this early in the evening. When she sang, I could study her. See if I could detect something different, or if it'd all been in my head.

Upon returning to the table, narrowly missing one of the cats' tails lying in ambush, I heard Cara speaking in low tones.

"She's so stubborn."

Jamie nodded. "I wish she'd let me help."

Bel cut in with a hand on Jamie's arm and a wide-eyed look. "That's not fair. She's doing what she feels is right. Having you get them in the door doesn't make it sustainable, and you have to see why taking money from you indefinitely would bother her. This isn't new."

"What's this?" I asked, taking my seat at the table to Bel's left.

"My great-grandparents. They should be living at Silverton Springs, but we can't afford to get them in. They were both in the hospital about a year ago and the medical—"

"I don't think Julian needs all the details," Bel said gently.

Cara's cheeks flooded a deep red. "Right. Well, anyway. She doesn't want Uncle Jamie's help, and neither does Grandma. I get it, but... I don't."

Her shoulders were hunched, and she fiddled with a crumb on her plate. I wondered if Quinn knew how heavily this issue weighed on her daughter. It didn't surprise me to learn Jamie had offered to help or that Quinn had refused. She'd mentioned something to this effect the other day, part of her diatribe on all that'd gone wrong for her that morning, but I hadn't realized the gravity or far-reaching consequences.

And though I'd known she had plans for the building and had wanted the income from the rent from the other tenants, she couldn't have paid it. So I didn't need this slightly guilty feeling I had when realizing my choice to buy the building outright might've affected her plans for her family.

"Well, uh, how's your mom, Julian?"

He must've been truly desperate to change the subject and save Cara any further humiliation to bring up my mother.

"She's still recovering but seems to be doing well. I visited a week ago, and we've talked every few days." Sounded normal enough, but Jamie knew better.

"And is she still as... delightful as ever?" he asked carefully.

I nodded. "As ever. Between detailing her plans for q-4, she has asked me why I haven't produced an heir yet, why I am living in Silverton at all—using colorful adjectives—and indicating that, as usual, the half of me that came from my father is poison and should be ignored."

The human half, she meant. The part of me that felt deeply and longed for more than what I had, more than what I could buy. More than she thought I *could* have, as evidenced by her repeated efforts to engineer engagements between me and her powerful friends' daughters.

Jamie shook his head, and Bel and Cara looked simply horrified.

"She's mean," Cara said. "You shouldn't listen to her, even if she is your mother."

"I agree."

I did. And I tried not to internalize her criticisms. I'd kept myself away from her for years, brushing past in quick exchanges that satisfied the minimal possible threshold for interactions. But she'd been sick this year, and I'd felt oblig-ated. She was my only family. She and my father had divorced when I was ten, but he'd been fifteen years her senior. He passed more than a decade ago, and I missed him with a soul-deep ache that would never fade.

I was all she had left, and vice versa. And that had become an unbearable reality. It'd set my globe spinning at a new tilt, and I'd decided to change things. More than I'd already been on course to change.

I'd started accumulating even more of Silverton. Maybe it was madness, but something in me felt greedy for the place to be mine. Quinn's building was the most recent in a long line of acquisitions in the area, and I had no plans to stop. The more I could do to improve Silverton and physi-cally hold and stake my claim here, the better.

Ally began asking for cookies, and Cara hopped up to help her serve them. The older girl was well-mannered, kind, and apparently quite talented. I found myself hoping she'd request time to play at the hotel so I could hear her and see for myself what kind of skill she had cultivated at such a young age.

"Hey. You good?"

Jamie's low words made me register that Bel had taken the baby, so it was just the two of us. "Yes. I'm fine."

He studied me a moment. "What's up with Quinn?"

I inhaled slowly, debating for a moment before saying simply, "I don't know."

His brow furrowed. "Should I be concerned?"

"If you feel her being around me is concerning, then perhaps. I do plan to continue seeing her." Now that I'd started, I couldn't entertain returning to what it'd been like before. Me wondering about her, but trying not to. Me listening to that voice and absorbing her presence from the stage when I could catch her, but never having a piece of it for myself.

Friendship with Quinn was the endgame, I reminded myself. It was for the greater good of all.

His brows jumped, then relaxed. He knew *seeing her* wasn't dating her. He knew for me, it meant actually seeing her. Insinuating myself into situations where I saw her, more like, but he might even know that.

"Be careful."

My jaw flexed and irritation shot through me, though he wouldn't see any change in my expression. "Will you tell her the same thing?"

His eyes narrowed. "Will I need to?"

"Hey, Jamie, can you take me home in like twenty?" Cara asked from a few feet away.

"Course. Just say when."

"I could take her. I'll be heading out soon anyway." I turned to Cara. "I could drop you, if you'd be comfortable with that. No problem if not." She didn't know me, though I assumed being invited into Jamie and Bel's lives signaled I was fairly trustworthy.

"Oh. Uh, sure. Thanks."

Jamie hadn't stopped skewering me with his ridiculous blue gaze. "You're not just going home? It's a five-minute walk."

I tossed my napkin onto my plate. "I'm heading to the hotel after this. It's not much past it."

Eventually, he gave up trying to read between whatever lines he thought I'd drawn, and we joined Bel and the kids in the kitchen. Jamie pulled Cara aside, clearly asking if she truly did feel comfortable with me taking her home, and she must've said yes, because minutes later, I was starting my car with her in the passenger side seat, cookie container sitting on her lap.

"So, you're like, a millionaire or something?" she asked as we drove down the winding path out of Jamie's—and my —neighborhood.

"Something like that."

She absorbed that. "What'd you do to make your money?"

People rarely asked so boldly. Most people searched online to figure out my roots, but Cara's unashamed questioning charmed rather than irritated. She was a kid figuring out the world, and though she was arguably surrounded by millionaires, she seemed to sense something about my life was different than Jamie's.

"I invented some things a long time ago, right out of college. I built a company and eventually bought a bunch more companies. Made good investments." It was both not at all and exactly that simple.

"What'd you invent?"

"In the very beginning, a few different parts that assisted with artificial limb intelligence, along with the programming and other necessary parts to allow better integration with a human body than there had been."

"Like people who lose an arm or something? Like soldiers?"

Her genuine curiosity made me keep talking.

"Yes, a lot of veterans. But other people too—sometimes people who never had a certain limb from birth, others who lost them in accidents."

"That's really cool. I mean, that's *important*."

Though I would never presume to accurately assess a teenager's moods, something about her words struck me as almost melancholy.

"It is. I don't do anything with all that now, nor have I for years. Sometimes, I think what I do now is rather unimportant."

When I glanced at her, she was gazing out the side window.

"I've always wanted to go to Juilliard. Get trained, then play professionally. But lately, I've been feeling like that's so..."

I waited for her to finish, curious.

She huffed. "So pointless."

"How could it be pointless if the point is to play professionally? That has a very specific and measurable end state." I turned up the narrow path that led to Quinn's house. I'd never driven up the driveway, never been this close to her home. My pulse increased.

"But like, what's the point in that? You helped people. You made someone's life better."

I stopped the car in front of a house so clearly Quinn's. I chuckled under my breath. Browned flowers sat abandoned in a pot, likely because she hadn't had time to attend to them since the freeze last week. A bright turquoise door made the whole place look ridiculous and cheery, and I could see a welcome mat which likely had something cheery or sarcastic scrawled across it. The small porch featured a wooden swing with cushions that'd been used.

A sudden, vivid image of Quinn swinging lazily flashed through my mind and sent my pulse spiking. I'd imagine it later, no doubt, however unbidden it was. The vision itself and the knowledge I'd remember it both should've alarmed me. But just now, I had to address Cara's concerns before she disappeared inside. She'd already opened the door.

"Cara."

She turned.

"Music has value and can make people's lives better. It *does* make people's lives better. It has done so for you, for your mother, and for many people the world over. Making something beautiful, even if it isn't functional, is part of what makes us human."

She clutched the container of cookies close but nodded. "Thanks for the ride." Then she shut the door and raced to the front. After unlocking the door, she sent a quick wave before disappearing inside.

I turned around in the tight space, then proceeded back toward the hotel, wondering if Cara had any idea how captivating her mother was when she performed. If she'd ever felt the lightness in her soul like I did when I heard Quinn's voice. If she had, I couldn't imagine she'd doubt the significance of sharing so much beauty and passion with the world.

CHAPTER ELEVEN

Quinn

The bar was absolutely packed, and though that made for good tips, I could've used a quiet night. As it was, the first set went great, and the constricted feeling in my chest had eased a bit.

After slinging drinks for my entire break, I checked my phone to see a message from Cara saying Grenier had taken her home and that he was nice.

Nice? Nice. That word hit me all kinds of wrong, but I couldn't refute it after everything he'd done. He was pushy and odd and still had that irritating sense of entitlement, like he was owed my responses or information or time, but yeah. I guessed in some weird form of the definition, he *was* nice.

I'd thank him when I saw him, and not for the first time tonight, I wondered if he'd show up. Probably not, after being at Jamie's. But... maybe.

My insides flipped, not at the thought of Grenier, obviously, but at the excitement to sing my next set. Chase and Angel nodded at me and moved toward the stage, and I grabbed one last swig of water before taking my place.

"We're back, everybody," I said, then plucked a bass guitar. "We're going to liven things up a bit right now—that okay with you?"

The crowd applauded, and hoots and hollers overlaid the clapping. Adrenaline raced through me, and I nodded to Chase. Angel counted off, and we were in it. I sang Alanis and Carpenters. We did The Rolling Stones, and the Beatles, and basically all our favorite rock covers. By the end of the set, some of my restlessness had calmed, and I felt high on adrenaline and the liquid joy that dripped into my veins when I performed. A pure cocktail of dopamine and serotonin.

As I was stepping down, a familiar silhouette caught my eye. Sure enough, Grenier sat in his usual chair with his eyes glued to mine. My fingers tingled as I approached the bar, poured a shot, and knocked it back.

"Whoa, Quinney. Gettin' all riled up. I like it," Brandon said, flashing one of his lady-killer smiles even as he poured a Guinness and somehow flirted with the girl in front of him at the same time.

I needed the liquid courage, though it likely hadn't been my best idea. I didn't drink often, and I didn't do it on a half-empty stomach. I'd lost my appetite for dinner the minute Grenier had walked into Jamie's house, and though I'd eaten what I could, I felt the burn of the alcohol all the way into my stomach and knew I'd been hasty.

Too late now, though. I only had about twenty minutes until my last set, and then I'd be folded back into the crush of the bar, likely slinging drinks until well after midnight if the current buzz in the room didn't deceive. I marched up to him and stopped when I bumped his knee with my leg. The low lighting, and honestly, the adrenaline, making me borderline jittery caused me to be even clumsier than usual.

"Ms. Darling."

My stomach dropped low. So low.

"Thanks for giving Cara a ride," I said, sounding pleasingly unaffected by that deep, dulcet tone of his.

"Pleasure was mine. She's a smart, interesting girl." He balanced his empty glass on one edge and rocked it side to side, not looking away from me.

A breathy, silent laugh punched out of me at his words. Why did I like that so much? That he'd said she was smart and interesting instead of beautiful or sweet? And why did it surprise me that he'd said that?

I reached for his highball, drawn to him as usual. "I'll get you another."

A beat passed, like it so often did with him. Like he had nothing else in the world to do but look at me, which was perfectly at odds with his energy and demeanor otherwise.

"If you like."

Woo. Nothing about that should seem sexy. It shouldn't. Me offering to take his drink and refresh it, and him saying that. But it hit me in the gut and made my insides twist.

Yeah. Shouldn't have had that shot.

"I'll be right back," I said and took the cold glass, exhaling sharply with pent-up energy as I paced back to the bar, certain his eyes were on me the whole way.

Five minutes later, I'd poured another of Grenier's drinks—an aged scotch that cost a ridiculous amount of money per ounce—and helped Brandon express a few items before carrying a small tray with me. I'd given Jeanine a nod to say I had Grenier, and she'd winked, fortunately unperturbed by my helping her out. It was busy, and she knew me well enough to know I wasn't trying to make a grab for her tips.

Under his watchful gaze, I moved to set the scotch on the small side table next to him. He took the drink from me before I could release it to the surface, and our fingers brushed when his closed around the glass.

My stomach took up a position on the US women's Gymnastics team and started a floor routine.

Had we ever touched? Could I possibly be more aware of this man?

"Thank you, Ms. Darling."

I shifted in my heels, wishing I'd worn something more sensible for the busy night. "You should probably call me Quinn."

He nodded. "Then call me Julian."

I swallowed. "Okay. Have a good night, Julian."

He speared me with that intensity of his for a few seconds before my brain kicked in and I forced myself to move. Stepping away, I finally broke eye contact and turned, but stopped when he spoke.

"Are you available for lunch Tuesday?"

My heart thumped as I slowly turned back to him. He still occupied the chair in that relaxed way he had here and nowhere else. Anywhere else I'd seen him, even at Jamie's, he'd seemed on alert, at least a little.

"Lunch?" I said brilliantly.

The stare. Of course. Because Julian Grenier did not strike me as a man who repeated himself, and here was proof.

"What time were you thinking? I'm at the shop, but I could get someone to cover, or even close if we keep it short. I—"

The slight shake of his head cut me off.

"No, don't close. See if you can get someone to cover. If not, I'll come to you."

My mouth dried out, and I silently begged my brain to get a grip. What was this? Another business meeting? A lunch date? Him coming to secretly check out the shop for some reason?

Although, why would he need to do that? First, his assistant had been in very recently, so she could've reported on anything he wanted to know. And second, he could walk in himself anytime he wanted.

But as far as I knew, he'd never been in. I only had one part-time employee, and he probably wouldn't have mentioned that Julian had visited unless he'd bought something huge. So maybe he had browsed around at some point.

"You—should I call your assistant? Or...?"

He stood in one swift movement, less grace and more efficiency, and whipped out a thin wallet. He pulled a card from inside and held it out me. "No, call me. Use the personal number there. I'll answer."

I hoped I didn't appear as stunned as I felt. But stunned, I was. I'd heard more than a handful of people talk about how impossible it was to get Julian Grenier's personal information. Kelly served as gatekeeper. It added to the air of mystery that surrounded him, and this moment did nothing to clear it.

I took the card, pinching it between two fingers all kinds of casual-like. "Will do."

Brandon shouted my name, and I saw him widen his eyes in a silent plea for help. The crowd had thickened, and he and Bobby were slammed.

"Better go," I said, then turned and left. I'd like to say I didn't speed-walk on the verge of a jog away from him, but I'd be lying if I did that.

I'd also like to say I spent the rest of the night—making drinks, singing through my last set—completely unaware of him in the far corner of the room. But that would most definitely be a lie. Every one of my senses had been stitched to him. He moved, I glanced up. He tapped out a message on his phone, I sensed it.

His eyes burned into me while I sang, and my chest tightened with anticipation and awareness. The last set was always slower, more ballads and angst, and I wished we could flip it and crank out something fast-paced and rushed. Something to mask the adrenaline just knowing he was watching sent through me.

By the time I stepped off stage, I felt wild, and only the still-bustling bar crowd kept me from going back over to Julian and... and... *what?* I had no idea what I'd do. I didn't even know how I felt beyond that odd, admittedly thrilling sensation that he was watching me and I didn't mind.

At all.

But after cranking out what felt like a thousand drinks, my hands on autopilot, the high from singing and our earlier interaction faded and embarrassment set in. He'd asked me to meet him for lunch and had given me his card. That wasn't date material. That was business-level stuff. He hadn't purposefully touched me. He hadn't flirted.

He couldn't help it if he had resting smolder face, and every look he gave felt like it'd sizzle right down to my bones if it had the chance. He couldn't be oblivious to how strikingly handsome he was, but that didn't seem to be something he ever leveraged. He wasn't like Brandon, who winked and smiled and gave little hot looks to the women he served. Julian was severe and serious and just... different.

And despite the fact that I should still dislike him, or at least it seemed like I should, I didn't. The part of my brain that had relegated him to *jerkwad greedy billionaire* status had been silenced by his actions. He'd helped me more than once, and even if some of that was a little off, he didn't seem perturbed when I got upset. He didn't take offense when I told him he'd done something wrong—he merely suggested I do whatever I needed to fix it. Maybe it should bother me he'd overstepped in the first place, but after his taking Cara home and even seeing him with Ally at Jamie's, I could tell.

All my defenses against a full-blown crush on Julian had been built up on the fact that he was a jerk. Selfish. Money-grubbing. Someone who'd built up a business so gargantuan he had more money than some small countries. That'd created a nice little barrier between me and anything beyond appreciating the salt-and-pepper streaks at the sides of his head or his perfectly trimmed stubble. Or how he wore a suit. Or how he held his glass of scotch.

Honestly, there were a million things to attract someone to him, but all that money had been an easy barrier. And that was still a stone wall to any *real* feelings. I couldn't sincerely date someone who was that different from me socioeconomically.

But the crush? It'd officially taken up root in my chest, because I had to admit it—Julian Grenier wasn't a bad guy.

CHAPTER TWELVE

Julian

Pluck sat between an ice cream and smoothie shop, Scoop, that I imagined would be out of business within a few months since no one wanted ice cream or smoothies in winter, and Keller Accountancy. The front façade had ridiculous charm with deep red brick and black trim on the windows and doors, as did the whole building, which included the accountancy business, Scoop, the flower shop Bloom, and two upstairs apartments on the Silver Street side. The horseshoe shape was capped with the accountants and the opposite side of the building lined the end of Lily Lane.

I'd inspected the building via images, a tour of the apartments and accountant's offices, but I'd never been inside Pluck. It'd felt like a forbidden fruit, and if I entered the place without a plan, I'd be in danger of knowing too much.

I already knew too much about Quinn Darling, and

against my better judgment, I liked her far more than she liked me. That disparity should prove troubling except I'd never had the experience before. The novelty of feeling something for someone who appeared to, at best, tolerate you? Intriguing.

Most often, my romantic relationships had felt more like transactions at best and money grabs at worst. That more than anything had resulted in an overwhelming disinterest for dating or attempting to find someone. Friendships came infrequently but I had solid ones—Jamie, Jack, a few others worth guarding.

But that'd changed. *I'd* changed since stepping foot in these mountains with Jamie all those years ago, and had slowly begun shifting toward something else. My mother's mindset toward life and her utter solitude save for me and her staff had driven the change home.

I didn't want to be a financially wealthy man alone at the end of his life. Yes, I loved money and the power it gave me—access, ability to make change, opportunity to build. But I had more money than I could spend in a lifetime even if I gave away half, and I did give quite a bit away.

What I wanted was more. Something like what I'd seen filling every corner of Jamie's house this past weekend. Friendship. Family. Belonging. Joy. Peace.

As much as these thoughts sounded like a Hallmark card, I'd long since stopped the tendency to feel ashamed of wanting these things. At nearly forty, I had no interest in pretending I was lost. I wasn't lost. Like I had my whole life, I knew exactly where I was and exactly what I wanted. My father had exemplified genuine love for me—I wasn't one of those men who'd never experienced it. And I loved quite a few of my friends, Jamie included. But romantic love? That was foreign to me and not something I'd imagined being possible.

Since moving to Silverton, I'd been watching and waiting. Sadie Miller had seemed like a possibility, particularly once she started showing her face more often. She was brilliant and certainly beautiful. She also came from an extremely wealthy family and based on everything I'd dug up, had no spendy tendencies. I could've cared for her deeply, I imagined. Especially after talking with her a handful of times about her business months ago, I believe I would've.

But would I have *fallen* in love? Unlikely. Falling wasn't calculated or planned, and I had a track record to prove I rarely did anything I didn't plan on doing.

All that said, the more I interacted with Quinn, the more my reactions to her were unpredictable and vastly different from anything I'd ever done, as evidenced by my *how can I help* approach thus far. The more a possibility of *something* brightened between us.

The challenge now was getting it.

I was going for friendship. This tack should work. As far as I'd seen, people rallied around each other in Silverton because they were friends, which made them genuinely care. I didn't need the people of Silverton to help me, but I wanted to fit. I wanted this place to become a part of that full life I'd allowed myself to pursue once I arrived here.

I pulled at the handle of Pluck at one minute to twelve. Regrettably, I did have a schedule for today and had no more than an hour to spend with Quinn. Whether she'd give me that much time remained to be seen.

She'd seemed more receptive to me lately, though. She didn't automatically snarl when we talked at the bar the other night. Maybe because I'd taken her daughter home?

Maybe because she'd started to see me as a person rather than a suit?

Whatever the change, I'd take it and capitalize on it, just like I would in any other scenario where I saw something I wanted and moved strategically to get it. Though it would've been miles easier, purchasing Quinn's friendship wasn't exactly up for option, so... here I was.

A bell chimed overhead, and I stepped through into a cluttered wonderland of music and instruments. Straight ahead in the back of the store, a man sat hunched over a guitar, picking at the strings and fingers flying. *Quite good*, I had to say.

Quinn sat next to him, beautiful head bowed, eyes shut like she needed to concentrate on what she was hearing. I couldn't see her face but wondered what the expression would be. I approached but stopped a good ten feet short of the pair, recognizing they were doing something and my interrupting would be unwelcomed.

After another minute, the man hit a final note, then one long strum that he let sing for a moment before dampening with his hand.

"Yeah, I hear what you're saying. It's definitely off in there somewhere, but I'm going to need to think about it. Also, I want to say your E string is old or something. You want me to restring it this afternoon?" Quinn tilted her head and the man nodded.

"That'd be great. I typically do it myself, but I have work. I could pick it up around five. You want to grab dinner after?"

My back stiffened, and though I made no sound, Quinn's eyes shot to mine. "Oh, hey, Julian. I must've missed the bell while Chase was playing."

"No problem."

This Chase person rose to standing and extended a hand. I recognized him from the bar, and as one of Quinn's bandmates, so to be fair I shouldn't be standing here calling him *this Chase person.*

"Nice to meet you. Chase Palmer."

I shot out a hand, bracing myself for contact. We shook, and I immediately relaxed when I felt his firm, dry grip. I didn't have time to discombobulate over a cold fish handshake, nor would I, but relief swept through me that I wouldn't be fighting the memory of such a sensation all afternoon.

"I've seen you at the club. You're quite good."

He smiled. "Thanks. Quinn makes us all look good."

My eyes met hers. "That she does."

She lifted the instrument and bustled behind the counter a few feet away. "I'll have it ready by five, Chase."

"Dinner?" he asked again.

I had to hand it to him—he wasn't going to miss taking his shot. Good for him, even if it did make him a little twit.

"Oh, sorry. I have to grab Cara from one lesson, get her to the other, and then—"

He waved her off. "No problem, just had to ask." His attention turned to me. "Back to work I go. Nice to meet you officially."

"Likewise," I said, relieved he hadn't hung around any longer and ridiculously pleased at Quinn's swift dismissal of his dinner offer.

I shouldn't have cared. I had no claim on her and no right to feel glad she'd rejected the man. Did that stop me? No.

I could admit it. I was a greedy bastard. I wanted her to see me and just me right now. She hadn't been able to come to me, so I'd come to her. Friends did this—they met for lunch. But I had no desire to share time with her bandmate.

"Give me a sec to write myself a note about this, and then we can eat out back, if you like?" Her eyes dipped to the plastic bag I held in one hand.

"Of course."

She scrawled on a small notepad using a purple pen with what looked like a fine tip. I wrenched my eyes away and chose not to think about how awful writing with fine-tipped pens felt, and instead took in the details of the shop. Brass and string instruments everywhere, sheet music papering an entire wall, and what felt like every possible space filled. Cluttered, but it felt like a quaint mess instead of a stressful one. Like if you stayed long enough, you'd find all the secrets instead of uncovering dust bunnies and garbage.

"Okay, all set. Ready?" She tipped her head to one side, a subtle invitation.

I followed behind the counter, wondering what it'd be like to wear jeans and a T-shirt to work and feel so completely at home in a space like Quinn did. She led us through a cramped back room, then out an exit to a surprisingly charming space behind the building.

"I saw this on the plans but didn't realize it'd been paved." Small red brick hexagons created a tightly woven patio almost the same size as the building itself.

"Mr. Corrigan did this about two years before he decided to sell. The former owners were all for it since he did it out of pocket. He'd planned to have little open mic nights here when Othello's was there." She nodded to the building that butted up against the back, which I recalled had sported a *Great Things Coming Soon* sign for more than a year, last I checked.

"You don't think it would be successful now?" I asked, taking a seat at the small glass-topped wrought-iron table across from her. The tabletop was probably the diameter of my forearm and the chairs looked unstable, but so far, they held our weight and likely, she'd sat here a hundred times or more.

"I don't have the bandwidth for it right now. Wish I did, but between weekends at the bar and other obligations, I just don't. My employee wouldn't be up to running something like that either."

She took the bag I placed in the center of the minuscule table and pulled out two sandwiches.

"Yours is number one," I said, feeling oddly off-kilter to be sitting in this quiet little courtyard, the patio scattered with orange and deep red leaves, this woman across from me.

This woman.

"So, uh, how—er, um, you know, how's it going?" she asked, then took a giant bite of her sandwich.

I blinked. "I'm not sure how to answer that."

She covered her mouth and laughed—at least, I thought it was a laugh. After a moment, she swallowed, took a gulp from her water bottle, and flashed a smile. "Sorry. I'm just, uh, nervous."

I chewed my bite and swallowed before asking, "Why?"

She didn't need to know that I felt as close to nervous as I ever did when around her. That sitting this close to her, all alone out here, felt like I'd won something and like I was right about to lose it, too. I hadn't realized, until right this moment, how seldomly I put myself at the mercy of someone else. In fact, I never did it, ever. But right now, I sat across from her, waiting for the verdict of whether she'd accept the gesture of this lunch.

"I guess I'm just not sure what you're going to say. I don't really know you, and I'm nervous you're going to decide to raise the rent after all, or—"

I waved a hand to stop her. "I'm not raising the rent. You've already signed the new rental agreement that indicates there is no raise. That's binding for you, but also for me."

She inhaled, then released the breath and with it, some of the tension that'd kept her shoulders stiff. "Okay."

We ate in silence, and I wondered how long she'd let it go on. I could handle silence, even a strained one, for hours. Days. Months. Not that I wanted silence between us—quite the opposite. But my natural inclination to push wouldn't serve me here, so I'd resolved before arriving to hang back and let her come to me, so to speak.

"So, not about the rent, then."

I smothered a smile by taking a sip of my water, then responded, "No."

She waited, clearly expecting me to expound. When I didn't, she pursed her lips, a determined expression crossing her lovely face. "Okay, so, why are we here? I mean, not to be rude, which I realize is a little new for us, but I don't get it."

"You don't get why we're having lunch together?"

Her eyes ticked back and forth between mine before her shoulders sank. "I'm sorry, Julian, but I'm missing it. Can you explain why we're here?"

I inhaled the fresh autumn air and a hint of her clean, feminine scent. Nothing nauseatingly floral or fruity, but clean and fresh and alluring enough that I suddenly imagined what it'd be like to track my lips along her neck and get closer to her so I could breathe her in. My pulse shot through the roof— *Not a productive line of thinking.* We were supposed to be friends. Nothing more. I wouldn't entertain those kinds of thoughts about her, however tempting.

My gaze jumped to hers, and relief struck inwardly when I saw she clearly hadn't read my mind. And of course she hadn't, but I wasn't used to having those thoughts about a woman, and especially not when she sat right next to me.

"Like you said, we don't know each other. So we're remedying that."

Her mouth opened to speak, then closed. Then opened. "Okay. Uh. Tell me about yourself."

She seemed so perturbed by my response and even asking her question. She looked adorable with her brow slightly furrowed, still confused at why we were here. I couldn't very well come out and say why I was here though, could I? Telling someone you wanted to win their friendship instead of just buying it out when the bulk of your exchanges had centered around disagreements didn't set a man up for success.

So, I decided to dive in, both feet. "I like to read but have been terrible at making time for it lately. I would rather eat a steak than anything else in the world, but don't let myself more than twice a month. I'm an only child, and my father died a little over a decade ago. I enjoy music a great deal, which is a kind of triumph as I tend to be extremely sensitive to noise."

Her mouth dropped open like what I'd just said had truly shocked her. I filtered back through everything I'd said —maybe mentioning losing my father so casually? Had I blacked out and told her I wanted to be her friend in order to belong here and find acceptance in the town? Had I said something I couldn't take back?

"What? What did I say?"

She shook her head just slightly. "Uh… nothing. I mean, that was great. I just kind of expected to get your resume and a list of all your financial holdings or something."

My furrowed brow asked the question for me.

"I keep doing this. I expect you to be this… I keep judging you. And it's not fair. I'm sorry."

Then she set her hand on mine, ever so lightly, and my stomach clutched. I yanked my hand back and tucked it under my thigh, all while watching her eyes go wide. Frustration crashed through me. She'd just touched me, and I'd done the opposite of what was expected of a friend.

"I—I'm sorry. I didn't mean to—I'm sorry." Quinn swallowed hard.

I needed to say something, but my throat had locked up. I nodded and willed my tongue to move. To reassure her she'd done nothing wrong—that it was me.

"Someone's in the shop. I'll be right back, if you're okay." Her gaze swept over me, checking for other signs of distress, I supposed.

I managed another nod.

"Okay. Be back in a few."

I scrubbed my hands through my hair and pulled at it, soothing myself and working to push away the frustration with my response. I had heard the ring of the shop's bell somewhere in the back of my mind—she hadn't made that up to escape this horrifically awkward moment.

I rarely had trouble with this kind of contact anymore. But I hadn't anticipated it, and obviously, I'd been more on edge than I realized. And now, I'd have to explain.

Five minutes later, she returned, arms crossed and tucked into her body like she was afraid she'd do something to upset me.

Damn, I hated that I'd put her on edge. "I'm sorry."

"You don't need to apologize. I shouldn't have touched you without your consent. I didn't—"

"You can touch me. You can. You don't have to ask. I just wasn't ready for it."

She'd shrunk herself up. She sat in the same spot she had minutes ago, but all her warmth and energy had coiled into itself and hidden away. I hated that my reaction had done that, but I hoped if I could explain, she'd understand. She'd unfold again, and I wouldn't have to start back at square one.

"I mentioned sensitivity to sound. I'm also sensitive to other things, one of which is unexpected physical contact. I don't often touch other people, and when I do it's purposeful, direct—things like handshakes that I initiate."

"Our hands touched at the bar. When I handed you the drink."

I could hear the unspoken question. Why hadn't I recoiled then?

Though normally I wouldn't have been quite so direct, I wanted her to understand me. "I wanted to touch you then —to connect with you in a way I wouldn't with strangers. Welcomed it."

"And just now, you didn't?"

"I wasn't expecting it. We haven't had a physical relationship—" Her cheeks burned red almost instantaneously, and I rushed to clarify. "Of any kind. Beyond a handshake. I didn't assume that our friendship at this juncture would include touching, and I'm sorry for startling you."

She grabbed her water and chugged down a few gulps like it would steady her. I needed her to speak and tell me if I'd just ruined any chance I had for anything at all with her. She might not realize how much I wanted more than polite business interactions, but now she at least knew I wanted some level of connection.

"Are you okay now? Is there anything I can do to make it better?"

I huffed a frustrated breath. "No, Quinn. I'm fine. Thank you. If you're not completely put off, I believe it's your turn to tell me about yourself."

She licked her lips, then smiled—small, but genuine. The tension in my back and neck eased slightly, and we both inched back into conversation and eating. Ten minutes later, my alarm buzzed in my pocket and I said my farewells. She thanked me for lunch and walked me to the door of the shop.

She didn't touch me. In fact, she'd folded her arms and braced them against her body, almost like she had to keep herself from doing so. When I exited the door and left her behind, I felt sick. Not because of what'd gone wrong, though plenty had—I'd been rigid before I'd pulled away from her.

No, it wasn't all the things that'd gone wrong that made me ill.

It was the reality that I barely knew this woman, and yet, I wanted to be her friend. No longer was this simply a way into favor with Silverton—I couldn't pretend that was all. Nor was it that fascination she'd always presented. No. I liked her—liked being around her—and I wanted to call her friend, have her inside my inner circle, as much as I'd ever wanted that with anyone.

And maybe... Maybe more, too.

CHAPTER THIRTEEN

Quinn

Julian Grenier occupied my every waking thought for the rest of the week. Well, except when I was working on Cara's winter formal dress because I couldn't think about other things while sewing that silky material, but still.

He was so... unexpected.

A bang on the front porch had me sloshing tequila over the side of the glass. "Come in!"

A cacophony of sound trailed inside as Sarah, Dahlia, and Sadie entered through the side door, chatting and laughing like there were ten of them instead of three.

"The principal told him, if he wants to date adults, he has to be at least eighteen. He said he turns eighteen next month, so then the principal had to further explain how it wasn't okay, even though I'm a substitute, and... *ugh*," Sarah said, her voice tinged with horror.

Dahlia cackled, and Sadie looked both amused and horrified.

"What's this now? You're trying to date at the high school?" I added lime wedges to the sides of pint glasses, then set them on a tray.

"Ew. *No.* I had a student who's a senior give me a note that I promptly reported to the principal. It was... inappropriate." Her cheeks darkened.

"Oh. *Oh*," I said, reading the blush for mortification rather than a pleased, sweet blush. Sarah was the queen of a blush—I'd swear looking at a menu could make her blush. But only because she had super pale skin. Whatever the case, she broadcasted her feelings pretty clearly, and this time, she wasn't pleased.

She nodded, taking the tray, and Dahlia came into the kitchen to grab the other tray I'd loaded up with chips and salsa and guac. Sadie handed me a fresh bottle of tequila and a bag of limes.

"You planning on getting crazy tonight?" I asked her.

She grinned. "No. Not especially. But I didn't think bread would go with our menu, so tequila was my second choice."

I liked that about Sadie—that her generosity came first in the form of her excellent bread. Dang, I was glad I'd gotten to know her these last few months.

"What's Warrick up to tonight? Is he gonna be okay without you for a whole evening?" I teased.

They'd been attached at the hip since summer. I figured wedding bells would be chiming for them any minute. It seemed like everyone was pairing up, though maybe that was just Wyatt and Warrick. Sarah, Dahlia, and I were still single.

I took a glass from the tray and settled into the sectional couch. Honestly, this couch was my pride and joy. Bright red and so soft it was ridiculous, made of some magical material that I'd been able to get red wine and dirt and blood and pen ink out of... seriously the best thing I'd ever bought. Seeing Dahlia sprawled on the other end, Sarah snuggled into the middle, and Sadie sitting in the overstuffed chair on the other side of the coffee table made me feel all kinds of warm and fuzzy.

Also maybe that was the tequila hitting.

"So I saw something the other day that I was wondering about, and I've been trying to figure out how to talk to you about it." Sarah said this calmly, but like she was tiptoeing up to a line I couldn't identify.

"I'm terrible with suspense and surprises. Just tell me."

She took a gulp of her drink, swallowed hard, and set it down. "It's not a huge deal. But I saw Cara talking to a guy out in front of the school, and I could've sworn it was your ex—"

The breath I'd sucked in at the word *ex* made my half-swallowed drink clog my throat. I coughed, then sputtered, working the fiery liquid down my throat and gasping for breath. All of this while my rage-o-meter cranked from *Life is good* to *Get the shovel!*

"I wouldn't be shocked. I'm pissed, but I wouldn't put it past him to try to insinuate himself into her life like that instead of doing it above board. Ughghg." I groaned in frustration.

Sarah gave me a pleading look. "I'm sorry, I figured you'd rather know."

"Yes. Absolutely. I need to call him and see if he'll fess up, but I definitely do want to know anything like that." I scrubbed a hand down my face. "This is like the month of men trying to drive me insane."

"He has to back off, right? He can't be doing that, can he?" Dahlia asked.

"I mean, he can talk to her. It's not like there's a restraining order. He's not a danger to her, he's just a big fat jerk. She knows who he is, but they don't talk, so I don't know if she'd be curious, or excited, or mad... I don't know."

And that was part of the problem with the way I'd been dealing with this. I wanted to protect her from hurt, so I hadn't talked to her. It'd been weeks since he'd first started reaching out, and I could tell he was getting more and more intense about it. But I hadn't wanted to expose her to him, to build her hopes up and then have him disappoint her.

"Can you ask her?"

Sadie's quiet question cut through my self-loathing.

"I should, right? Even if it might hurt her?"

She nodded. "I'm sure it's hard. I can't imagine wanting to protect her, but knowing you need to talk to her about something that might hurt her. But loving her and showing her respect mean doing that, I think."

I didn't know her whole story, but part of Sadie's past involved her parents basically ignoring her history with anxiety. They didn't want to make their lives, or hers, harder by talking about it. So in the realm of parental communication, Sadie's words meant something. Also, she was just one of those people who spoke rarely enough that when she did, it was always worth listening to.

"I will. I will this weekend when we have some time together and she doesn't have to deal with school or lessons or anything else." She was at an extended rehearsal for an upcoming recital tonight, thus the perfect timing for a little girls' night in.

"What was it that you said about men driving you nuts this week? Who else is besides Chuck?" Dahlia asked.

I exhaled slowly, wondering how much to share about the whole Julian thing. Then I remembered, I really wasn't a secret keeper. I wanted their take, which was part of the reason I'd invited them here instead of planning on eating out. Also, I didn't have cash for eating out with drinks, so this worked better.

"So... Julian Grenier owns my building. He was going to raise the rent, but I asked him not to, so he said he wouldn't. Then he was really nice to me at dinner at Jamie's, he gave Cara a ride home, and we had lunch two days ago for no reason..."

I looked up to find them all blinking back at me, varying degrees of surprise on each of their pretty faces.

"For no reason? What does that mean?" Sarah asked, carefully setting her drink back on the coffee table.

"Well, I thought he'd set up the lunch as a meeting to review the new lease, even though I'd signed it last week. Then he said it wasn't. And that he just wanted to get to know me. Oh, and he bought me a new dryer and paid for Chip to come fix my pipe." Couldn't forget that little gem, which still made me want to shrivel up and die a little.

"Wait, what? You told me you'd gotten a new dryer, but you conveniently left out that Julian Grenier paid for it."

Sarah and I had grown close since she'd gotten back. We'd been friendly in high school, even if not actually friends, but we'd really clicked since she'd gotten back earlier this year. I hoped she wasn't hurt I hadn't told her the whole truth about the dryer, but I hadn't known what to think, and reporting on it before I'd figured out my own feelings seemed odd.

"I'm not keeping it. Obviously, I can't."

"Why obviously?" Dahlia asked. Sadie's head tilted like she had the same question.

"Are you kidding? I hardly know the man. I can't go accepting gifts like that. Or... I mean.. he said he didn't want anything from me, just to be friends, but that's pretty unbelievable, right?"

Wasn't it? No one paid that much money for something and didn't expect a fairly large return for it.

Surprisingly, Sadie spoke first. "I don't know. I've talked with Julian a few times in the last few months, and he's always super direct. I feel like he's almost honest to a fault. He says what he wants, and he means what he says. So if he says he just wants to be your friend, I would actually believe him."

We all digested her words for a few moments before Sarah spoke again. "So your lunch this week was..."

I swallowed, knowing she wasn't asking for logistics of what we ate. "It was different."

Wasn't that the truth? I'd been terrified I might've offended him by touching him. I didn't know if I'd ever felt so awkward, and my foot-in-mouth disorder tended to place me in awkward situations not irregularly. But afterward, he'd explained so matter-of-factly, and my heart had twisted in my chest. And it hadn't been bad. It hadn't been pity. It'd been with empathy and longing to only do things that made him comfortable.

And I could still hear his voice—rich and low when he'd explained why he hadn't startled when our fingers brushed last weekend. *I wanted to touch you then... Welcomed it.* My heart flipped despite the part of his explanation about connection that made it all a little less sexy and more friendly. That was all he'd ever indicated, wasn't it?

"Do you... like him?" Dahlia's confused tone aptly embodied the feeling in the room.

"I have no idea. No?" I swallowed. "Maybe?"

Sarah bit her lip to hide her surprise. "I can see it. I can. He's hot. And super smart. And not exactly polite but courteous in his own way."

Sadie jumped in. "He is. Plus, he's actually very generous. I guess you've gathered that personally, but the offers he made me were ridiculous. Really terrible business deals, which I know he isn't doing accidentally."

I nodded. "I heard he paid one and a half times asking for my building. I'd thought that was all a bid to steal it from me, but now..."

Now I'd come to terms with a few things. First, I couldn't have bought it *and* maintained it, let alone made the upgrades Kelly had listed out as scheduled for the coming months at one of our first few interactions before I'd even sat down with Julian. Even if I'd been approved for the loan, it wouldn't have made sense for the owners to sell to me when someone else had cash in hand. And second, I wondered if Julian had given so much over because he'd known the owners were retiring. They were moving to Florida in search of warmer weather, and he'd sent them off with quite a blessing.

None of what I'd learned about him in the last few weeks added up to the picture I'd had of him in my head. It was like I'd imagined him one way based on evidence I'd had, but since I'd actually interacted with him, I'd discovered the evidence had only been partial.

"Now, you might be about to date a billionaire?"

A thrill shot through me. "What? No. Date?"

Sarah tucked her lips between her teeth to smother her

smile again, and Dahlia and Sadie gave me looks like they knew I was ridiculous.

"You aren't attracted to him?"

I snorted. "I mean, I have eyes."

All three of them shared delighted smiles and a few laughs.

"What? He's all serious and sexy. It's irritating. And it's... I don't know. I can't figure out if I like him or if he's just thrown me for a loop enough that I'm off balance and easily toppled. It's like the next thing he says is going to nudge me over some unknown edge, and I can't tell what that means."

"I think that means you like him, friend," Dahlia said, then raised her glass in a silent toast.

Sighing, I slumped down into the couch. "*Aahhghhgh.*"

We all laughed at my dramatics, but Sarah had a look that said she had something to say, so I raised my brows at her, waiting.

"I'm just saying. You've got a hot billionaire who seems interested. This doesn't seem like a problem."

I chuckled. "It's ridiculous. Plus, I honestly don't know that he's attracted to me. He hasn't mentioned dating or anything romantic. Not really. It's all been—gah, he's so direct, but I feel like there's a crazy amount of room for interpretation. All he's said is friendship, and I'm inclined to believe him even if my brain gets other ideas."

"So ask him what he means. Or just ask him out." Dahlia shrugged a shoulder like that would be no big deal.

Like walking up to Julian Grenier wouldn't take every bit of guts I had. Like I even knew if I wanted to go out with him and—*was I really even thinking about this?*

"I say at least make sure he knows you'd be up for it. It sounds like maybe you've been a little cagey. So now, make sure he can see you're at least up for seeing what might happen."

My stomach flipped.

Sure. Yeah. Just tell the bossy, kind, superhot billionaire that I maybe kind of wanted to see what happened.

Cake.

CHAPTER FOURTEEN

Julian

Quinn seemed nervous tonight.

One of the things that made her such a joy to watch was her ease on stage. She didn't get ruffled by shouts or requests, and sometimes, she took them and slayed them. She had such an easy way with people, though I would bet she didn't see herself in that light.

But tonight, she looked like she hadn't slept. Or maybe she'd been crying? Something about her face seemed... off. Still painful to look at and not be close to, of course. Her full lips shaping the words of each song, her bright white teeth, and the way her brow furrowed on high notes. Yes. Confirmed. Gorgeous. Not news—any person attracted to women would've noticed that.

But her makeup couldn't hide the shadows under her eyes, and in them. At first, I'd thought I was seeing something, but when she teared up during a song in the second set, I knew. While Quinn was passionate and unleashed on stage, tears were an aberration. She kept it together, touching the emotion like she scooped her hand down into water from a slow-moving boat, coasting along and dragging at the feeling, but not pulling it into her.

Tonight, she got drenched in it. I cursed not knowing her better. If I did, maybe I'd be able to read her more clearly and know without having to ask. That's what friends —real friends—were for. Maybe I'd suss out the problem and fix it before another cursed tear fell—based on my typical reaction to her in any state of agitation, who knew what I'd do to stop her?

My eyes followed her every move. Maybe I shouldn't have allowed myself the pleasure—normally, I at least attempted to keep to myself unless she was singing. That'd become more difficult, but tonight, it proved impossible. Completely.

By the last song of her second set, my heart had grown heavy in my chest. Her voice rang out, soulful and beautiful, pulling every person in the room into the whirl of longing and grief and pure angst of the song. By the end, my hand pressed over my suit on the left side, like it might soothe the ache there.

The audience erupted into applause and she smiled. Chase, the guitarist, and the drummer both waved, and Chase dipped his head to say they'd be back in twenty while Quinn practically ran off stage.

My pulse picked up, the urge to follow her as she slipped into the kitchen and out of sight churning in my blood. Technically, I could go into the kitchen if I had to, but I had no desire to interrupt the dining room's last hour.

Plus, she wouldn't have stayed in there, I didn't think. More likely she'd snuck through to escape into the back hallway, away from the crowd of the bar.

I stood, straightened my jacket, and fixed my tie as I walked. Men and women alike eyed me as I moved quickly from my chair at the back of the bar to the exit. There wasn't all that much space, the bar being fairly intimate in size, and yet the popularity of these weekends with Quinn singing made it feel crammed with parishioners seeking her voice.

Down one long hallway, around a corner and down another, I slowed my pace as I came to find her pacing in front of the double doors making the back entrance. One arm tucked under the other, her gaze focused on the ground just in front of her feet where she walked. She glanced at her phone, scowled, and punched through the right-side door.

She hadn't seen me. Maybe for the best. She might simply need air after an overwhelming day. But before the door shut, I heard her say, "Whatever you have to say, just say it and be done."

Her tone rang cold and sharp, a blade against the person approaching. I'd heard a version of that tone before, when she'd been on the ropes about the rent, accusing me of being a greedy jerk buying up her town. Alarm shot through me as I waited, wondering what this was. Who would meet her outside the hotel? Anyone she knew even remotely well would meet her inside, wouldn't they?

I shoved open the door and stepped out to find a man holding her wrist in what looked to be a painful grip based on his white knuckles and Quinn's gritted, "I said, let go of me."

"Remove your hands from her," I said, when the man didn't instantly drop her hand.

His attention shot to me. "This is none of your business."

"Someone touching another person without their consent *is* my business, especially when it happens on my property. Let her go. Now."

He dropped Quinn's arm and held up both hands, a smirk rising to his face. "We were just talking."

"You haven't actually said anything yet, Chuck. And this proves the point—have your lawyer call mine. If you think you're going to spend time with Cara after putting your hands on me like that, you're delusional." She folded her arms and tucked them close to her body.

I stepped closer to her, wanting to shield her but definitely not about to touch her. Just... needing to be a bit closer in case she needed me there.

"She wants to get to know me. You really going to keep your daughter from knowing her father?" He took a step back and sneered.

"*You* did that. Don't ever forget it—you're the reason she doesn't know you."

Moving in front of her, I closed it down. "Time for you to leave."

The man, Chuck apparently, left in a whirl of expletives, peeling out of the place where he'd parked with a squeal and a colorful hand gesture. We watched him go in silence.

We didn't speak for long minutes, her attention in the direction the car had gone and mine on her as discreetly as possible. She shivered, and I registered the chill of the late-October night and her inappropriate clothing. As she often did, she wore a black dress with capped sleeves and a hem that ended at the knee. It fit her body very well but would likely do very little to ward against the cold.

"Come. Let's get back inside." I pulled open the door and waited.

Her eyes hit mine then, and hit was the accurate word. I abandoned the door and stepped to her, my hands at her shoulders. I wouldn't have touched her, especially not after that idiot's hold without her permission, but she looked like she might fall over.

"Quinn. What is it?"

Tears sprang to her eyes and she struggled to swallow. "Everything's falling apart. *I'm* falling apart."

Pain for her sliced through me. I shook my head. "No. No, you're strong. You're doing fine."

She answered with a shake of her own, dejected and slow and so far from any version of her that it made my stomach turn.

"I'm not, though. I can barely make rent. My grandparents need to get more help. My mom is exhausted and I can't help her. And Cara hates me. She thinks—" She sucked in a breath and clenched her jaw, breathing through a tide of emotion. "She thinks I've kept her father away all this time. She believes him, and I... I can't..."

She tipped forward and her forehead hit my collarbone. My instinct told me not to pull her close, though I wanted to. She was seeking comfort from me. *Me.* Every part of me wanted to reach out and console her, assure her everything could be fixed.

I had resources. Endless resources, compared to most. And I would use them. "What can I do?"

I had to do something to fix this. I could.

Please let me help.

She breathed in, her shoulders rising and falling. The place where her head touched my chest through my shirt and where my hands held her shoulders were our only connection. It felt oddly intimate, her leaning into me, though the pressure where she rested was minimal. Slight enough I knew she wasn't actually leaning on me—like she needed the connection and a moment for herself without allowing herself to fully rely on me.

That was Quinn Darling in a nutshell. She knew herself, knew what she needed, and wouldn't allow herself to lean on anyone to get it. But damn, how I wanted to give her whatever she needed. In this quiet, full moment, she'd disarmed me completely.

How could I be surprised? At this point, nearly every interaction I'd had with her had done the same.

I'd been kidding myself that we could be just friends. It was all or nothing with this woman.

But did it mean... Could I...?

No. Nothing could happen there. I knew that perfectly well, didn't I?

She loosed a sigh, then pulled away. I dropped my hands immediately, not wanting to push or pull or do anything to make the moment harder on her.

"I don't know. Probably nothing."

Determination shot through me. "I'm sure there's something."

She tucked a strand of hair behind her ear and her eyes searched for clarity in the darkness. The security light cast a yellow glow from above the doors, and she let out another weary breath. "I don't think so. It's my mess."

Perhaps that was true, but it didn't mean I couldn't help. And it sounded like the financial end of things would be the starting place. But I couldn't figure out a way to help beyond simply shoving a check in her hand, and she'd die a thousand deaths before accepting that. I'd need a plan, and before that, I needed her back into the heated building before she froze out here.

"Let's get inside."

I held the door for her and she ducked in, still not looking me in the eye. I don't think I'd seen her green gaze but for a flash when I'd first walked out and told Chuck to unhand her.

Just outside the kitchen doors, I stopped and ducked my head, silently asking for her attention. She gave it to me, those expressive eyes slaying me with their sadness and worry.

"You're an amazing woman, Quinn. You are surrounded by people who love you who will not stand for that man's lies. And if you want, you have me at your disposal. I'll do whatever I can to help you, if you can think of a way I can."

Her lashes fluttered as she absorbed my words. "Thank you."

"If you have time, come early tomorrow. Meet me at my office. Any time before your shift."

Her brows furrowed, but she agreed. "Okay. Sure."

"Good." Then I opened the kitchen door, and she slipped through without another word.

I couldn't solve all her problems. I couldn't change the fact that her ex was an idiot or that her daughter felt betrayed. But I could figure out a way to infuse a little cash into her situation, and I'd figure that out in the next twenty hours.

I already had an idea brewing, and now I needed to work out the details. To be honest, it wasn't new. I'd considered this angle before, but now I had the perfect opening, and I just needed to finesse it before we met tomorrow—if she'd come. I'd wanted to approach her about this anyway, and she'd just given me the push I needed.

I had to help Quinn. On a gut level, I *had* to. And if she'd let me, I would.

CHAPTER FIFTEEN

Quinn

Cara was asleep by the time I got home and she left before I woke up. If I hadn't checked her bed to confirm she was there, I wouldn't have believed it. But she'd been curled into a little lump under the covers, looking for all the world exactly like she did when she was three. She still clung to the same scruffy old bear.

She'd escaped to help my mom with my grandparents this morning, so I couldn't even be mad and hang on to that more manageable emotion. It made me proud that she wanted to see her great-grandparents and help out with little things. My mom was so worn out, and Cara knew that. Even at fourteen, she could see.

My heart was now a ragged, ugly thing. Something that'd been bunched up and tossed in a corner. How did I prove to her that Chuck had chosen not to be a part of her life without making all of this so much worse for her? I could show her the paperwork he'd signed. I could tell her stories of times he'd said he wanted to be in her life in the past and then flaked out completely. His desire to be here now didn't mean he'd become a new man who could be a father, or who even wanted to be. To me, it merely meant the whim to insinuate himself into her life, or worse, that he'd figured out something he could get from her, or me, and this was his angle.

Maybe I needed to give him more credit, but fifteen years of this bull and I didn't need to learn the lesson again. That was why John Wallace, my lawyer, had become my next best friend.

And then, there was Julian. What the crap did I do with him?

I'd been numb as I took the stage for my last set last night, but not so much that I didn't notice he hadn't returned to his usual seat. In fact, I hadn't seen him again at all last night. He'd done more than his duty—he owed me nothing as it was. And even though I didn't think Chuck would've done anything more than grab my wrist, relief had hit hard and fast when Julian had arrived.

As off-kilter as he made me, he also gave me this feeling like he'd reinforced my backbone. It was the oddest thing, because I'd never been accused of not having one, and yet Julian showing up had bolstered me. He made me feel stronger. Something in the way he spoke up on my behalf but not for me, or instead of me. He didn't storm in and punch Chuck or berate him. He commanded him to release me, nothing more. And later, upon reflection, that'd been kind of hot.

That thought right there made it clear how mixed up about Julian I was. I liked him. For as much as I'd thought I hated him at one point, I... didn't anymore. He wasn't the villain in my story, though I'd tried desperately to peg him with that title when I'd found out he'd bought the building.

I couldn't pretend that was the reason everything was falling apart. It just was. Life was kicking my butt and it had honestly nothing to do with Julian Grenier. In fact, he'd already given me one break on the rent, and any other owner likely wouldn't have done the same since it hadn't been raised in years.

I didn't know what he wanted, but a half hour before my Saturday night shift started, I knocked on his office door. It stood wide open, and Kelly had long since gone home, if she'd ever been there on a Saturday. Weeks ago, I would've assumed Julian was the kind of employer who worked his employees to the bone. I would've imagined him the kind of man who demanded his staff remain at work as long as he did, ready at his beck and call.

Now I knew better, and that left us completely alone in this executive wing of the hotel.

"Quinn. Come in, please."

He stood behind that giant desk and closed the lid of a sleek laptop. I wondered what he did on there—what actual work he performed on the computer. An odd thought, really, but I had no idea what he did day to day other than he generally seemed busy and on a tight schedule.

Except lately, with me. And clearly, his Friday and Saturday evenings weren't all that tightly packed, because anytime he was in town, at least that I could tell, he sat in the same chair in his bar until the end of the live music and then left.

But day to day, I'd witnessed him countless times fast-walking from place to place like he'd only allotted two minutes and seven seconds to move from location A to B, and if he slowed, everything would be off. It couldn't actually be that bad, but I did recall Jamie commenting on how regimented and carefully scheduled Julian's life was.

He rounded the desk and walked to the same seating area where we sat last time I'd been summoned to his office. "Have a seat."

This all felt oddly familiar, and yet we'd traveled such a distance since that meeting weeks ago where he'd presented the new lease and I'd ended up begging him not to raise the rent. In another life, maybe even a year ago, I would feel shame crashing around me at that memory. Not anymore, though. Not having to increase my rent payments meant that much more for the medical bills. That much closer to getting them into Silverton Springs someday.

I took my place in the same chair I had that first time, hands in my lap. I genuinely didn't know why I'd come, except that he'd asked me to and at this point, I wanted to see what he had to say. He drew me in, and even though I didn't love admitting that, I had to. He'd been nothing but kind, if a bit odd about it, and maybe I needed a little kindness in my life.

He unbuttoned his suit jacket and sat. His deft fingers on the button and that careless way he brushed aside the material when he bent to sit made my stomach dip. *He really is so stupidly handsome.*

That thought did not belong here, nor did the observation that his facial hair seemed thicker and his hair hadn't yet been messed with like it usually had by the time he arrived at the bar.

A record scratched in my mind and I shook away those thoughts. When on earth had I started noticing the quality of his beard or the set of his hair?

It's been a while now. Just admit it.

Oblivious to my internal idiocy, Julian took me in for a

moment before crossing one leg over the other and leaning back in the chair. "How are you?"

"I'm fine," I said automatically, nerves crawling up my throat now that his attention rested so fully on me.

His brows dropped low. "You've recovered since last night? Has he bothered you any more?"

Ah. I didn't imagine he'd asked me to come here last night simply in order to make sure Chuck hadn't grabbed me against my will again, but it did make sense he'd want to confirm I hadn't been harassed again. "No. And I got ahold of John, my lawyer, so we're meeting next week. It should be fine. Chuck did actually leave me a long-winded and mildly-genuine-sounding apology for touching me and being so harsh."

He studied me, and even though I wanted his attention, if I was being honest, it also made me antsy. Last time, I'd had a plate of delicious scones and fruit between us, but this time, nothing separated his hawk-eyed gaze and my fidgety fingers.

"And your Cara?" His tone softened with these words.

My heart kicked out in response to her name, and his saying it so gently. Like he knew this, more than Chuck, was my soft spot, and where it hurt the most. "We haven't talked. I'm hoping tomorrow."

He nodded. "She loves you dearly. You'll get through this."

I blinked back at him, completely floored by the thoughtful reassurance. Nothing callous or flippant—no. Julian gave me two sentences that I could cling to. That I had been clinging to, despite my doubts.

"Thank you," I managed, though my throat felt tight.

He nodded and watched as I struggled to swallow. Dang, his intensity was a lot. Between the high emotions of the last two days and his unexpected approach here, my chest fluttered nonstop with pent-up emotion.

He stood, buttoned one button on his impeccable jacket, of course, and extended a hand to me. My stomach flipped at the gesture. It was particularly meaningful for him, I now realized. When touching could feel so bad to him, his choice to invite contact seemed momentous. Of course, he shook hands with people all the time, and it'd sounded like the key was preparedness. That's all this was too, I was sure, but it didn't stop my heart from revving into a sprint.

My hand slipped into his warm, firm grasp, and I stood. He was tall, definitely over six feet, but with my heels, we had only a few inches of difference.

"I have an event this coming week," he said, low and steady, still holding my hand.

That fluttering in my chest gave way to full-on flapping. An event? Why would he tell me this unless he was going to invite me? Or maybe ask me to sing, but I doubted that was it, based on the approach. Judging by the way he still held my hand, firm but not hard.

"Oh?" I cringed internally because that sounded so lacking when it emerged from my mouth, but I hadn't figured out what he meant, and running ahead accepting an invitation to something would be a nightmare of embarrass- ment if he actually planned to ask me to sing. Or bartend, *ugh.*

"It's black tie."

"Fancy," I said, and my hopes sank. If he did ask me, I couldn't afford a dress for a black-tie event. The last time I'd worn a floor-length gown had been in the birthing room, although that had really only come to my knees. Before that? Senior prom.

"I'd like you to accompany me."

Slight pressure on my hand made me step forward. We were inches apart now, by far the closest we'd ever been. Even last night when I'd rested my head against his chest, I'd leaned over to do that. Our bodies had been at least a foot apart. It'd been intimate in a way, but I'd been drowning in fears about Chuck, about losing Cara, about all the crap piling up on me. I'd needed connection but had been afraid to reach out and hug him, fearing making him uncomfortable.

But with his hands on my shoulders, he'd initiated. And when I'd leaned into him, he could've stepped away. Far less of a trap than a hug would've been, though I wished he would've wrapped his arms around me. In that moment, it didn't make sense for it to be Julian, but he'd been there and it'd felt right.

Shaking all that off and working to ignore how the air felt like a too-tight guitar string between us, I fumbled for an answer, hoping I didn't betray the odd mix of hope this might actually happen and disappointment the black-tie element caused. "I—I, uh, I'm not sure I have anything to wear."

He dipped his head a half inch. "I'd pay you, of course."

I blinked.

I'd pay you? What?

"What?"

His brows lifted a touch. "I'd pay for you to escort me to the event. I wouldn't expect you to come for free."

I stiffened and pulled my hand away, then stepped back. "Escort?"

He held up the same hand I'd just dropped. "Not that kind of *escort*. Perhaps a better word would be accompany. And I mean, I'd pay you to go and perform. To sing. And I'd find you an appropriate dress too, of course. All expenses incurred would be my responsibility."

My insides had frozen when that little shoe dropped. The one that said, *No, he's not asking you out on a date. He's offering to pay you as a performer and possibly an actual escort.* The fuse of outrage and disbelief lit low in my belly, but I still couldn't fully fathom this. "What would you... want?"

A shadow passed over his face before his eyes met mine and it slipped away. "Simply your time at the event itself— there will be a live band, so you'll only need to arrive and do whatever it is you do to prepare. It's out of town so it'd occupy something like thirty-six hours all told. I was thinking something around five or ten thousand as compensation, considering you'd likely have to miss one or more days at Pluck and would have to make arrangements for Cara."

My insides hollowed out and my mouth dropped open now that disbelief had overtaken me in full. His gaze narrowed on my expression as though it surprised him. As though he genuinely expected me to be thrilled by this proposition and not mildly offended by the use of the word escort. Granted, he'd backed off from that, so all this was? A gig.

"That's a bit high for a few hours of singing, especially if I'm not bringing my own band."

"It's a simple business arrangement from which you benefit. You perform, then circulate the room and I introduce you to people. I imagine it's quite a bit more money than you make in a weekend at the bar and would assist with some of your financial stresses."

Shame and embarrassment punched at my gut, but that dynamite stick of rage had finally burst in my chest.

"How dare you? Seriously, what in your mind thought paying me off to do who knows what with you would be an okay thing to even say out loud? Is there actually a job here, or is this just a weird excuse to hire me as your arm candy or something? I don't know what kind of sick billionaire circles you run in where you think you can just buy people to get them to do what you want, but I am not for sale."

I forcefully tucked my jacket around me, then stepped back and rounded the chair. Time to get gone, and fast. I could take a minute to put this behind me before I started my shift, and then I could avoid Julian Grenier indefinitely. I could blur out his section of the bar. I would insist on dealing with Kelly, not him, for anything to do with the building. I would make sure Jamie knew Julian and I were not going to sit at his table together anytime soon, and he better not try to change my mind.

"I'm not trying to buy *you*, Quinn. Just your time—your talent. It's no different from a consultant or—"

"Or a prostitute? Because that's how you're making me feel right now, and I honestly have no idea whether you mean to or not. You're mixing in a few hours of singing with something you're terming *accompanying you*, and then you're paying me that much money? Maybe that's something you're comfortable with, but I. Am. Not."

And of course he didn't know, but all of this sent me right back to Chuck's suggestion that he give me an "allowance" to "treat myself" to nice things while he was in LA, and then he'd come see me whenever his work brought him to Salt Lake. Gag.

His face dropped, those words finally penetrating that thick, ridiculous skull of his. "I—"

"Don't bother, okay? Have yourself a lovely evening,

Mr. Grenier, and please leave me alone. And just in case it's not clear, my answer to your very generous offer is *hell no*."

I whipped around and stormed out, ramming my shoulder into the doorframe in my effort to just get out as fast as I could. I clutched at my shoulder while rage-walking down the hall, refusing the tears that begged to escape. If I cried, it would be because I'd just jacked my shoulder on the dang doorframe and not because of what he'd just said.

Not because I'd thought we were maybe about to start something, and he'd just put a cold, hard end to it.

CHAPTER SIXTEEN

Quinn

Grenier didn't show at the bar, thank goodness. And yes, I'd reverted back to thinking of him as Grenier because that's who that man was. Julian was someone else entirely, and apparently, he'd left the building long before my meeting with Grenier.

I sang angry girl songs all evening, albeit jazzy, funky versions that suited the bar's mood. The ladies' night out crowd filling the bar loved them and cheered me on in my righteous indignation wailing.

But by the time I wiped down the counter after another long night, I was left with two harsh realities. First, I definitely had a crush on Julian, and now that had to be over. It was over.

And second, I could really use that money. Whether it was five or ten thousand, that would be an insane leap forward for me. For my whole family. And I absolutely hated myself for getting stuck on that, like money was most important in life. It wasn't, but at the same time, what a necessarily evil. Would it be so wrong to take him up on it?

Yes. Yes, it would be. Because I was not a professional escort. And though he'd seemed offended by my suggestion that he wanted to pay me for sex, he certainly wanted to pay for my company. And what did that even mean? What universe were we living in where that was even a thing? Yes, he'd included a few hours of singing, but did he have any clue how out of whack his pricing was? Maybe if he'd only suggested singing, it wouldn't have hit me so wrong, but *crap*, the more I sat with it, the more this reminded me of Chuck just throwing money at me to get me to do what he wanted.

Most of the anger had worn off via the singing, at least for tonight, so by the time I reached my car, I slumped into it and wished I didn't have to drive home. I started the car, then gasped when a sharp rap on my window nearly turned my heart to petrified wood. That it was Julian Grenier standing outside my door did nothing to calm me.

Rolling down the window two inches, I practically barked at him. "You cannot do that to a woman late at night in a dark parking lot."

"It's perfectly well lit."

I glared at him, and he straightened.

"Fair enough. But I wanted to give you this. Please read it. I hope it'll make sense of what I—what we were talking about earlier. I'm afraid I did a bad job of making clear what I had in mind, and I hope you'll at least consider reading this."

He stuck a cream envelope into the crack of the window and waited. I eyed it with suspicion, certain I didn't want to read whatever was in there and yet equally sure I needed to read it immediately or risk losing. Losing *what*, I couldn't have said, but it felt so clear right then. So I pinched one corner of the envelope, then tossed it onto the seat next to me.

"I'll consider it," I said, knowing full well I was about to drive home and read it the second I got inside.

"That's all I ask." He stepped back, eyes still on me. "Drive safe, Quinn."

My stomach flipped at my name on his lips. I cranked the key to fire up the engine and drown out this tangle of feelings. Again, he'd done the unexpected and reached out right away. He hadn't hidden away and pouted that I didn't say yes, but he also hadn't forced me to avoid his heady gaze in the bar all night. He'd struck the chord between assertive and respectful—unless his letter was a repeat of the earlier proposition, in which case he really did need to learn he couldn't just do whatever he wanted.

The drive home slipped by quickly now that I had this incentive. I focused on the beams of my headlights and made myself promise to read the letter and then assess my feelings. As it was, I felt wrung out from singing through the gamut of anger, indignation, frustration, and hurt all night. Disappointment had dragged at me, too, and admittedly, this letter on the seat next to me had abated that, at least for now.

I hardly remembered pulling into the driveway or unlocking the door to get inside. I couldn't have said where I left my purse, and I didn't bother shucking my jacket, instead sinking onto the couch and tearing into the thick envelope to find one neatly tri-folded piece of stationary with a sturdy-looking capital G in the middle and nothing else.

It fit him, as did the precise lettering that filled the page beneath it.

Quinn,

I apologize for my poor attempt to explain myself earlier. Under no conditions should you imagine I was attempting to solicit your company for anything other than conversation. I would never hire someone for a physical interaction, whether you or otherwise. You insinuated perhaps that was something I did regularly, and I feel it necessary to make clear it certainly is not.

All that said, I hope you'll consider my offer, particularly because hearing your voice at the event would undoubtedly guarantee its success. If you're that underpaid at the bar for what you do, perhaps we need to have a conversation with the hotel management as your shock at the rate was troubling.

I won't presume to know the details of your financial hardship beyond what you've shared and hinted at. If the benefit of this brief, professional arrangement would ease any of your stress, I hope you'll consider saying yes. If you have any conditions under which you'd say yes, please only list them and I'll execute them as you wish.

I want the best for you, Quinn. I don't know how else to say it, so there it is. Please let me know by end of business Monday if you're amenable to the idea with this additional information. If so, we'd leave before noon Wednesday and return before Thursday evening.

Rest well,

Julian

.   .   .

I reread the letter twice before anything other than the pounding heart in my chest made itself know. Slowly, like water colors bleeding on a page, I absorbed the words. Flashes of emotion burst in my head—relief, frustration, anger, shame, embarrassment, thrill... confusion.

He'd *handwritten* me a letter like an old-timey correspondence. Not a text or an e-mail, or even a phone call. He'd scratched out a fairly lengthy note to me, his tight, controlled writing tracking across the page and spelling words I wasn't sure what to do with.

My thumb swept over the date at the top right of the letter. Something about knowing he'd sat down and written this for me, his full focus on the paper and lines of text, made my heart circle around like a cat preparing for a nap in the sun and snuggle down in a warm glow.

One letter, and I felt no clearer about the man, or the situation, than I had earlier tonight. Actually no, that wasn't quite right. I'd felt offended, angry, and sad earlier. Now, I just felt an unfortunate twist of disappointed and hopeful.

"I want the best for you."

What was that? Just like a handful of times before when he'd been so kind and sweet, that line hit me in a soft place I hadn't shielded against. Maybe it was a protective instinct I brought out of him, which I didn't love but wasn't the worst thing. It didn't mean he had feelings for me, and everything else about the situation pointed to his *not* having feelings beyond that odd desire to help me. Maybe that came with the first billion—wanting to play financial savior.

But could I actually go through with it? Could I look myself in the eye if I let him pay me that much money to sing for, what, max five hours? However much he refused to call it an escort, that's what I'd be if the price tag remained that high. I might not tuck him into bed, et cetera, but it wouldn't be much better.

Especially because, if I were honest, part of what hurt about all of it, once I got past the fact that he'd proposed it in the first place, was that this seemed like a pretty clear signal that he didn't have any real feelings for me. So all my little flutters and silly thoughts were just that—girly nonsense I'd let grow from the barest of fertilizer in the form of his kindness.

Instead of agonizing any further, I readied for bed and promised myself I'd decide tomorrow. I didn't want to spend the next two days debating. I didn't have the emotional bandwidth for that, frankly. I needed to tell him no and be done with it... or tell him yes.

I decided I needed reinforcements, especially after Cara had refused to say anything but that she had promised to help my mom with breakfast this morning and "Grandma will call you later."

It'd felt almost like a threat, though that didn't make sense. My mom knew Chuck, and she knew me, and she knew Cara. She'd do whatever she could to help us fix things. I'd made Cara promise we'd sit down later, so I had that to look forward to and dread. But until then, I had a few hours to work through this mess in my gut over Julian's proposition. Settling that would set me up even better to have our mom and daughter talk later.

Sarah had been the only one free this morning since Dahlia was busy, Calla was in LA recording, and Sadie worked until about ten today. We met in Rise and Shine's cheery yellow atmosphere, and I ordered a croissant, a slice of the pumpkin chocolate chip bread, and a black coffee. Sarah had grabbed a seat in the bustling café before I'd arrived a few minutes late, as seemed to be my perpetual habit.

"Okay, I'm ready. Lay it on me," she said, toasting my bright blue mug just as I set it on the table.

I'd texted the group to ask for advice this morning, so she'd come prepared to give it. Thank goodness, because I just wanted to get into it and make a decision.

"Julian offered to pay me to be his date to some fancy event this week. Then he tacked on that I'd be singing at the event for a bit, too."

Her brow furrowed as she swallowed a sip of coffee.

"Like... thousands of dollars and buy a formal gown to wear."

Her mouth dropped open. "Um..."

"Yeah."

We stared at each other, and she took another drink of her coffee. Her wide brown eyes were almost comedically big as she gulped the hot beverage. "So. Does he want you to—"

"He clarified it wouldn't be anything physical. Just a weird gig-date combo. And he also said he made the offer because he thought it would help me." Disappointment sliced through me again and my cheeks heated.

"Help you financially, I guess. But I thought you guys were kind of circling each other. About to finally go out."

I chuckled humorlessly. "Finally?"

"I haven't even been back here a full year, but anytime I've been in the room when you both are, his eyes are on you."

My stomach flipped. "Prior to very recently, it was likely due to a predator circling of prey dynamic."

She gave me an unimpressed look. "I doubt it. I can't imagine buying your building was something he had to think about very long or hard at all. He's drawn to you, for sure." Her brow furrowed and she set her mug down very carefully. "But Quinn..."

The hesitation in her words and pain on her face told me what would come next. "I do need the money. I hate to say that out loud—you can't know how much—but even more than I did a few days ago, I do."

She grabbed my hand. "I wish I could help."

"Me too. And I know you would, too."

Sarah was the kind of person who'd give you the shirt off her back or shoes off her feet, no question. She showed up for people, and she had a generous heart. But she had her own struggles, and this wasn't something she could solve for me.

"So what are you thinking about all this?"

I let out a huge dramatic sigh and twined my finger in my ponytail.

"I think I might do it." Gah, my cheeks burned admitting that. But when I glanced up, instead of judgment or surprise, I saw understanding.

"I don't blame you. I can't pretend to understand what's going on there for him, but if he's said there'll be no physical obligation, that's one level of protection. I just don't want you to get hurt. But hopefully, you can focus on the performance piece of things and minimize whatever else is there."

I gave her a thin smile. "Same."

The truth was, I would be hurt. If I did this, I'd effectively close the door on any interest in actually dating Julian for good, if that'd ever been an option. Shoving aside all the insanity with my grandparents, the pressure I felt to change things for them and my mom, and the mess with Cara right now, just this would still hurt me.

But weighing it out told me that hurt feelings was the lesser of two evils, so I had my answer. And soon, Julian would have his, too.

CHAPTER SEVENTEEN

Quinn

The slam of Cara's door put a perfect little exclamation point on my failed attempt at conversation. And even though she'd said words that should've reassured me, the whole stomping away with door-slamming situation left me unconvinced we'd made progress.

When I'd joined her for lunch at my mom's, she hadn't outright ignored me. My mom had made her best effort to do the thing where you're talking to one person but sort of talking to the other in order to get the first person to speak. Things like, "Cara was just telling me she aced her reading comprehension test, weren't you, Cara?"

And Cara had played along, answering less sullenly than she had in days. Grandma peeked out from her recliner and winked at me, clearly aware of the drama. Pops kept quiet in his chair, reading whatever large print suspense novel had topped his stack from the library.

After a few hours of helping my mom straighten up, swap laundry, and change the sheets like I usually did on Sunday afternoons, Cara and I rode home in silence until I couldn't take it.

So I jumped back into where we'd left off Friday when it all unraveled. "I don't want to keep you from knowing him."

Her head whipped to me. "I'm not an idiot, okay? I know you don't like me talking to him, and Grandma told me why."

Her voice did that thing where it got small and tight at the end just before she cried, and my heart squeezed.

"I don't want you hurt, Car. I love you. If you want to know him, you can. But let's go easy at first. You don't owe him a thing, okay?" I pulled into the driveway and slowed to a stop.

Her door cracked open before the tires settled. "I get it. I'm not getting hurt. It's fine." Next, she was out of the car, into the house, and just as I entered, slamming her door.

It reassured me, at least to some degree, that my mom had been the bearer of bad news when it came to Chuck. That Cara had been told something concrete as to why I might not be willing to trust him with her beyond spitefulness or other nonsense. If I stripped away all my feelings about the man, I was left with just a simple fact. If his being in Cara's life was a good thing, he could stay. If at any point it became anything less than good?

He'd be done.

I scoured my own house, making sure I scrubbed every inch of the kitchen and bathrooms before I finally fell face-first into bed. I probably should've offered to go into the bar tonight. I could use any extra weekend cash, especially a busy one like this. Especially after Mom had slid me the new crop of past-due envelopes that'd arrived yesterday.

I'd learned a lot about bargaining with medical debt collectors this past year. Easily my most alluring skill. Not something I could list on a resume, but I'd found it helpful and knew it was keeping the wolves at bay. Having a lump sum like a few thousand dollars to throw at these people would get us through the end of the year at least. And that pushed me over the edge, if I'd been on one. Honestly, I hadn't. I'd decided earlier, but this confirmed it. We needed the break, and if Julian wanted to play benevolent billionaire by paying me to be his date for a day or two?

More power to him.

On Monday morning, I gave myself a minute to relish the quiet house and then sucked it up and called Kelly. She put me through to Julian instantly. We'd never spoken on the phone before, and hearing his curt hello made my stomach clench.

"Good. I'll see you Wednesday, then. Kelly will forward you a packing list."

"Okay. I have terms."

A pause. "We'll discuss them on the ride there."

I swallowed and hoped he couldn't hear it. "Okay."

"It will be, yes."

I wanted to say something else. I wanted *him* to say something else. I wanted this whole thing to go away, and yet I was already counting on the money despite myself.

"Okay. Well..."

"I'll take care of all the details."

"I—okay." Ugh, could I say anything else?

There was a pause, a shuffling of papers, and I thought I heard Kelly's voice muffled on the other end like maybe she'd peeked in to give him a message.

"See you Wednesday," he said, then hung up.

Within minutes, Kelly sent a packing list. It didn't go right down to the underwear and sock level, but how incredibly detailed. I wondered if he'd made it, or she had. Either way, did he have a packing list too? Hard to imagine Julian referencing a list. I'd seen him in such particular circumstances, and never actually working. He moved away from his desk whenever I met him at his office, and he didn't seem to be working at the bar.

I'd read somewhere that he'd grown up in a wealthy home, but that he'd built his own empire. So not like he'd simply inherited the money. Maybe on this little trip, I'd get a better feel for what he did for work.

Readying to head into Pluck, I messaged Sarah to thank her for her listening ear and to tell the group I'd accepted the offer. I'd filled Calla, Sadie, and Dahlia in on the essentials earlier.

Lots of clapping ensued. Calla had submitted her vote and said she was glad to hear I was accepting help. But I needed to tell Jamie. For some reason, I'd put it off instead of going to him first. Normally, if someone knew more about a situation than I did, I wanted that person's advice. But the fact that Jamie was close with Julian—as close as anyone other than Kelly seemed to get, anyway—had me shying away from my old friend.

I called him while opening the front door to my shop, one earbud in my ear so I could still hear other things as needed.

"To what do I owe this honor?" Jamie's voice came loud and clear into my ear.

"My calling you? It's not that unusual, is it?" I fiddled with the system I used for checkout, firing it up despite the unlikelihood of needing it anytime soon. Most of my customers came later in the day unless by appointment.

"The last time we spoke on the phone instead of texted was sometime after my first album release."

I barked a laugh. His first album had come out right around the time Cara had been born. "That is a lie."

He grumped a noncommittal sound. "Whatever. You've got an agenda, so lay it on me."

I chuckled at him, wondering if little Jamie had kept him up last night or if he'd just gotten old enough to be perpetually slightly grumpy. Generally, especially after he'd patched things up and gotten together with Bel, he was downright cheery.

"I'm going to an event with Julian."

"Nice. Glad he asked you."

I blinked. "You knew he was going to?"

"He'd mentioned the event and you in the same few sentences, so I put it together."

I stared at the computer screen, wondering what that meant. "Uh, okay."

"I think you'll have fun, Q. It's not like you're shocked he asked. I know—" He cut off and must've muted the phone, because the line went soundless but the call stayed connected. A few seconds later, he returned. "Anyway, good for you. Enjoy it. I know you've had your doubts, but he's a good man."

My mind scrambled around for purchase. What was he going to say when he muted? Why had he cut himself off?

Whatever information he'd neglected to share felt essential, and he was keeping it to himself. Gah!

"What were you going to say? Before you muted?"

"What? Oh, nothing. But I have to jump off. Have fun with Julian and be nice."

My mouth dropped open, though no one could appreciate the shock. "I'm always nice."

He laughed, open and hearty. "Right. Talk to you soon, Quintastic."

"*Ugh*. Later, weirdo."

His chuckle cut off when the call ended, and I sat there, staring at myself in the shine of the glass display case. "*It's not like you're shocked he asked.*" Did he mean he asked like he was interested in making a business arrangement for this event, or romantically? I hadn't mentioned that Julian was paying me, and Jamie hadn't let on that he'd known. Most of his comments sounded like he thought Julian had invited me as his date. And I supposed he had, but in a business-arrangement way.

I hated that I wanted Jamie's words to mean Julian was interested in me romantically. I didn't have time to deal with these feelings, and I'd always been pretty good about not following after someone if they weren't emotionally available. I had no interest in an unrequited love story.

But this was better, wasn't it? I didn't have time for *any* love story. Julian might make me feel restless and excited, but he also kind of drove me insane. Letting myself feel the things that were worming their way into my heart and mind wouldn't get me closer to my goals of paying off my grandparents' debt and getting them into Silverton Springs. But keeping him as a business associate would.

Resolved to banish all squishy feelings for Julian, I focused on inventorying the newest shipment of sheet music that had arrived on Saturday and that I'd ignored at the time. I didn't think about the man, the financial crap-storm, or how much I needed this break. I definitely didn't think about how Julian would look in a tux or what kind of party we were even attending.

CHAPTER EIGHTEEN

Quinn

One bag slung over my left shoulder and a shabby backpack over the other, I entered the terminal of Silverton's tiny airport and glanced around for Julian. Kelly bustled over, hand apparently extended to take my bag.

"I can get it, but thanks," I said, wondering if she typically carried Julian's bags, because that was just weird. She was like twenty-five and half his size.

"Julian's in a meeting on the plane. Go ahead and use the bathrooms or whatever you need, and you can get settled in the car. Just hand your bag to the driver, Scott. He'll just be another five minutes, and you'll leave right on time. Thanks for being a few early." She smiled, then ducked back to the iPad in her hand, swiping wildly and probably doing ten things at once.

The instructions had indicated I had to be on time. We weren't flying, but apparently, Julian was arriving home from one trip and jumping right into the car to make this other event. That need for promptness more than any of the other details had made me nervous because I tended to run on the early end of late. I didn't run fifteen minutes late, more like three to five. But for someone like Julian, that was no doubt an eternity. He struck me as a ten-minutes-early-is-late kind of man, and I couldn't help feeling he'd added that instruction since he'd noticed my propensity for showing up a few minutes past time.

I'd tricked myself into seeing the required time as ten minutes earlier than it was, so I'd only been five minutes late for my own deadline, and five early for his. *Phew*. I didn't want to begin this trip having him wait on me.

Scott smiled broadly from the sparkling black Range Rover parked just outside the terminal. I hadn't thought about how we'd be traveling but had called Kelly in a mild panic when I'd seen the meeting place. She'd assured me we weren't flying, which relieved a bit of the pre-event stress. I didn't particularly relish flying in a tiny plane, but more than that, I was not mentally prepared to leave the state with Julian. Don't ask me why that would make a difference—a three-hour drive versus a three-hour flight—but it did. This was all forcing me out of my depth, which I already hated, but to deal with being so far from Cara and my grandparents... *no*. No.

"Have a seat, ma'am. Julian will be here in a few."

Scott held the door for me, then shut it once I slid in. *Wow*. The leather seats were soft as butter. I ran my hand along the cushion next to my thigh. I'd been in nice cars any number of times, but probably none as nice as this. It wasn't flashy, but I loved the sturdy feel of it.

I liked big cars, so I welcomed the fact that we wouldn't be driving in a town car or even limo. We were in the mountains here and heading to what had to be a location some-where else in the mountains. Though it was only late October, snow and ice were almost a guarantee if we were out late enough. I had a long enough list of things to worry about, so I was perfectly happy that picturing us plummeting off the side of a canyon road due to poor traction didn't need to be one of them.

That list, as I settled my backpack by my feet, grew longer. Now that I didn't have to focus on getting here on time, all the things I'd worked to ignore came flooding in. What were we doing? Where, exactly, were we going? What was the dynamic between me and Julian, and what did I do with my feelings for him, however muddled they were?

The door cracked open on the opposite side, and Julian slipped in, eyes on his phone. "I've got a meeting in ten minutes and will be working most of the way to the house. Can you briefly outline your amendments so I'm aware of them?"

He focused on his phone, energy buzzing as though he'd hung a shingle over his head that read *BUSY* in bright red fluorescent. His charcoal gray suit hadn't wrinkled on his flight, and his white shirt appeared pristine and crisp as ever. The tie knotted at his throat looked like it belonged there. I guessed it kind of did.

"Sure. Do you want bullet points, or are we actually going to have a conversation?"

His eyes finally flicked up to mine like he'd registered he was being rude, and that sign blinked off. He breathed deeply enough that I could see his shoulders rise and fall, and his face smoothed out from that more severe focus he'd had on his screen to something I might call calm.

"Conversation is good. Bullet points are acceptable, if you prefer."

"I don't know why you're paying me so much, but you obviously know I'm not in a position to refuse. But since you are, I want you to give me as much to do as possible. I don't want to feel like this was a favor or a charity thing, even though I'm not stupid enough to believe it's not. But, just... I want you to get your money's worth."

He absorbed my words for a moment. "Do you have any suggestions?"

"Well, I made a set list long enough to fill about five hours—all songs most decent bands would know. Plus, I can do whatever assistant-y things Kelly would normally do. Carry your bag or whatever. And—"

"Kelly doesn't carry my bags."

"Oh. Okay." Now I felt both awkward and relieved. "Well, I don't know what else you might need for this, but other than singing, obviously, and I can... clean. Organize. I'm an excellent sock pairer."

I could swear he hid a smile with the purse of his lips. "I'm quite adept at pairing my own socks, believe it or not. But even if I weren't, this trip isn't long enough to require laundry services."

"Right. Yeah. I'm just... I'm nervous."

"How can I help?"

A jolt of anticipation and something else I couldn't quite identify streaked through me. He'd said those words more than once to me now, and it always came as such a surprise. "I don't know. I guess tell me what we're doing? Any idea how long I'll be singing? Where? For whom? I'm in the dark here."

"Kelly didn't fill you in?" He looked surprised.

"Uh, no. She seemed to talk like I already knew, so maybe she thought you would've."

His brow furrowed slightly. "My apologies. I didn't mean for you to be so uninformed. We're attending a private movie screening at a friend's. It's late tonight."

"Which movie? And which town?"

Humor lit his eyes. "Jack McKean's latest. And it'll be up in Deer Valley."

I gulped. "Who is your friend?"

One brow jumped. "Jack McKean."

I pressed my lips together and breathed in a slow, controlled breath. *Ho. Ly. Crap.* Holy crap. "Is it the—"

"Yes."

"But it doesn't premiere until—"

"Right. This is a director's cut."

"Didn't he direct and—"

"Yes."

"So you are friends with—"

"Yes."

I made a face. "You don't actually know what I'm going to say. You should let me finish a sentence."

His brows rose. "*Karrigan's Muse* movie. Next year. Act. Jack McKean. Were those the answers to your questions?"

I narrowed my eyes at him. "Okay, so you did know what I was going to say, but it's still really rude."

He chuckled low, and a thrill spiraled up from my belly straight to my brain and hit me with a lovely little burst of dopamine. *Wow.* That was the first time I'd heard anything close to a laugh from him, and it almost made him give me a full smile. I shouldn't like that so much, but oh... I did.

"Fair enough. I didn't expect you to care about Jack

McKean. You're friends with one of the world's sexiest men already. I thought you'd be immune."

I laughed loudly at that. "Jamie is like my brother. Cousin, at least. I get that he's beautiful, but I feel no attraction to him. I've never met Jack McKean, but he is..." What was the word for someone so strikingly handsome and apparently genuine, based on all the press?

"He's exceptional," Julian put in.

"Yes. *Yes.* The man is gorgeous, yes, but he's an amazing actor. And the fact that he's not a big fat jerk in real life, so say the rumors, is just... so appealing." I may have sighed a little dreamily. Because seriously, Jack McKean was the stuff of fantasies. Face. Body. Style. Movie roles to both please the masses and win awards. He was just ridiculous.

"I can confirm he is all that and a bag of organic, locally sourced chips."

I gave him a smile. "Well, that's good to know. Can I ask why you are paying me to sing at your friend's premiere and essentially be your date to an event at your friend's house?"

That businesslike mask filtered down over his face like a drop curtain, and he reached for his phone. "I need to prepare for my call, if you don't mind."

"Oh, sure. Do your thing."

Talk about a shut down, wow. I don't know what I expected, but it wasn't that. So far, Julian had been straightforward about everything, at least once I'd asked. Granted, he'd done plenty behind my back with hiring Chip and the dryer thing, plus buying the building. *Okay*, so he wasn't exactly upfront, but he wasn't evasive once I called him on it. Odd.

"I'm here."

His low voice drew my eyes. He sat with a tablet in his lap, earbuds in both ears, squinting down at whatever displayed there. My gaze trailed along his close-cut stubble that served to highlight the strong line of his jaw more than hide it. What'd seemed sharp and almost dangerous in their severity when I'd seen him the first time years ago became more human, more familiar, and to my dismay, more appealing.

He cut me a glance and our eyes locked. I smiled and hoped he wouldn't notice the blush creeping up my neck to my cheeks at being caught watching him.

And then he did it. He smiled. Just a half smile, but it reached his eyes. Our gazes held a moment longer, and he nodded, returned his attention to the screen, and said, "Yes. Agreed."

Heat sizzled in my chest from only a partial smile, and I hoped he'd answer my question. When he finished the call, he'd tell me what I was doing here, and maybe I wouldn't feel so much like a woman without a map.

CHAPTER NINETEEN

Julian

How do you tell a woman you want to know better that you've paid her to come with you to an event to alleviate the financial pressure in her life because you could tell it was swallowing her whole and you couldn't fix anything else without sounding like a raving overstepping lunatic?

Well, you don't.

My last call ended two minutes before we arrived, and Quinn didn't lose a moment.

Hands on her lap and curiosity bursting from every pore, she asked, "All done?"

"For now, yes."

"Can you talk to me?"

"Yes, though we'll be arriving in minutes." My hope was futile, but I had to try to put her off.

"That's fine. Can you tell me now?"

"Tell you?" The *purposefully obtuse* game would buy me a minute.

"Yes. Can you tell me why I'm here?"

I studiously tucked my tablet into its case and set it on the seat between us, then thought better of freeing up my hands and held it on my lap.

"You're here to sing before we see the new movie. There will be some socializing before, then we'll all go dress up and there'll be some photographers, then—"

"Photographers?"

I detected a twinge of nerves. "Don't worry. It's extremely unlikely they'll use any images with you in them. This is all a big publicity stunt for Jack, but he managed to make it happen on his own terms with people he knew."

She looked skeptical. "Won't they want pictures of you? I'd think people would be fascinated to know that you and Jack McKean are friends."

I considered that. "I suppose you're right. Normally, I do whatever I can to avoid the media, but I didn't require anonymity to attend, so that may mean you'll be photographed with me. If that concerns you, please just—"

"Should it concern me?" Her head tilted to one side, elongating her neck.

My eyes dropped to the delicate slope where her collarbone dipped, then jumped back to her face. "That depends on a few factors."

Her eyebrows rose, clearly not expecting that answer. "Like what?"

"Like whether you mind that we will be romantically linked. Whether you are bothered by having your photo published, and likely information about your store in Silverton. They might even ferret out your connection with Jamie, but that's unlikely as he won't be in attendance."

She inhaled and seemed to be digesting my words. I hoped that, at the very least, the first item didn't cause her concern. She hadn't known she might be photographed—indeed an oversight on my part—but she had to have known she'd be linked to me romantically. At least in appearance. If that proved to be problematic for her, I'd certainly have my answer for whether the money was the only incentive here.

Because a part of me had started to hope... Perhaps she'd get used to me, though that same part of me disliked the idea immensely. How many other women had tried to do just that for the sake of being tethered to me and, more importantly in their eyes, my bank accounts?

I shook off that thought immediately because there was little I liked thinking about less than being used by people to get what they wanted. Though it drove me insane, the fact that Quinn refused to use me made me like her even more. I suspected the minute I told her I had no need to pay her for this little outing, that there wasn't actually a need for her to sing tonight, she'd refuse the money. Prideful, yes, but honorable, too.

And that was the crux of it. Against the grain of my plans, I'd started to hope for a friendship with her, being accepted by the town, but also, something else. Something more. The way Quinn had looked at me more than once, it would be stupid of me to not acknowledge something might be there behind those expressive eyes. Most of the time, women saw me and their interest reflected dollar signs. Quinn hadn't given even a hint that she wanted my money, and she'd come under the guise of the gig.

Unless she proved me wrong. And I'd never wanted to be right more. This little outing, while ideally assisting her financially, would also be a litmus test for Quinn. Despite appearances, did she have interest in my financial situation? When surrounded by some of the most beautiful people in the country, would she be loyal to the person who brought her?

And no, it wasn't a perfect way of knowing her every motive since I'd gotten her here under false pretenses. That detail would flush itself at some point, and I'd deal with the fallout then. Until that point, I had a front row seat to Quinn at a veritable buffet of beauty and privilege.

"We're here." Scott pulled into the driveway as he spoke.

Quinn hadn't answered, and when I glanced at her, she seemed steeped in thought. I didn't relish the idea that she dreaded any of the things I'd listed she should consider here at the eleventh hour, but it did buy me another segment of time I could reasonably *not* respond to her larger question.

When the car halted, she startled and gave me a wide-eyed look.

"It'll be fine. If at any point you are unhappy with the way things are going, you are free to leave."

Again, I hated the thought, but it needed to be said. Especially considering that, at some point, it would be very clear things weren't as I'd originally claimed, and she may well want to blow out of here the minute that happened. I was counting on one or many things about the evening keeping her here when we got to that point, but until then, I'd observe her like a hawk.

"I'm not leaving."

Somehow, I maintained a somber face and nodded once, then focused on my phone to avoid smiling at her. She'd think I'd gone insane, but her stubborn determination surprisingly delighted me. Yes. *Delighted.* One of her many charms.

Scott extended a hand to Quinn. Seconds later, Jack swung open the door to a garishly large house and beamed. I snuck a glance at Quinn and found her fiddling with her backpack, unaware that one of Hollywood's A-list Oscar-winning actors had come out to greet us himself.

"You look old," he said, hand outstretched to me.

I took it, and he pulled me in as we both patted each other's shoulder. All firm, predictable movements, and comfortable. No doubt I'd have some skin-crawling episodes later, so I might as well enjoy the absence of it here. I hadn't seen Jack in person long enough to have a conversation in over a year. He looked good, and closer to happy than I'd seen him in a while.

"You look older," I returned as usual, smiling back at him, then stepped aside to gesture to Quinn. "This is my friend, Quinn Darling. And Quinn, this is Jack."

Quinn's mouth hung open for a moment as she looked back and forth between us, and my smile dropped. She *was* stunned by him. Of course she was. I'd had a similar reaction the first time I'd seen him—maybe not exactly, but a kind of awe that a man could be that spectacular in person. I could admit it—he was beautiful in all the classical ways Americans liked their men, but more masculine than they actually came. The slight British twinge to his words that slipped out occasionally, especially when a few drinks deep, charmed all the more.

"Nice to meet you, Quinn." Jack extended his hand to her.

She took it, shaking her head like she needed to clear out the fog of Jack's beauty. "Sorry. Hi, Jack. Nice to meet you. I was momentarily stunned into silence because I don't think I've ever seen Julian smile before."

Jack's eyes lit and he gave me a look I read as completely

delighted, though maybe I'd hallucinated all this. It seemed too good to be real. Surprise—this was starting to be the tone where Quinn Darling was concerned.

"He's quite pretty when he smiles, isn't he? I've told him more than once that he should do it more often." He slid me another look and winked.

My attention darted back to Quinn when she spoke again. "I agree completely."

Our gazes met and it hit me. She really meant it. She hadn't been shocked into an open-mouthed daze by Jack, but by my fleeting smile.

Anticipation lit in my stomach and began a slow burn.

I couldn't have blamed her if she'd fallen head over heels for Jack on sight as many women did—or really, as what felt like everyone did. But that she remarked on me...

"Well, let's get inside so you can relax and decompress a bit before the insanity begins."

He maintained the cheery tone, but I knew this kind of thing wore on him. He'd all but begged me to come last week when he'd called, and I couldn't refuse him something I could very easily make happen. Once the location shifted from LA to just three hours south of Silverton, I'd happily accepted.

I extended a hand for Quinn to precede me. She looked up and gave me a smile so bright and pleased that I coughed like it'd choked me. Warmth flooded my chest as I followed behind her and Jack. Soon, I wouldn't know which way was up, if she kept so easily affecting me. Strangely enough, I looked forward to more of that.

Someone approached him and spoke in low tones, then darted away. At least six other people bustled around the house.

"Sorry it's crazy in here. I'm going to have to run deal

with something, but if you head down that hallway, I think Louisa is down there, and she'll help get you settled. I'll see you in a bit." He jogged to catch up with the woman who'd given him the message.

More than ready to get away from the busyness of the space, I plowed ahead toward the hallway he'd gestured to.

"Ah, Mr. Grenier. You will be here, and Ms. Darling, you'll be just across the hall, there. If you need anything, don't hesitate to call the number listed on the information card in your room. Your bags will be delivered momentarily. My name's Louisa, and I'm happy to help with anything you should need during your stay."

I nodded, and she turned on her heel and paced away. I sensed Quinn looking at me, so I turned to her. She reached out and grabbed my arm just below my elbow, then released it like she'd been burned. She needn't have worried—something had switched in me after that first unexpected touch. No crawling skin or pit in my stomach—only awareness where there'd been none.

"Sorry. Reflex, I guess. Is this his house or a hotel?" She gazed up, up, up to the ceilings that were, not surprisingly based on what I'd seen thus far, painted with aspirational imitations of Michelangelo.

"It's a rental home, lucky for him. The staff is his, or at least Louisa is, and I recognized at least one other person, but Jack's not here long term. Due to the event, they're probably treating it more like a hotel. It's certainly big enough to be one."

"You don't like it?" she asked, tilting her head.

"It's too big. Doesn't feel like a home. As you said, it feels more like a hotel." Even the décor, which had come pre-staged as Jack had warned, felt more like the impersonal touches of a display than the reality of a home.

"Isn't your house in Silverton about this size? I can only imagine what your home in LA is like." Her green eyes watched and waited for my response.

"My home in Silverton is certainly not this big. My house in LA is irrelevant." It was a monstrosity. I liked it well enough, but part of the reason I'd sought out Silverton was to feel at home in a way I never had. I was getting there. I didn't need to worry about the LA property feeling like I belonged if I wasn't there any more than I absolutely had to be.

Quinn hummed. "I guess I should go relax and get cleaned up. Things start up at five?"

I nodded, an anxious twist in my gut making me shift on my feet. I should tell her now.

"Okay. Well. See you in a few hours."

She nodded, then turned, but I grabbed her hand. White hot energy and sensation shot up my arm, almost painful in its intensity. Her smooth palm against mine, our fingers locked, sent my pulse sprinting.

"For the record, don't apologize if you touch me. *When* you touch me. You are welcome to do it whenever and however you like."

She blinked and opened her mouth like she might speak, but instead tucked her bottom lip between her teeth and nodded. After a beat of heady connection—gazes, hands, and what felt like heartbeats—she slipped out of my grasp and through her door.

I watched her door shut, then entered my own room and prayed I'd be able to keep her around. Whatever I needed to do, I wanted to keep her, under any guise. I wouldn't even get to pretend she was mine to begin with.

But maybe... Just, maybe...

CHAPTER TWENTY

Quinn

With my tattered suitcase came a garment bag. Somehow, I'd completely forgotten about the dress. I mean no, I hadn't forgotten, but I'd spaced that he'd said he'd have options for me. I'd imagined choosing something before we'd departed but somehow had completely forgotten about that. I'd given Kelly my sizes, but nerves crawled up my throat as I unzipped the bag. *Please let one fit. Please let one fit.* The chant repeated in my mind until I pulled out three long dresses.

My heart raced at the sight and it finally clicked. I was in Jack McKean's house about to get ready for a black-tie event, and in my hand I held three gowns, all of them worth more than what I paid Julian to rent the store and my mortgage payments combined.

I hooked the hangers of each dress over the bar of a double-doored closet with bright lights inside and gaped.

One had thin threads of clear and silver beads all over like a flapper dress that dropped below the knee and featured a dramatic V-neck and little black bows on the shoulder. Interesting and very unique, and depending on how much cleavage actually showed, potentially quite elegant or maybe super uncomfortable. The second was a rose blush shiny silk sheath with tiny little straps that crisscrossed in the back and a cowl-style neckline. I suspected that wouldn't work because this was one that required stick-on bra magic, and I had none of that and wasn't about to go braless in front of cameras and... well, anyone. No, thanks. But I'd try it just for fun.

And finally, a black gown with a halter neck that led to panels that crossed high on the chest, then widened in an x to cover the breasts and attach to the waist that draped down gracefully. There was a hole that would show skin, but it'd all depend on the fit whether it ended up being revealing and kind of too much or dramatic and just right.

I loved the black one, but that was my usual go-to for singing gigs, so I made myself try on the other two first. Both beautiful, but I landed on the last one. The little triangle of skin that showed at my midriff was a little sexy, but not as revealing as I'd thought it'd be. I felt good. Thank you, Grit and Warrick.

I felt great, actually, and a little burst of anticipation for Julian to see me like this warmed my chest. And then I remembered he hadn't answered my question.

So far, he'd evaded responding to my question of why he'd brought me—why he needed someone with him for this event with his apparently very good friend Jack. He'd always looped that in—this wasn't just a few hours of singing. I'd be with him for some of it, too, and he wouldn't say why. It'd felt purposeful, and yet, I couldn't be sure. His meeting had started the first time, and we'd been pulling into the driveway the second.

As I pondered what his response might be, I went through the process of getting ready. I'd made sure my hair was clean and ready to style but hadn't done much in the way of hair and makeup since I'd wanted to make that call based on my dress. The next hour flew by as I styled my hair into a sleek twist. My bangs swooped to one side and fortunately seemed to feel like behaving so I didn't have to hairspray them to within an inch of their lives. As the evening progressed, little wisps would slip out, undoubtedly, but for now, the style was simple, but hopefully chic.

I kept my makeup to what I usually did since I needed to feel as comfortable as I could in a formal gown, and part of that would be feeling confident the rest of me felt like *me*. Smokey eyes, dark lashes, a touch of berry pink to my lips, and a spritz of the perfume I associated with going out, aka a scent I loved but rarely used—I was ready.

Oh, but shoes. I peeked into the bag that held three boxes, each presumably to compliment one of the dresses. The names on the box made my heart sprint, which didn't make any sense because I didn't care about labels, but I knew the names Choo, Louboutin, and Blahnik. If those were the names of the shoes, that likely meant the dresses were similarly branded, and therefore, whatever I wore was worth far more than even my imaginings.

No. Nope. I couldn't do thousand-dollar shoes on top of everything else, especially because even fancy-pants shoes would cause blisters the first time wearing them, and I was not about to be hobbled by performing in four-inch heels tonight. I didn't even open the box, because I was a red-blooded woman and if they were as gorgeous as I guessed,

I'd be unlikely to resist and pay for that folly later. My old reliables would have to do.

After slipping my feet into my own worn-in black pumps, I felt as prepared as possible. They were three and three-quarter classic black heels with a slight point to the toe, and I could run in them if I needed to. I could stand for hours since I did that every weekend, and I suspected there'd be a lot of standing around before we ever sat for dinner or the movie or whatever else would happen tonight.

I'd brought a little clutch but had no idea if I really needed it, though I'd want to refresh lipstick and at least have some Chapstick. Plus my phone. Cara would kill me if I didn't try to steal a photo of Jack, even if it did make me a little lame. We were staying here at the house, so did I? Or no?

It was this little question that tipped me from the Lala-land of preparing to the halting realization of what lay ahead. Somewhere in this house was Jack McKean and probably some blazingly gorgeous starlet as his date. No doubt there would be other faces I'd recognize from the movies or music, and while I prided myself on generally keeping my composure in the face of fame since I'd had a fair amount of practice with it once Jamie found it, a current of nerves still ran through me. I'd sung for all kinds of crowds over the years, but the intimacy of this one could prove to be unique among my experience.

But more than all of those swirling thoughts came one crystal-clear one. Something I couldn't ignore or simply go along with before I hobnobbed with all of these fancy folks and maybe even had my photo taken.

I needed to know why I was here. I couldn't pretend I understood or even knew why Julian had chosen me to be here like this—in a room across from his instead of grouped with the musicians or wherever the staff would stay. I didn't want to think through what it meant. So I straightened my spine, pulled my shoulders back, and grabbed my clutch, thankful we'd be inside so I didn't have to figure out how to stay warm in this relatively skimpy outfit.

Shutting my door behind me, I glanced left to right as though my next move was something clandestine. My body seemed to think it was, anyway, because my heart had started pounding in my ears and my throat felt dry. I should've had some water before I left, but too late now, because I'd already knocked on Julian's door.

He opened it seconds later, and his gaze slipped over me, then met mine. "Come in."

I swallowed hard, feeling stuck to the floor outside his room. "Uh, okay."

But I didn't move.

"Are you all right?" He inspected me more closely, a slight furrow between his brows.

I cleared my throat. "Fine. Yes. And thank you for the dresses. They were all beautiful."

His eyes bored into mine. *Gah.* He'd dialed up the intensity to ten thousand tonight, and the striking tux made him even more... striking. *Ughghg.* He'd scrambled my brain, and all he'd done was look at me and invite me inside.

"Come in," he said again, swinging the door wide.

My feet unstuck themselves, and I moved past him quickly, like being close might burn me. I didn't understand why I'd gone from feeling prepared to on the verge of a heart attack, but all I could say was that seeing Julian all dressed up like this had messed with me on more than one level.

"I'm glad you liked the dresses. You chose well."

I turned to see his eyes lingering on my exposed back.

The straps crossed around my neck, but the halter left everything from that strip of black material to the base of my spine exposed. I could admit, it was sexy. I also had to be honest and say I liked that he seemed to want to look. That might've been part of the reason I'd chosen this dress, but I would've wanted that with any one of them.

"Thank you," I said, remembering he'd said something and I should respond. And then, because it needed to be said, I added, "You look very nice."

He approached with a small velvet-covered box in his hand and held it out to me. "Thank you."

I raised a brow.

"One last thing for tonight." He opened the lid of the box, and I felt like every cliché because I gasped at the sight of the sparkling diamond teardrops.

"I—those are beautiful."

"They'll compliment the dress and your hairstyle. But the most beautiful thing is certainly the woman who'll wear them." He forced the box into my hand and moved to a small table that held a pitcher of water and other decanters presumably stocked with liquor. He poured two small glasses of water and handed me one. "To you."

I shook my head, nerves and something I might call ecstasy—except that didn't make sense—simmering low in my belly. "To the success of Jack's movie."

He nodded, seeming pleased, and gently touched his glass to mine. We both drank, though he took a small sip, and I gulped mine down to fortify my nerves. The water didn't do much in that way, but it did help my throat not feel so dry. Just in time, too.

I straightened my spine but dipped my head to one side as I fastened one of the earrings in, then the other. "So, I need you to answer my question."

He took my now-empty glass with the barest brush of our fingers, then moved to the small table, where he tipped the pitcher of water to the side and refilled mine. "What question is that?"

I exhaled, wondering if he was being purposefully oblivious or if I had asked him other questions that he'd avoided answering. I honestly couldn't remember because the main one had been foremost on my mind. "The question about why I'm here. Why you need *me*."

He nodded, handing me the glass. "I needed a date. I don't like to appear single at events like this."

"Events with friends?"

He pursed his lips, which I couldn't help noticing looked firm and appealing. Not plush or inviting like Jack McKean's, but then everything about Jack had that vampire quality, like he'd been crafted especially to glamor humans into his favor. Julian's more severe form of beauty created a push-pull, a feeling of forbidden, like he was fruit that shouldn't be tasted.

I'd always had great sympathy for Eve.

"I have an unfortunate history with women wanting to... become attached to me. When I go to events—big or small—this can become more of a problem if I'm alone."

He sat on a cushy-looking pure white couch, and I wished I could join him. But no. I was not about to sit during this conversation or until I had to in this dress.

"But aren't all these people friends of Jack's?" My voice shook, betraying my nerves and this new crush of wanting.

"In one way or another, and in theory, yes. But there are different definitions of *friend*, and Jack's agent has an agenda with this little gathering. I am likely one of only two real friends he'll have here. And I suppose you, by extension, though you've only just met."

I turned that thought over in my mind. I mean, sure, I'd happily be Jack McKean's friend. But the idea that he'd planned this intimate gathering that wasn't actually intimate seemed odd. More importantly, Julian's statements about women wanting to *attach themselves* to him made me particularly restless.

"So I'm here to be a bodyguard of sorts. But you could've just asked me, right? We're... friendly enough, aren't we?"

Heat hit my cheeks like a slap, which I hated, so I turned away and wandered past the bed to the windows. The view from his room was gorgeous and full of nearly bare fall trees and stalwart pines climbing the slopes of mountains that would soon be filled with skiers and tourists for the ski season. Not unlike back home, and yet so very different because this area had always been for the upper crust.

"We are," he answered after a moment. A slight rustle told me he'd stood, and nearly silent pats on the carpet brought him closer. He stood just behind me when he said, "I wouldn't have been asking for a fake date, though."

I swallowed, or tried, then took a drink of water to ease the way while my pulse scampered. "What would you—"

"Something real."

I nodded, victory and happiness lapping around my chest in time with my beating heart. I turned quickly enough to find his gaze on my back again, and when his eyes met mine, my stomach dropped low. "You could've asked."

"Could I?"

His response came quiet and with what I thought might be humor, though his mouth gave nothing away.

I nodded, my heart in my throat. "Why did you make it a contract, then?"

This was what didn't make sense. Maybe he hadn't realized I would be open to going out with him. I'd been pretty prickly whenever I found myself near him, but that was just kind of me sometimes. And I thought he knew that by now, didn't he? But he'd led with the date, then the singing, so it all folded into something businessy.

He sniffed and looked out the window in front of us. The sunset was on my side of the house, but we could still see the pink, purple, and orange left high in the little streaks of clouds. It'd be full dark anytime now.

I saw his redirected attention for what it was this time, though. "Julian?"

"Yes?"

Irritation spiraled up my spine. He was avoiding this, and I'd had it. "Why aren't you just answering me? You're driving me nuts."

He inhaled and let out a long breath through his nose before turning back to me. "I offered to pay you because you could use the money, and you wouldn't take it if it was a gift."

A heavy hand pressed against me, causing a collapse in my chest, and I stumbled back, then paced to the opposite side of the room. I shouldn't have been surprised— really, I wasn't, and yet it hurt. I ached with this news because I *had* needed the money. Of course I had, and he knew that thanks to my begging for no rent hike and the whole dryer debacle. But worse than his knowing I needed the money was the reality that it'd been a pitying move.

"I was afraid of that," I said so quietly I wasn't sure he'd heard me. The volume hid the shudder of anger that rippled through me. Then a realization clicked into place. Jack hadn't said a thing about me singing. I hadn't met the band.

Louisa hadn't given me instructions about sound checks or warming up. "Am I even singing at this thing?"

His jaw flexed, and the minuscule shake of his head sent fire through me.

"I could've told you it was canceled last minute."

He'd lied. He'd purposefully deceived me in order to get what he'd wanted. He'd overstepped into my financial situation like he had before, but this felt so messed up. All of that mixed with the toxic disappointment that he'd prioritized offering me money and lying about this being work over simply wanting to help me... It messed with my head.

"Don't do that," he added softly.

The command chafed, and I heaved a slow exhale to find calm. A futile effort though, and my tirade showed exactly that when I opened my mouth.

"Don't do what? Be upset you wanted to pay me out of pity? That you got me here under the pretense of a job and you needing a date and I'd be doing you a favor, but I come to find out it's because poor little Quinn needs cash?" Ire geysered up from my belly, searing my heart and landing squarely in my brain, burying all ability to be logical.

"I don't pity you, Quinn. There's nothing pitiful about you."

He crossed to me where I stood by the door. I snorted an ugly false laugh.

"Sure. That's why you were paying me to do exactly nothing. Because I'm so damn admirable? Because I'm just that amazing?"

He nodded. "Yes. *Yes.* You are admirable. And you shouldn't have to toil like you do. And I could help that, at least a little. I knew—"

"You knew I wouldn't say yes if I'd known that. You lied to me, and while some part of my exploding brain realizes you were being kind and generous, I don't want that from you. I don't need it. Understand me very clearly—I will not take your money."

His jaw hardened as his eyes darted over me. He looked so much more handsome in that tux with his serious hawk face and his probing eyes. It made me want to punch him. Or push him. Or...

Or...

Something in the air charged and shifted as he stepped right into my space. My back against the door, he set one hand to the right of my head and dipped his chin, eyes blazing and more expressive than I'd ever seen.

"What do you want from me, then? What can I do?"

My breathing had been rapid, but now, it outright raced like I couldn't catch it. My mind whirled and my heart clenched. "I want... I—"

And then I did it.

I grabbed the lapels of his tux, pulled him to me, and kissed him.

CHAPTER TWENTY-ONE

Julian

Nothing had prepared me for Quinn's lips on mine.

That said, I couldn't claim I hadn't longed for it. Despite my insistence that I wanted her friendship, of course I'd always forbidden myself to even think of this. Even dreaming of someone, more than a fleeting yearning, could feel like robbing them of their consent, so I had never ventured there.

But tonight, after everything that had happened so far, that fire in her eyes and the flush to her neck and cheeks sent heat through me. I allowed it to, and it lit me up. So when our lips collided, flames burst to life.

Truth be told, I'd never wanted anything the way I wanted Quinn Darling—I acknowledged it now. My body had known, but I wasn't a man who paid heed to his base instincts when my brain had always provided the more rational path in any situation. Having Quinn at arms' length had been something, had caused a bit of a stir inside. Not enough, but better than the nothing I'd had for every other minute I'd lived in Silverton or been away. Far better than before I knew she existed, before she'd dropped like water over the ink on my page and blurred every clear line I'd ever drawn.

Her hands at my neck urged me closer as she took from my mouth, a kiss so comprehensive, I couldn't imagine what might be better. Then I stepped closer with her pull and pressed against her so she was trapped. I held her to me, one hand at her bare shoulder and the other at the curve of her waist.

The contact sent tremors of sensation through my mind, synapses firing into small revelations with every press of her lips, every slide of her hands against my skin.

This was no ordinary kiss. Not like anything I'd ever had, not that this came as a surprise. Quinn's kiss was passion and fire, but it was fury too. While I disagreed with her assessment of what I'd done, I was beginning to understand. If I told her that her reaction to my lie had proven me right, and now, that I wanted her more than I ever did, she'd end the kiss.

I did nothing but kiss her back. I wanted to say her name. I wanted to pull her back and look in her eyes to see the desire there—desire for *me*. Not my name or my money—the money might've made this very occurrence less likely. In fact, I knew it did.

However angry she was, part of it was that I hadn't simply asked her. I'd considered it but thought this was the better offer, both for her and me. For her, she'd benefit, and for me, I'd guarantee she wouldn't change her mind. We'd chug along easily as friends, the job going away in a poof of smoke worth nothing more than a shrug since what was done was done, and here we were so why not enjoy the time. Yes, I understood the problem more fully now than ever, but I couldn't regret it if this were the outcome.

She tilted her head, deepening the contact and sending need spiraling through me. Now that I'd consciously opened the floodgates, the emotional vortex swallowed me whole, though Quinn, she consumed me entirely. No denying it now. I leaned closer to her, loving the feel of her, how she pressed back and arched into me. Her grip was firm, her lips demanded. And all I wanted to do to with this woman was obey her whims.

"Mr. Grenier? Mr. McKean has requested to speak with you."

The knock and voice speaking in a clear, raised volume rang like a shot and Quinn froze. Her eyes opened wide, and though the heat hadn't extinguished, I saw the moment when she came fully back to herself and remembered she was mad at me. She pressed her head back against the door, at which point I realized she couldn't escape with me pinning her to the panel.

"I'll be a moment," I said, uninterested in another rap on the door to sledgehammer between us even farther. Quinn already appeared to be removed from the moment, though she stood right in front of me, chest rising and falling, lips stung and perfect.

She's perfect. That echoed through me, a fact discerned from seeing her like this on the heels of so many other fiery ones.

"Certainly. I'll be just down the hall to escort you."

Presumably, the woman retreated far enough not to overhear my next words. "Do you need a minute?"

She licked her lips, which drew my gaze, but I forced

myself to refocus on her eyes. The furrow between her brows hadn't fled. But she didn't speak, only nodded.

"Would you like me to wait for you?" I didn't want to crowd her or set her off again since I knew instinctively that whatever came next had to be entirely up to her and could go either way. She needed to forget about my way of getting her here and focus on the very strong case we'd both just made for our being together.

"No. I'm fine. You go ahead and I'm going to, uh, check my makeup." Her index finger traced along the edge of her bottom lip.

My eyes followed the movement, a crush of longing to kiss her again flooding me strongly enough that I stepped back. "Very well. See you in a few minutes."

She opened the door and walked straight across to hers and shut it. I glanced in the mirror and noticed her lipstick giving away our encounter, so I wiped it off. Some part of me wanted to leave it there so it was clear to everyone attending the event that she was mine. Like a primal urge to be marked by her.

But that could end up being less romantic and more uncomfortable, likely especially for her. I didn't know what chance I had with maintaining Quinn's interest in a room full of Jack and his ilk, but time would tell. Now that it'd happened, I could admit this was one of several scenarios I'd wanted confirmed by bringing her here, even if I hadn't real-ized it initially. Her reaction told me exactly what I wanted to know—she wasn't falsely indignant or simply demurring. She didn't want the money.

And the fact that she'd kissed me?

I smiled to myself before straightening my jacket and heading to find Jack.

He was waiting for me in the kitchen, shoveling in appetizers from a tray while waitstaff zipped around him, readying as much as they could in the final minutes before more guests would arrive.

"There you are. I thought you were going to meet me in here ten minutes ago. I've been nervous eating." He popped another canape into his mouth and chewed like he hadn't eaten in a week.

"Settle yourself, McKean. I got held up."

His brows rose. Normally, I would ignore that and not say a thing, but he knew I had a thing for Quinn based on the mere fact that I'd brought her along, and I felt like making an official declaration about our kiss to the whole party. I wouldn't, of course, but I could mention it to Jack.

"Quinn and I had words."

His eyes widened. "I'm listening."

"She's upset about something. Very upset." And she was gorgeous with that fire in her eyes and heat in her cheeks. It might've made me a cliché idiot, but she was stunning when infuriated. I wouldn't want to be on the receiving end of that very often, but since I knew why she was upset and felt the problem could eventually be solved, it hadn't been as disconcerting as it might've been.

"Why do you look pleased by this? You're a strange man, Jules," he tutted, then tossed another little appetizer into his mouth.

"First, don't call me Jules. Second, you should save some food for your guests. And third, it wasn't because she was angry. It started because she was angry, and then she kissed me like the world was on fire."

That got him. A big smile flashed across his face before he wiped his mouth with a napkin and tossed it into a nearby trash can. "Well, that *is* interesting."

I nodded, too pleased with my news and his response. It

might make me a sap, but frankly, I didn't care. A man had to face hard facts, right? I knew she could very well hate me even more than she did before we'd established this... whatever it was. If she felt embarrassed, or like I'd coerced her, I'd be done for. I had blocked her in, hadn't I? She could've slipped to one side, and I couldn't imagine Quinn being intimidated by anyone, even if I had a few inches on her despite the high heels. Still.

I never did things like that. Being someone like me, someone people wanted to trap or have an excuse to sue, meant I *never* made physical overtures. Paired with my dislike of touching or being touched unless I initiated and had a purpose for the contact, I simply didn't do such things. But Quinn had drawn me in, fly to fruit, and I couldn't resist getting close and seeing what she'd do with all that fire in her eyes.

I did this in business fairly often—pushed enough to encourage a response from a development team or board. But never had I done it in my personal life like I'd been doing with Quinn, or like I did today.

And I'd never been more pleased with the result.

"Jack, people are arriving." The woman I recognized as his right hand and surrogate mother-slash-assistant clicked in on heels in a long golden gown, looking lovely and a bit rushed. "Take a drink of water before you head out, and when you flag, remind yourself it's just an hour before we sit and watch your performance. And hello, Julian."

She glanced up at me, then back down at her tablet, doing three things at once aside from talking.

"Nice to see you, Anita," I said, because it was. She'd gotten Jack through a lot, and seeing him look so healthy and relatively at ease, especially before an industry event, gave me a sense of relief I hadn't realized I'd needed.

She winked, then clicked back out of the room toward the entrance. Jack dutifully gulped down half a glass of water and then settled those unnerving blue eyes on me.

"I'm looking forward to talking to Quinn. I'd like to get a feel for her." He turned and slipped through the entrance to the kitchen and down the hallway leading to the front door.

I followed close behind. "You don't need to do that. She's good."

"I'll be the judge," he said without looking back at me.

"I've already judged. I don't take this lightly, as you know."

Just before the hallway opened to the opulent entrance, he paused and pinned me with his gaze. "You know as well as I do that you can't trust yourself with this girl. You've just ravished her in your—"

"I didn't *ravish*. What am I, a nineteenth century duke? We kissed. *She* kissed *me*."

He raised a brow. "Fine. You want to get with her—"

"Oh, perfect. Make me sound like I'm going to try to sleep with her and leave her before she wakes up." I stretched my neck to one side, the collar of my shirt chafing.

He pointed at me. "See? You have it bad for her. Which means you're not objective. Which means she could be like so many before her, and just after your—"

"*So many* before her? You realize who you're talking to, right?"

He chuckled and shook his head. "I do. You're one of my best friends, whether you'll admit it or not. And I'm going to check this girl out because I know Jamie Morris has known her his whole life and he's a paragon of judgment on the matter, but *I* am going to see for myself. Now if you'll excuse me, I'm an extremely popular person and the host of this party, so if you don't want to greet everyone with me and *my* date, then go find your own."

If looks could kill, he'd be laid out on the polished wood floor about now. As it was, my unimpressed glare did nothing. He flashed another smile, straightened his bowtie, and spun away.

That Jack thought of me as a best friend warmed me. I wasn't an effusive man. I didn't fawn over people, but I did collect the good ones and keep them. And while he didn't need to check up on Quinn, part of me liked that he wanted to. He'd seen enough trouble in his personal life, not unlike the kind I'd had, so he'd feel better about it if he talked to her.

Quinn wasn't after my money. She wasn't interested in using me as a means to an end. I'd learned that lesson, and learned it again.

And ironically, I wanted her to use me. I wanted her to want anything from me, because to this point, she'd wanted nothing—not really. The kiss gave me hope, but no assurances. And I hadn't gotten this far in life on hope, so I'd have to work on the latter.

Plus, there was the small matter of getting her to take my money—my assistance—now that she'd seen through my plan tonight.

CHAPTER TWENTY-TWO

Quinn

Jack McKean was so beautiful, it was hard to look at him. I'd forgotten just how word-stealingly handsome he looked somewhere between slipping into a designer gown and kissing Julian Grenier's face off.

Taking a steadying breath, I worked to relax myself while approaching the movie star. I couldn't think of him as simply Jack or Julian's friend because his good looks and polish were so out there compared to real people. It was almost obnoxious, except he was directing one of his thousand-watt smiles at me and extending a hand like he was glad to see me, and I doubted anyone could resist being a bit mesmerized by him when he did that.

"Quinn, you look lovely." He held out a hand and cupped his other over mine when I shook it.

He had nice hands. Nice everything, really, but wasn't that to be expected when a person was literally paid to maintain their looks? Notably, I felt a twinge of nerves, but no butterflies. Nothing like what permeated every part of me when Julian touched me, even casually. Perhaps because the contact had been so limited. Well, until twenty minutes ago and that kiss.

"Thank you. You look very handsome, though I don't suppose I need to tell you that." I smiled back at him because the gleaming smile he still wore required the response.

"Oh, I'll never say no to a compliment from a beautiful woman. But tell me, how'd you end up here?" Something shifted in his expression and moved from full-on charm to a sharper sparkle in his eye. Almost like all that gorgeous physical glory hid a darker, cutthroat side.

Maybe it did. I didn't know the man. As much as I was beginning to trust Julian, I didn't truly know him either. That was part of the problem, wasn't it? So how could I know if this guy wasn't some kind of crazy predator who'd invited us all to his house to dine on his Hannibal Lecter-style meal?

No. I didn't really think that. But the question sounded specific and geared to find out something. I just didn't know what. "Hmm. Well. I got into Julian's car and Scott drove us here. Then you answered the door and invited us in. Do I need to show an invitation?"

He chuckled gamely. "Of course not, no. I'm well aware of why you're here. I only wanted to hear your version."

"Why am I here, then, Jack? I'd love to hear *your* version." I wondered what Julian had told him, if anything.

He tilted his head to one side. "I hardly think it's fair if I go first."

If I hadn't been wearing a formal gown that required me to stand up straight, I would've crossed my arms. Instead, I fiddled with the clutch. "All right. I'm here because Julian asked me. Why he did that, I don't really know. I thought I knew, and now..."

I sighed. This man didn't need the nitty gritty of my mixed-up feelings for his friend. He definitely didn't need to know I'd been stupid enough to buy that I'd been hired to sing at the event but had zero contact with the band or planning team. I'd done more than one house party and should've known, but *yeah. Idiot.*

His eyes softened. "Now?"

"I'm not sure. But I'm glad to be here. Thanks for welcoming me."

His brows dipped, and he reached up like he might run his fingers through his hair but stopped like he'd been chastised for doing that very thing. "Listen, Quinn. I'm not trying to be an ass. Jules has had a few rough breaks with women, which I'm sure you could guess. I don't want to see him hurt."

I blinked at the frank words. "I don't either. Not that I think I could, but I assure you I have no nefarious motives with him."

His stark blue eyes shifted between mine and he nodded as though satisfied with something. "Good. And for what it's worth, he doesn't have anything but good things in mind for you."

I opened my mouth to say something, but that wording halted the words in my throat. It sounded like he might be insinuating Julian was my benefactor. Really, he hadn't said anything that would lead me to believe Julian had feelings for me beyond his over-reaching insistence on throwing money at me. But the idea that I could hurt him contradicted all that.

After more than a beat, I summoned a broad smile. "That's good news."

He nodded, and then someone grabbed his arm and pulled him away. Before I had a chance to feel lost or wonder what I should do with myself, Julian approached and offered his arm. I looped mine through his and worked to control my breath and heart. They'd both taken off the second I'd seen him, and after that conversation with Jack, I didn't know how to behave.

Actually, that wasn't true. The conversation was odd, yes, but it was the kiss. I'd kissed him but *oh, baby* had he kissed me back. Passionately enough that my understanding of Julian Grenier had been blown to bits. I usually saw this man as ice, but I must've forgotten ice could burn, too— sometimes worse than fire.

If we hadn't been interrupted, I couldn't say where we would've ended up. We might've just stayed there, pressed together and pinned against the door, kissing like we'd finally found each other after a long separation.

"Did Jack say something that troubled you?" he asked, his voice low so we wouldn't be overheard by the small crowd of people huddled around Jack a few feet away near the door.

"He asked me why I was here." I glanced over at him, then followed when he led me farther from the group to the side of the room.

"What did you say?"

I swallowed, wishing for a drink. "I said I didn't know."

His gaze traced over my lips, then slid up to meet my eyes. "I'm sorry I've made a mess of this. But I hope you believe me when I say you're here because I want you here."

I nodded and tore my eyes away. He was just so dang intense at close range, and here he was saying that so clearly, right to my face. I didn't know what else I expected because other than the one question he'd skillfully avoided until half an hour ago, he'd always been direct.

Maybe that was why anger spiked again at the memory of how he'd lied to me about the contract. My brain had flatlined after the kiss, the flood of endorphins and desire pummeling all my indignation into a placid pool of amazement and confusion. But now, I remembered. He hadn't asked me to come as his date because... why? He'd wanted something real, he said, but he'd used the contract as a way to make it happen. Either he wanted to control the situation by leveraging the money and contract, or he pitied me and did the same. In both cases, my anger felt justified. I shouldn't feel bad for him or worried about him, but Jack's words stuck in my side. I wondered what "rough breaks" he'd referred to, and whether I'd ever be able to ask Julian about them. We'd very rarely spoken about his personal life.

"Do you believe that? I won't settle for a misunderstanding on this. I want you, Quinn."

My stomach swooped low and butterflies fluttered frantically in my chest. Not "I want you here," but "I want you." That only threw another log on the fire of hope, confusion, anger, and the general feeling I was out of my depth with this man. "Okay. I believe you."

He held my gaze for another few seconds, right until I thought I might burst and plead for mercy from the intensity. "Good."

"Obviously enough, you're not paying me a cent."

He frowned, but said no more since a flurry of chatter rose and broke the heady moment between us. Turning to face the door, I exhaled some of the tension in my chest and then saw several stars walk into the room, including Bri

Williamson, the world's favorite pop star, and Jenna Halter, one of the funniest women in Hollywood.

"Oh, good. I love her," I said, more to myself than Julian.

"She's lovely. I'll introduce you."

I smiled over at him. "I've met her once before when she visited Calla a few months ago."

Julian nodded. "Of course. Well, if you'd like to meet Bri, I can introduce you." He studied me, clearly waiting for an answer.

"Sure. He's not really my flavor, but I'm glad to meet him."

He made a light sound, more like a huff than a laugh, but thrill raced through me. It had been a laugh, however small and hidden. "What?"

"He's not your *flavor*?" One of those strong brows arched.

I bit my bottom lip to keep from smiling, then said, "Yeah. He's obviously gorgeous, talented, and from what Calla has said, a real quality human being. But he just doesn't do it for me."

A flame lit in his eye. "No? But Jack does?"

My heartrate kicked up. "Jack is a stunning man. I got caught in his tractor beam of charm and beauty earlier. But..." I swallowed down a whole pile of nerves, amazed at what I felt coming. "He doesn't do it for me like I thought he would in person."

The room seemed to shrink to just the two of us when Julian dipped his head. "That's a shame."

His eyes hadn't left mine, and I slowly came to register we weren't standing side by side with linked arms, but instead facing each other with his hand on my waist, the pads of his fingers just barely grazing the bare skin of my back, and my hand on his wrist over his suit jacket.

Heat and sensation chased each other out in waves from the contact at my side. "Not such a shame. I can't imagine dating someone in the public eye like that."

His thumb swept an arc over the skin of my stomach through the smooth material of my dress, and then he released me. Shutters came down over his expression, and all that heat and delicious tension evaporated, leaving me wondering what I'd done wrong. I'd been so close to telling him I liked him, so none of these other men, however handsome and appealing, didn't hold sway for me.

But he offered his arm, then led me into the crowd without another word. And though no one else would know, his expression seemed more guarded around the eyes than before. He was always serious and stern, but now he held himself a quarter turn tighter on that well-controlled dial.

Something about my comment had bothered him, and rather than say anything, he just ignored it. He must've grown used to having his way in conversations. And he could live like that for now, while he introduced me to famous people and Silicon Valley fancy pants.

But soon, I'd ask him. Because I wasn't going to deal with another round of not knowing and not understanding. We'd get through tonight, and then I'd corner him in the car on the drive home tomorrow and I'd get him to talk. About what just happened. About what he wanted from me—really. And maybe about those tough breaks.

Julian might be used to getting his way, but he had no idea how stubborn I could be.

CHAPTER TWENTY-THREE

Julian

Quinn was a natural. Maybe thanks to her lifelong friendship with Jamie, or maybe because of her innate sense of self and comfort in her own body, she charmed everyone she interacted with. I had no right or claim on her to be proud, but I felt it anyway.

She remained unfazed by Jenna, Bri Williamson who gave Jack a run for his money on the beautiful people list, and even Juliet Christensen, a friend of mine whom I hadn't seen in years.

"Julian, it's so good to see you." Juliet kissed each cheek with her baby soft ones, then beamed at me.

"Likewise. Let me introduce you to Quinn Darling. She's an extraordinary singer and musician. She owns a music shop in Silverton that outfits all the local schools with instruments and music as well as many top tier musicians, and is generally an excellent human being, much like yourself."

Juliet's blue eyes lit with warmth, and she shook Quinn's hand with both of hers as I continued. "Quinn, this is Juliet Christensen. She's head of several organizations, a philanthropist of many colors, and is serving as a Goodwill Ambassador for the United Nations."

Quinn's eyes widened. "Wow."

I smiled inwardly because making Quinn speechless didn't happen often.

Juliet patted her hand, still holding Quinn's gaze. "It's so nice to meet you, Quinn. A friend of mine visited Silverton this time last year and is planning to get back there soon. I'm dying to join her after some other travel I have coming up. She mentioned the amazing live music at the hotel lounge and said Silverton is basically a dream."

"I highly recommend it." Quinn smiled back at Juliet, unable to resist her genuine brightness.

"Quinn sings at the Silver Ridge Resort bar on weekends, and it's not to be missed. Make sure your friend—"

"It's Maddie Reynolds!"

I nodded, pleased to hear this. "Of course. I was out of town for much of her first visit, but I'm pleased to hear she'll be returning."

Juliet sparkled back at us. The woman was just one of those people whose inner beauty, as damn cheesy as it sounded, absolutely matched her outer beauty, and both were stunning.

"Folks, we'll be starting the film in five."

The announcement came via Anita as she whirled around the room, alerting everyone to the impending change.

"I better go find my date. See you after, I hope."

Juliet turned and walked off to find whoever was lucky enough to be here with her. Undoubtedly someone not good enough. I'd set her and Jack up ages ago and they'd gotten along well but reportedly had no chemistry. In the end, they both enjoyed each other so much that they'd stayed friends.

"She's just a little impressive," Quinn said, staring after the woman. "Are all your friends billionaires, A-list celebs, and model gorgeous?"

"No. Of course not. But that is the gathering of people here, so it may seem like it." I glanced at her to see her brow furrowed. "What?"

"I am a fairly confident person, but I feel very much out of my depth here. I'm not—" She swallowed, then released a breath. "I'm not like these people."

I took her hand and led her to the side of the room, frustration rising. "You're better. You wouldn't know how to be fake if someone paid you."

And then I winced, because that ran along the lines of what I'd asked of her coming into tonight. Fortunately, her anger with my deception seemed to have faded. She rolled her eyes and bit that bottom lip that called to me, then glanced around again before speaking.

"You're right. I'm not fake. But none of the people we met tonight seemed fake. Maybe that's because they're just that good."

I shook my head. "No. I only introduced you to the people who aren't. There's a handful of clingers in here who do whatever it takes to be in places like this—in a room with the *who's who* or whatever you want to call it."

Her green eyes flicked back and forth between mine. "Sounds exhausting."

I wondered if she meant for the people hanging on, or

for the people already in the room. I suspected both were the case, though I only knew it from my experience and I could confirm. Yes, it was exhausting.

"You two are sitting by me. Let's go." Jack nodded toward the theater door, and we followed obediently.

As we walked, I placed my hand at the base of Quinn's spine. I'd done it twice before during the social hour, and each time, she hadn't balked or moved away. She'd let me touch her there in that proprietary, personal way, and even this third time, it sent satisfaction racing through me.

For a woman who'd decried the public life of Jack McKean not an hour ago, she certainly managed the socializing well. I wasn't actually surprised, but it made that twist in my gut when I remembered her reason for not wanting Jack wrench even further.

My life didn't have as many public interactions as Jack's, but I *was* a public figure. Occasionally, I did interviews, and every so often people recognized me. Depending on where I was, I required security. I made attention-grabbing lists of all kinds of things, and in the end, not all of my life was my own. Far different from true celebrity, of course, but still not tucked away in Silverton all the time.

Not like the life she seemed to want. And that, more than anything up to this point, set me back on my heels.

That was the strangest, clearest realization of my life thus far. I felt more for this woman than I did for anyone other than my dearest friends, and naturally, the feelings were different. She'd pummeled right through all the tidy compartments of my life, my usual responses to attraction and interest, and she'd taken me by the neck. She had me completely, and I couldn't pretend it had anything to do with friendship or Silverton. *She* had me.

Her anger over my lie made sense. It did. Her reaction

to it threw me in the best possible way. And the fact that she could stand in this room full of people she recognized and names she knew and not be lured in by any of them, but stay by my side? It might be a little pathetic how rare that was, especially since she didn't stick to me because I out-earned all of them by a hundred times, save Juliet. And she seemed absolutely repulsed by my money.

But being put off by the fame and publicity didn't bode well, either. Again, I wasn't Jack or Jenna or Bri or even Juliet, but I'd had my share of problems due solely to fame. I'd had many others due to my financial status and people wanting to leverage knowing me to their advantage.

Jack pointed at two seats in the middle of the home theater and we each sat, then he did.

"This is a very large home theater," Quinn said quietly.

"It's obnoxious, right? I don't want my house to have one of these whenever I settle down."

Jack's response sounded tired, and one glance told me he was giving himself a minute for the shiny *Publicity Jack* to take a breath.

"Oh, right. Julian mentioned it's a rental," Quinn said.

"Yep, crazy enough. I've been here about two weeks, and I'm not sure how much longer I'll keep it. I mean, I have the lease for six months but it's just so freaking huge." He shifted in his seat and passed out smiles to people as they found their seats.

"I told you about the lots in my neighborhood. You need to come see them."

He leaned over the armrest, eyes raking over Quinn before settling on me. "Think I could find more than a house there?"

I caught his meaning, as though he hadn't papered it

over his expression for all to see. "Remains to be seen, but you won't know if you never step foot there."

His eyes narrowed, then one side of his mouth kicked up into an expression I'd come to know as a harbinger of mischief. Sure enough, he leaned back but spoke to Quinn. "As a lifelong citizen of Silverton, do you think it's possible for an outsider to truly belong in Silverton? To be fully accepted and adopted into the community?"

"I do. I can think of several examples of that easily. Mia Morrison moved in and started working at the library. She ended up marrying Danny Morrison, a local. Wells Bryant-Morrison has a similar story. And Jonas Bauer is probably the most fish-out-of-water version of someone from outside fully settling in. He's a bit like Julian in that he came in and a lot of people thought he was taking over, but he ended up being great for the community." She glanced at me, then back to Jack.

"Good to know. And what about you, personally? Do you welcome outsiders, or are you someone who longs for the simpler times in Silverton?"

I stifled a sigh. Could he be more obvious? Not that Quinn didn't already know I liked her, but the man needed a knock to the head. He might as well have asked her if she liked me, check yes or no.

"I resisted a lot of the changes a few years back—the resort, the revamp of the theater, and a few other things. I was afraid it would change the nature of the town, not just the façades of buildings or the skyline. But I've come to embrace the changes and see the growth and expansion as really great."

Jack rewarded her with a smile. "Good answer."

"So you're thinking of settling somewhere in Utah? Is that it?"

Jack's eyes flicked to mine, then returned to Quinn, and I braced for whatever came next.

"Not unlike Julian, I've always wanted a place that felt like home. Truly like *my* home. I've been kicking around different places for years but haven't been at the point where I could really invest. I'm jealous Jules has found that, and it makes me antsy for my turn."

Quinn hummed but seemed to carefully avoid turning to see me. "I hope you find it."

"Thanks. Me too."

"Ladies and Gentlemen, *Karrigan's Muse*." Anita announced the movie, and everyone in the room quieted.

Since this was a director's cut and a private screening, no previews played. The lights dimmed, the music swelled, and I didn't stop being completely aware of every shift Quinn made. That people sat on every other side of me didn't chafe like it might've without her there, her light, fresh scent teasing just beyond my full grasp.

I wanted to take her hand in mine so badly, but I kept mine clasped together to resist indulging. And Quinn didn't notice my odd pose because she was completely engaged in the movie. She gasped and laughed and cried at all the right moments, I assumed, because everyone around her did the same.

Jack was a black hole of energy, no surprise. Few things made him coil into himself like watching his own movies, but it was part of the gig. He'd unfold as the light came up and probably enter hermit mode for the next few weeks to recover from being on all night. I didn't know how he did it and thanked God I didn't have the same obligation to be charming and open with people.

The credits rolled and everyone stood and clapped. Jack

nodded graciously, a perfect mix of humble and pleased with the recognition.

And then the night slipped by so fast, it was like I'd been knocked out and came to just as Quinn slipped her hand into mine when we rounded the corner to our hallway. Or maybe this was the contact I'd been wanting but had been too cowardly to attempt. Her palm against mine, her fingers clasping over my knuckles, felt like the most sensual, personal, consequential thing that'd ever happened to me. Even more than the kiss hours ago, because it came after a night of being exposed to my unenviable social skills.

"I had fun tonight. And while I do not endorse your method for getting me here, I'm glad I came."

We slowed to a stop in front of our doors and turned to face each other. My heart pounded a rapid beat in my chest, neck, and temple. "It was my honor to have you with me."

Her eyes softened, though they hadn't been hard before, and she stepped closer. Instinctively, I brought my free hand around to her lower back and steadied her as she leaned up on her toes and placed a slow kiss to my cheek.

My eyes shut at the contact, but I opened them quickly so I wouldn't miss anything. I couldn't go lax with this woman.

"I'd like to really kiss you again, but first, you're going to talk to me." She stepped back and disconnected our bodies and hands.

"I can do that."

One of her brows arched. "Good. Clear your schedule for the car ride home. I've got a list of questions for you, and I want answers, Grenier."

I couldn't hide the charmed smile at those words. I couldn't pretend I didn't like this side of her—I did. She didn't get runover by my bullheaded approach to things.

She didn't let me off the hook. And so far, she didn't let me go, though she had no idea just how on her hook I was.

"It'll be my pleasure."

She'd passed the test. She'd blown it to bits. And now the way ahead was even more clear than it had been before.

CHAPTER TWENTY-FOUR

Quinn

I met Julian out front at ten the next morning. He'd texted after we'd gone our separate ways to say he and Jack were going for an early run and that I should sleep in. Part of me had wished he'd knocked on my door and told me to my face, because I probably would've kissed him. Or let him kiss me. He looked too dang good in that tux, and I'd squandered the chance to do anything about it.

Jack had an interview going by the time we left, but I'd seen him earlier and thanked him. He'd given me a sparkly smile, then told me he hoped to see me in Silverton soon. Good luck to the women of Silverton when that one arrived, and with him, Calla, and Jamie all making their homes in town, we'd have reporters camping out on street corners any day now.

I shuddered at the thought while buckling my seat belt.

"Are you cold?" Julian shifted forward and tapped the display to increase the warm air and started my seat heater.

"Thanks. Actually, I was just thinking about what would happen if Jack moved to Silverton."

His head turned sharply to me. "What did he say?"

"He just said he hoped he'd see me soon. And it's not like I'm running in his circles, so I took that to mean he might actually take you up on the offer to visit and check out our little resort town."

"Ah. Yes. We'll see what happens." His eyes stayed on mine for another moment before they dropped to the tablet in his lap.

"You're not starting to work, are you?"

"Am I not?"

I chuckled. "Valiant though your efforts to avoid talking to me may be, we have some things to discuss." I leaned over my elbow where I'd placed it on the armrest that separated our seats.

He did the same, bringing our faces inches apart. My eyes dropped to his mouth, and my stomach flipped when I looked up to see his gaze had done the same, dipping to mine.

"What do you wish to discuss with me?"

If those weren't flames in his eyes, I didn't know fire. *Wow.* All those times I'd thought he was a cardboard cutout in a suit, something sterile and aggressive and so business-minded that I'd doubted he could spell the word passion let alone embody it? Yeah, I'd been so, *so* wrong.

In truth, I'd known that for a while now. I'd seen him transfixed during our sets at the bar. People devoid of passion didn't sit for hours and just listen to live music.

"I want to know you," I said, honesty pushing a flush to my cheeks.

His gaze shifted from heated to something softer. His eyes took a pass at my face, a look I might've seen as cherishing, and then he leaned back. "Ask away."

I hadn't expected it to be that easy. "Well, uh... where are you from? What's your family like? Do you have siblings? How do you know Jack, and—"

"Did you plan on letting me answer any of them?"

I shot him an unamused glare, then silently swept my hand out as if to say *be my guest*.

One of his eyebrows flared up. "I was born in California, attended boarding school on the east coast, went to college at MIT at just shy of fifteen, then pursued a doctorate at Cal Tech, and not long after that began my company."

My mouth dropped open. "Boarding school? College at fifteen?"

His brow dropped low. "I assure you I'm not embellishing."

"No, I didn't think that. It's just... *crap*. I mean, I guess it makes sense, knowing the little about you I do, but I didn't realize people actually lived that kind of life. I'm just..." I trailed off, not sure how to verbalize the oddly squiggly mess in my chest at this brief bio.

"Don't spare me, Quinn. You're just *what?*"

Heat rushed to my cheeks yet again. "I know I'm out of my league with you, but I don't think I realized it was all that much more than professionally and financially. But now I'm realizing how short-sighted that was. You're a genius. And, *ugh*, I'm an idiot." I dropped my chin to my chest, suddenly overcome with embarrassment.

This was not a feeling I often felt. I owned who I was. I hadn't been thrown by the financial disparity between us, though the difference between our lifestyles and livelihoods was laughable at best. But realizing he was so far above me in every possible facet of life?

His hand grasping mine brought my attention back to him.

"You are not an idiot. Don't say that."

I swallowed, my throat tight and eyes pricking. I inhaled sharply, forbidding the tears any more progress. "I feel that way."

One stiff shake of his head attempted to wipe away my words. "You, Quinn Darling, are magnificent. And yes, there are many differences between us, but the ones that concern me have nothing to do with numbers."

"Oh, good, so you're worried about this too?"

His eyes shifted between mine, and he grabbed my other hand. "Yes. But not for the reasons you are—or at least the things you just mentioned."

My heart was strapped to a rollercoaster car ticking up, up, up. I could see the crest coming and I had no way to stop the rickety ride and keep myself from plummeting over the edge into the reality of whatever he'd say next.

When he read my panicked expression, his concern deepened, judging by the furrow in his brows and the downward pull of his lips. "You are so full of passion and life. You're caring and generous in ways I never imagined those first few times I saw you, when I thought you were the most beautiful woman I'd ever seen."

The little car dropped, and my heart swooped low, falling fast, but instead of terror, it was thrill that came with his words. "I don't think of you as someone who's prone to exaggeration."

One side of his mouth tipped up, and his eyes warmed. "I'm not. I've been interested in you since the second I saw you. Nothing so prosaic as love at first sight, but I was more drawn to you than anyone I've ever met."

I wondered when that was—how long ago, exactly? I'd met him maybe three years ago. Or a little less. "Why didn't you just ask me out?"

"You wouldn't have said yes."

"How do you know?"

"I know."

"But how could you know when I'm not even sure what I would've said?"

His lips thinned with his skeptical glare. "If you don't know, I can't help you. But I can say that I'm fairly certain you would've said no. Normally, no doesn't scare me. I asked Sadie Miller with the full anticipation of her negative response. But with you, I couldn't bring myself to attempt when I knew I'd fail and potentially close the door on anything between us."

So many questions formed, then dissolved in my mind. How long had he felt this way? Was he being serious? If he'd actually thought all this, why hadn't he just asked me to come with him instead of the stupid gig ruse?

And more than anything else, what did he mean by telling me this now?

"So..." Too many thoughts crowded in, and I couldn't decide which to ask for.

"So, what I'm not concerned with is when I started college or your net worth versus mine."

I huffed a laugh. "I'm pretty sure people in my tax bracket don't refer to it as *net worth*."

He gave me another flat glare. I beamed, delight at seeing him so expressive and responsive to me flooding my senses and apparently addling my brain.

"My point is that my concern is centered on the kind of people we are, and in that, there is true disparity."

That sobered me. "In what way?"

His gaze swept over my face, and he reached up to tuck some hair behind my ear, the pads of his fingers coasting gently along my cheek bone before completing the move. My heart twisted at the tenderness in the action and the care in his expression.

"You're all warmth and goodness. You love your people fiercely, and you fight for them. You have a family who quite literally depends on you, and you're working yourself to a breaking point to make sure they're taken care of." His thumb swept over my hand. "I'm not like that, Quinn."

I considered his words, but the response came without much thought. "I'm not sure what you mean, specifically, but it seems to me that's not true. You care for your people—all your staff are devoted to you. Your friendships are strong and evidently long lasting. And based on the way you've been with me, you're ridiculously generous."

He shook his head. "You're different for me. I'm not like that with everyone."

Sadie's words bounced into my mind. "But you are. Sadie told me you offered to buy out her business and franchise it—how generous the offer was."

He'd also asked her out, though. Maybe he'd had feelings for her too.

"What's that look?"

"What look? I'm just sitting here."

"You're thinking about Sadie."

The man was too observant. For someone I'd often considered to be rather obtuse, he read me well.

"I just realized that you might've had feelings for her, which might've—"

"No. I did make her a business proposition, and in light of how you looked at me, I did ask her out. But I—no. She's beautiful, and odd enough I thought we might have something if we tried, but I never had feelings other than professional admiration for her."

My chest hadn't stopped fluttering. If I wasn't achingly familiar with atrial fibrillation thanks to Grandpa having the condition, I'd be worried my heart was actually beating irregularly. Every time I started to doubt or feel upset, Julian slid in with another searingly honest comment.

How was I supposed to react to this news?

How was I going to come to terms with everything that'd happened in the last twenty-four hours?

I had no freaking idea.

"Have I upset you?"

His low-spoken words penetrated my mental spiral. I looked up to see him studying me, his intensity no duller than it ever was.

"No. Or, I don't think so. I honestly never thought you were interested, so it feels a little crazy to hear you talk about it like this." My voice shook, so I cleared my throat to hide it.

"I'll tell you whatever you want to know to set your mind at ease. But make no mistake—I noticed you since I saw you on my first trip to Silverton when Jamie showed me the site for the neighborhood. And you haven't been far from my mind at any moment since, despite my best efforts at times, truth be told."

I swallowed. *Gulp.* This was the kind of crap girls dreamed of hearing, but I couldn't process it. Apparently, he'd broken my little brain's mainframe with his honesty, and I didn't know whether this was the best news, or something else entirely.

"Quinn, look at me."

I turned my head to the side to find an imploring look on his face. I knew in my gut the man didn't make that expression regularly.

"I know what I want in my life. I have every possible material need met, but I want more than nice things. I've been drawn to you from the beginning, but I haven't known more than what I could pry out of Jamie or gather myself until the last few weeks. I want to know it all. Like you said —I want to know you."

Emotion pricked my eyes as the tension in me unlocked. Knowing he'd thought I was beautiful or talented from the beginning was a lofty compliment, but this? This was the gift. That he wanted to know me like I did him. Far more than satisfying some physical urge or base desire for possession of something seemingly unavailable, he wanted to know me.

I crushed my eyes closed and exhaled slowly, forcing the fear crawling up my throat to shove back down. It'd been a long damn time since I'd let someone in, and I wasn't sure I knew how to do it anymore. Not someone who was more than a friend. I'd made several great friends in the last year and had let those women in more than I had anyone I'd known less than my whole life.

I hadn't been close enough to any men to let them in since stupid Chuck. And while I never thought I loved the guy, he'd reacted so terribly to the pregnancy, my choice to keep Cara, and the fact that I didn't let him off the hook to make him feel better, he'd hurt me. I hated the weak, broken feeling that'd haunted me during the pregnancy and on and off for years when he'd pop back into my life trying to toss money at a situation like it'd cover all his sins.

If I did this with Julian, knowing he wasn't just casually interested, I'd be at risk.

Now I just had to decide whether I believed he was worth it.

CHAPTER TWENTY-FIVE

Julian

Quinn seemed to decide something about me, or us, or the situation—whatever—and her demeanor shifted. She launched into rapid-fire questions that I couldn't connect to our larger conversation as they seemed so simple, but since she hadn't rejected me entirely, I complied.

"Black olives on pizza—yes, or no?"

"That's fine."

She nodded. "Do you eat leftovers, or do you have to have something new to eat for every meal?"

My brows raised as I considered. "I rarely have leftovers, but I don't mind them. I'm certainly not against them."

"Sports?"

I tilted my head to one side, not sure what she meant.

"What about sports? Who are your teams?"

Huh. I hadn't imagined she'd care that I was part owner in a European football club, but I didn't mind telling her. "I'm part owner in a French soccer club. I'm often approached about floundering NFL teams, but I prefer college football to pro—what? What's wrong?"

"I meant what sports do you like to watch or play." A breathy chuckle escaped.

Entirely without my permission, my cheeks heated. "Ah. Right. Well, I never played sports, as I was always the youngest and smallest in whatever grade at whatever school, but as I got older, I ran and did other things. Several of my patents—er, never mind."

She placed a hand on my arm. "No, tell me."

"I love the Olympics. And the Paralympics. Several of my patents are for parts of robotic or artificial limbs that some athletes use."

A smile grew on her lovely face with every word I spoke, and a match lit in my chest. The heat spread with her grin.

"You are kind of unbelievable. You know that, right?"

I frowned, wondering if I'd sounded arrogant. I was a confident man but didn't want that to be something that put her off. She didn't strike me as a woman scared away by a bit of overweening confidence, but now that I'd decided to factor her in, I couldn't ignore the twinge of unease the comment caused.

"I don't mean to brag. I have interest and investment in a lot of areas. It helps diversify my assets but also keeps me busy."

"You don't strike me as a man who needs help staying busy," she said, her eyes still crinkled with her smile.

The woman was painfully gorgeous at close range and happy. I wanted to put that smile on her face all the time.

"I do, really, or I go do crazy things like insist on land-scaping my friends' new houses."

She laughed loudly at that. "I have always wondered how you ended up doing that for Jamie."

"I know better now. I've done some of my own houses, but most of them came ready-made and I just made improvements. I think I got a little overconfident about that—"

"Gasp! Did you just admit—"

"Never mind. The point is, I'm glad Aidan Wallace stepped in and fixed the mess I made with the hedge selection, and I fully admit to learning a great deal in the wake of my ignorance. I also promised both Jamie and Aidan I wouldn't do any more landscaping work and now happily and avidly recommend Aidan's services whenever I can."

She nodded approvingly. "Good. He deserves it."

"That he does." Wallace was a good man and did excellent work—exactly the kind of person I liked to recommend.

"So, tell me more about the patents you mentioned. I want to understand." She bit her bottom lip and squeezed my arm before sitting back, ready to listen.

So, with no small sense of wonder about her curiosity, I told her. And she asked questions which morphed the conversation into other facets of her life and mine, and before I knew it, Scott had turned into her driveway, and I registered that we'd been talking for three hours.

Three. Hours.

I'd never spoken to *anyone* for that amount of time. Ever. It simply wasn't efficient or interesting or necessary and therefore had never occurred.

But this afternoon had felt essential and fascinating and important. If anything, I wished for more, though as I became aware of the wheels halting, my body drooped with exhaustion.

"Listen, Julian." Quinn had unbuckled and scooted to the edge of her seat.

I moved to unbuckle, but she stopped me with a hand on my arm yet again.

"No, you don't need to get out. I just wanted to say..." She swallowed, and her eyes flicked up to me. "I wanted to tell you that you should ask me out sometime."

She slipped out the door next, and Scott handed her the bag he'd retrieved from the trunk. As quick and capable as my brain generally tended to be, it sluggishly registered the permission she'd just given me as her front door closed behind her.

Scott re-entered the car and began driving when I finally jumped into action. "Wait. Just a minute."

I exited the car quickly and walked the path to her door, knocking the second I reached it.

She opened it immediately, concern stitching her brow. "Did I leave—"

"Go out with me. Tonight."

Her face lit with a glorious smile, and she chuckled. "I can't tonight."

"You just said I should ask you out."

She huffed another laugh. "Yes. And I do want to go out with you. But I've been away, and I need to check on my mom and grandparents. And more importantly, I need to see how Cara's doing."

I nodded, dousing the disappointment with appreciation for her devotion. This kind of care for her family was like unearthing a diamond while digging for granite. I already knew there was value here, so much worth, but discovering the astounding beauty of her soul threatened to gut me with wanting her.

"Can we figure out a time this weekend? Let me get back in the groove here, and I'll see you at the bar on Friday? We can choose a night next week, if you're in town?"

I nodded quickly. "I'll be here. And yes. You say the word, and we'll determine the day."

She smiled, biting her lip to contain it a bit, and I lost that grip I kept on myself around her. I reached for her, my hand cradling her jaw, and pressed my lips to her. The curve of her cheek and the warmth of her skin made sparks erupt on the surface of my palm, and heat pooled in my gut when she opened her mouth just enough to deepen the kiss for a few seconds before she pulled away.

"See you Friday, Julian."

I nodded, and retreated to the car, restless with energy and longing.

"Seems to have gone well," Scott mused aloud from the front seat.

"You shouldn't have been watching."

He did a poor job at stifling his laugh. "You're right."

He glanced at me in the rearview, and I laughed too, pleasure and anticipation coursing through me at the reality of what he'd said and why.

She'd told me to ask her out. I did, and she'd said yes. I'd kissed her, and she kissed me back. "But yes. It did go well."

Quinn had given me her permission. She felt it too— whatever it was between us. I could let it run and see where it took me, despite the uncertainty of not knowing the outcome. Sometimes, a degree of the unknown was required —a better result came from risking more than one had before. I understood this, with Quinn, would be a risk like I'd never taken before.

It'd taken long enough but now, I was ready and willing to take it.

Scott pulled out of her driveway, and we made it to my house in record time. The cluttered thoughts about Quinn, about where we'd go for our date and what day she might select, sifted to the back of my mind as I reviewed the last of my upcoming tasks. I still had a full day of work ahead, despite it being early afternoon.

Exiting the vehicle, I entered the house and nodded to Carol as I fired off a text to Kelly about the afternoon's schedule. I'd work from home the rest of today, unwilling to go to the office and waste the time in the car, even just a few minutes.

After sending, I sank into my chair just as Jamie called. "Yes?"

His laugh rang out in my ear. "So I've reached impatient work Julian already? I would've thought you'd still be reveling in your time with Quinn. From what I understand, it went quite well."

"How could you possibly know that?" I shifted items around on my desk unseeingly.

"Jack texted."

I sighed but found no real irritation. "The two of you could start your own gossip site."

"Not true."

"Completely true. Especially considering you both pretend like you don't talk all the time. I know better."

They didn't often cross paths despite both being in Hollywood, but they'd met when Jamie and Whit Grantham recorded a song and subsequently won an Oscar for best original song for a movie starring Jack. Incidentally, he'd also won Best Actor that year. Apparently, they didn't hit it off then, but the bromance struck up not long after Jamie moved back to LA with Bel years back. It felt a little bit like worlds colliding when we all realized we knew each other.

"Don't be salty about this. Here's the good news. Quinn's one of my best friends, and I'm one of yours. So is Jack. He approves of her, and obviously I do too. You've got a big ol' crowd of support for you two."

This pleased me, but the feeling held an edge of wariness. "Don't push this on her. Please."

The line was quiet for a few seconds before Jamie's throat cleared on the other end. "If I hadn't thought you were serious, now I know you are."

"Because I asked you not to push her? That's a perfectly normal request."

"Yeah, but you said please."

I chuckled despite myself. "You're an idiot."

"I'm delighted to hear you capable of levity, *Jules*. Let me know how it goes. We'll be back in town for Thanksgiving, and you better have something to show for these next few weeks."

I wondered what I could show for that amount of time. As someone infinitely capable of evaluating business timelines and calculating other aspects of the projects I cared about, I'd never felt like this. I'd never felt so much anticipation for simply seeing someone, much less being near them. I wanted to be with her in every sense; I wanted to know everything about her. I wanted everything from her, and I wanted to give it right back. As if, by letting the dams crack, they'd blown open right away and everything was flooding through now.

"I'll see what I can do," I said, hoping that'd satisfy him.

"See that you do. Be smart."

He hung up and I considered his words. *Be smart.* One thing in this life I had confidence in was my intelligence, but somehow, that metric didn't seem to be the one he meant. And every interaction with Quinn had showed me that I couldn't rely on what I always did. I'd decided I wanted something different, and I'd need to do things differently with her from here on out. No more contracts or engineering her loyalty. She'd proved once and again that didn't work—didn't apply.

I'd have to figure that out as I went.

CHAPTER TWENTY-SIX

Quinn

"**G**et to work, Darling. Those limes won't slice themselves."

I shot Brandon a fake glare and finished tapping out the text to my mom, confirming my grandpa was feeling okay. The last two days had been insanely stressful, and I was honestly relieved to be here at work. Singing would help. The noise and distraction would drown out the sinking sensation that everything was about to blow up in my face.

My grandpa's doctor wanted to change his heart meds, and the new medication that would ideally mitigate some of the side effects we suspected were making him feel worse wasn't an affordable one. Yes, in theory, it'd be covered by insurance, but in reality, it wasn't—the reason we'd tried the first and second options, though his doctor had indicated this third one was his first choice.

Grandpa understood the challenge this would pose—a

daily medication would add up. So he'd insisted he try the others that had more coverage. But he'd been just shy of miserable.

We got him the new meds this month, and hopefully, it'd only be another day or two before he felt a bit better. And I had approximately twenty-eight days to work out how we'd tuck that expense into the budget before we had to refill the medication and face the payment again.

Added to that was the upsetting episode of sundowner's my grandma had had yesterday during which she couldn't recall my mom's birthdate and became unusually agitated. She'd done that a few times before, but not in a while. I was a mess. As the evening wore on, my mom had called and the shaken quality to her words as she explained Grandma's confusion and upset as she'd readied her for bed made my heart pinch. As was typical, she'd been clear-headed and bright-eyed this morning, though, so that was good.

But how long could my mom handle that? And would it remain confusion at the end of the day, or was this the first sign of something else? Grandma would need to visit the doc soon too. And I had to figure out how to get them into Silverton Springs.

Shoving my phone into my pocket after willing my mom to respond and getting nothing for over a minute, I washed my hands and got to work on prep. I couldn't control the cost of medication, or how my grandpa's body responded to this new one. We'd just have to wait and see if it was a better fit. I couldn't control how my grandma's brain aged or the fact that right now, there was nothing we could do to help that but love her and be as attentive as possible.

And I couldn't control the other thing stressing me the hell out—Chuck. His lawyers had indeed contacted mine, and John Wallace had called me yesterday to update me on everything. Chuck wanted regular visitation. He'd said at this time, he wasn't going to petition for custody, but—

That's where the red haze of rage had washed over my vision, and I'd sunk to the floor. *Custody?* Was this man serious? He'd spoken to Cara a half dozen times *in her life,* and he was waving that around like the next step after taking her out to lunch a few times would be having her live with him?

I could be dramatic, sure. I really did know this about myself. But when I'd said, "Over my dead body," in response to that news from John, I think he and I both knew I meant business.

"Where's your head tonight, Quinney?"

I exhaled, trying not to feel the annoyance at the nickname for me. I wasn't in the mood to have adorable baby Brandon hit on me. And his little nickname for me wasn't flirting, of course I knew that. But sometimes, his twenty-three years seemed so simple. He was single. He had two parents who were still married, or so I thought based on what I'd gathered. He had a handful of siblings who were all healthy and either lived locally or visited often. He had game and loved bartending, so his social life was tight.

The kid wouldn't know what to do with my messy pile of financial challenges and teen daughter drama and baby daddy frustrations. He definitely wouldn't be able to access the fear that tightened my throat and made me gray out sometimes as it got so intense when I thought of losing any one of my four precious family members.

"I'm all over the place. Sorry. It's been a rough couple days." I stayed focused on the limes, thankful he didn't approach.

"That sucks. Sorry. Hopefully, it'll get better."

I stifled an eyeroll at the thought that it even *could* just simply get better. It wouldn't unless I did something to change it. My mom and I could barely pay the bills and keep my grandparents cared for. Cara was heading for total heartbreak with her dad, and that killed me. None of this would magically improve with the passage of time except maybe if I could find a few minutes to make progress on Cara's dress.

But I wouldn't be telling Brandon that. "Thanks, B. Hopefully, singing it out tonight will help."

I could see his thousand-watt grin from my peripheral vision. "Good plan."

For the next twenty minutes, we focused on prep as people trickled in. I never minded singing to an empty room, but Chase and Angel much preferred to have an audience. I tended to get lost in the music and could feel that coming. I wanted an escape into song desperately.

Chase wandered in, guitar in hand, a bit later. I poured him a drink while chatting with a couple who'd taken their seat at the bar and promised to come over for checks in five. We never did much of a soundcheck since we were the only ones who used the stage and amps the majority of the time, but it was still wise to check. No one wanted feedback looping right as we kicked off a song.

After filling a handful more drink orders, I shucked my apron, knocked back half a pint of water, and took the stage. Within minutes, the music worked its magic. The ropes that'd knotted around my rib cage loosened with every song, every note of harmony Chase sang with me, every bridge and chorus. By the end of that thirty-minute set, the lounge had filled to the brim, my own reserves had been replenished, and I truly felt lighter.

Nothing would improve with moping. I knew that as well as anyone, but shaking off the dread and even sorrow that had gripped me lately had gotten more challenging. Adrenaline pumped steadily through me and carried relief right along with it. The high from performing wouldn't last forever, but the fact that I could feel better, even for a few minutes, almost made me want to cry.

I signaled to Brandon and Kyle, the other bartender who usually worked weeknights, that I needed just a minute, and scuttled through the back and out into the hallway. After slipping into the bathroom, I walked back inside the lounge through the main entrance just to see.

I hadn't let myself look closely enough to tell if Julian sat in his regular seat. We were supposed to talk this weekend about our date, and the dangling carrot of that encounter had gotten me through some of the moments in the last few days. Having something to look forward to—not just singing, which definitely didn't solve all my problems, but seeing Julian—had given me a light at the end of the tunnel.

A thrill raced through me when my eyes met his. He sat back in the chair, elbows resting on either armrest, glass dangling in one hand. I took in his mussed hair, that slightly thicker beard, the rolled-up sleeves and missing tie. The top button of his shirt had been unbuttoned.

"Hello, Ms. Darling," he said as he straightened a bit and nodded to the chair next to him, one of the only free ones in the place.

"Hello, Mr. Grenier." Apparently, we were keeping this formal.

He shook his head slightly, but in clear disapproval. "I like when you call me Julian."

I chuckled lightly to cover the sweet heat that flooded my belly. This was flirting, and he'd never done it overtly. He was always business or pure wall-destroying honesty.

There hadn't been a middle where we flirted and tested the waters.

The kiss at Jack's, and the other kiss at my doorstep, had proved we had chemistry physically. But whether we'd actually get along still felt opaque. We'd talked for hours on the drive home and the time had flown, but we were so different. So deeply different in every way, from upbringing to education, from personality to lifestyle.

"You started the formal thing, *Julian*."

His eyes glittered in the low light, and one side of his mouth slid up ever so slightly. "I didn't want to assume, especially while you're working."

My smile grew full and stupidly charmed. "Fine, then." Next, the nerves hit, but I swallowed them back. "Are we talking about…"

I was not a shy woman. I didn't know if I had a shy bone in my body, but I felt a blush rise to my cheeks.

He nodded. "Most definitely."

Something crashed at the bar behind me, and I whipped around in time to see Brandon and Kyle scrambling to handle the crowd. "I better get back. Will you be here for my next set? We could talk when I take my break after for a few minutes, if that works."

"I'll be here."

Momentarily caught in the snare of his gaze, I stared back at him. The intensity on his face was softer tonight—no less stomach-flipping, but somehow curbed to welcome me in. As though it'd shifted from the usual focused brilliance of a flashlight and had now bloomed out into a spotlight causing everything around us to blur and glow.

Shaking myself from the daze that making eye contact with Julian evidently caused, I shot him one last smile and hurried to help at the bar.

CHAPTER TWENTY-SEVEN

Julian

Quinn's set ended with her genuine, pleased smile. I liked that one since it signaled she knew the songs had gone well, and as always, they had.

As she exited the stage, she nodded and smiled, said a few thank-yous, and finally found refuge behind the bar for a moment. Though I couldn't see her because of the crowd sitting at the bar top and where she stood, I could easily guess she was drinking down a water. Very occasionally a beer.

A minute later, she stepped around the customers seated at the end of the bar, and her eyes found mine. She tipped her head to the side, and I rose to my feet immediately. Her smile, especially when it came from my doing something right, was also a favorite.

I wove through the tables and out the main exit of the lounge, then down the long hallway that would take me to—

"Thanks for meeting me out here. It's just so crowded in there, and I didn't want to deal."

She walked forward with her hands clasped behind her back. I'd never seen her do that before.

"Perfectly all right." The rasp in my voice spoke to the long days I'd worked and more so, the ravenous anticipation of being alone with her.

Instead of speaking, her gaze met mine and held. "Take my hand."

I complied instantly.

Her soft, warm hand clasped mine with sure pressure, no creeping, tedious sensation in me but just a surge of genuine comfort. She pulled me after her, just around a corner into a slightly dim section of hallway. Her back against the wall, she dropped my hand and stretched out her arms.

Smart man that I was, I didn't need any more invitation than that. My palm slid up her arm and cupped her shoulder while she wrapped herself around me. At least, that's what it felt like as her hands sifted into the hair at the back of my head and she urged me closer. Soon, our lips met in a searing kiss that sent sensation fizzing from my head to my feet.

I felt out of my mind. Literally, the feeling of her hands on me and mine on her made it feel like the most pleasant possible version of a break in my brain, except nothing had shorted out. All synapses were firing in gleeful detonation at her touch, her kiss, the low, satisfied sound she made when I deepened the kiss.

But we stood in the hotel's hallway, not in a closed room —we had no privacy. And if she kept pressing me against her and kissing me like this, it wouldn't stay appropriate for long. In fact, we'd already crossed that line, and if I stumbled upon a couple in my employ in this position, I'd likely have to give the person a warning.

I slipped away from her mouth and kissed along her jaw, my fingers dragging against the arch of her spine. "We have to stop."

"Yes, we do," she said and nipped at my neck.

I pulled back to find a dark smile glittering back at me. "We're supposed to talk about going out."

She shoved against me, just barely, but I took the cue and stepped back. A forlorn expression slipped past her face, but she nodded. "Guess we should. I have to get back soon. My boss is a real hard ass."

I scowled. "I'm not actually your boss. You know that, right? I do assist with managing, but Silver Ridge Resort is more of a side project. I like having an office here, people know me, but I'm not really—"

She grinned. "Yes, I do know that. You being my actual boss would've made this whole thing even less appealing."

"Even less?"

She made a face like she'd been caught. "I just mean it would raise the stakes even more."

I didn't want to talk about the stakes. I wanted a time and date. "Okay. How about Sunday? You work tomorrow, right?"

She blinked as though this startled her. "I do. But I can't Sunday. I do family dinner with my grandparents and Cara. I—"

"That's fine. Monday?"

"I'm actually hanging out with my grandparents so my mom can have a night off."

Warmth and affection washed over me in waves. "That's kind of you."

"It's—not. She deserves it." She glanced away, and the

muscle in her jaw flexed like she must've been gritting her teeth.

"What is it?"

Exhaling, she looked everywhere but me before finally giving me her eyes again. "They're struggling. My mom and my grandparents. And I feel I can't do anything about it."

I held her by her shoulders, giving her a hard stare I hoped she'd read as truthful and insistent. "You're doing everything you can. You're working yourself into exhaustion. You're providing physical and emotional support. And you've raised a daughter who's doing the same. Quinn, you're remarkable, and your family is lucky to have you."

To my horror, her eyes filled, but she blinked the tears away with sheer determination. "Thank you. It doesn't often feel like that lately."

I wrapped my arms around her then, unable to stop myself from holding her. I wished this hug could imbue her with comfort and assurance. It felt futile—like not enough. But she sighed against my chest and laid her head on my shoulder, and I realized maybe it wasn't so useless. It didn't solve any of her problems, but hopefully, it helped her know she had a friend and ally in me.

And maybe something more. If she wanted it.

"At the risk of seeming like I have a one-track mind, can I take you out Tuesday?"

She chuckled against my neck, sending a shiver through me, then pushed away. "Yes. Tuesday should work."

I'd make it a perfect night. I'd already planned as much as I could, and knowing how worried about her family she was, I'd gotten a few more ideas about how to make the night memorable. *Special.*

If I didn't know Quinn was something special, I'd be incredulous. Had I ever wanted to make a woman feel special? I racked my brain and couldn't recall caring much about the outcome of any past interactions with women unless it had something to do with business. I'd never been so invested in a person.

I just had to hope that when she realized it, it wouldn't send her running.

CHAPTER TWENTY-EIGHT

Quinn

After a weekend full of highs and lows, a Monday packed with frustrations, and a Tuesday I'd titled *Purgatory*, Tuesday evening arrived with snow flurries and so much anticipation, I thought I'd never been so nervous.

"Are you seriously still pacing right now? You're crazy." Cara eyed me from her seat at our small dinner table.

"Stop heckling, child."

She rolled her eyes and returned to her giant bowl of spaghetti. While I maintained a mildly perturbed façade, the fact that she was making fun of me tinged the whole night in a glow I couldn't look away from. We hadn't had any major breakthroughs, but something had shifted in her. Maybe she'd taken my mom's words to heart and recognized that Chuck wasn't some tragic figure kept from her, but a man who'd failed her repeatedly with full knowledge of what he was doing.

Or maybe, quite simply, the tides had turned. Sometimes in parenting, you wait for the phase to change. Kids and our relationships with them are constantly shifting based on their development and outside pressures, plus whatever we as parents have going on. After this long in the game, I knew that, though the whole situation with her dad ratcheted up the stakes and intensity by a thousand. That she'd sit here in the room with me, looking me in the eye and chatting was downright impressive after the weeks we'd had.

"I get that he's good-looking. I mean *ew*, he's old, but like, not all that much older than you, right?"

The look on her face said the thought of contemplating her mother's age as compared to her upcoming date's age made her feel mildly squeamish.

"I think he's a few years older, but not much."

She chewed another large bite as I paced to the front door, then back toward her. "Okay, so that's good. And obviously he's like, crazy rich."

I cut her a disapproving glare. "That is not why I'm going out with him."

She gave me a *duh* look. "Obviously. I've known you for more than half a second, so I know you're not gold digging in Julian's pockets."

I didn't know if I should be horrified or amused by that statement, so I just nodded in acceptance. "Do you have an objection here? I thought when I mentioned it this weekend, you were good with this."

While my fourteen-year-old daughter didn't get to decide my dating life, things were upside-down enough for her right now. I hadn't dated much over the years, so this was new territory for us in some ways, especially since she knew Julian.

"No, not at all. Honestly. I like him, actually. He's weird, for sure, but like, in a nice way."

I chuckled under my breath and resisted the urge to check the window to see if he'd pulled into the driveway. *Weird, but in a nice way* seemed like an apt descriptor of Julian on the surface. He was much more than that, but most of the words I'd use to describe him weren't ones Cara needed to know just yet. *Passionate. Surprising. Thoughtful. Gorgeous.*

Still five minutes before he was supposed to be here, but my nervous energy had propelled me around the house all day, and the closer I got, the more antsy I became.

"Mom, seriously. Just sit down. He'll be here soon. Isn't he like, super punctual?"

I studied her, but she'd ducked her head. "I don't remember telling you that. How do you know he's like that?"

She focused on her spaghetti with the intensity of a food critic. "I may have talked to Uncle Jamie about him."

"You did? When?"

"Um. Sunday." She lifted her head cautiously and met my gaze. The grimace told me she worried I'd be mad about this revelation.

"What did Uncle Jamie say?"

At this point, I was fairly sure he was Team Quinn and Julian. If anything, it seemed like he was more worried I'd hurt Julian than he'd hurt me. That was fair considering I generally affected an air of being unhurtable, particularly romantically. I hadn't gotten wrapped up in someone since Chuck and had learned that lesson well. The idea that I'd genuinely feel for Julian probably didn't even occur to Jamie.

She blew out a breath. "Let me think. He said Julian's a

good man. He said he's odd, but mostly because his brain is so big."

I laughed. "He is very smart."

"Yeah, I knew that already."

"Any other thoughts from wise old Jamieson?"

She rolled her eyes. Considering how long we'd been talking, I was shocked this was only roll number two.

"He said he's pretty sure Julian really likes you and that he trusts him with you. He isn't sure about your end of things." She eyed me like squinting at me through her light brown lashes might help her figure me out.

I crossed my arms and leaned against the wall. "And you're good with me going out—"

"Moooom. Yes. Seriously. I'm not five. I want you to have a life. I know that getting one involves dating guys and... whatever." Her eyes shot around the room, and her cheeks bloomed pink.

Oh.

"You know I'm coming home tonight, right? I'm not staying the night with him." Though at some point, if things went well, that could very well happen.

"Yeah, whatever. It's fine, and I'm happy I can help Grandma tonight anyway." She shoved the remaining tangle of spaghetti around in her bowl before setting aside her fork.

Warmth suffused me. Somehow, I'd raised a warm, loving, generous kid, and I couldn't have been prouder. We'd had such a rocky few weeks, and I missed her. She shoved out of her seat and moved to clean her bowl at the sink. I waited until she'd set it in the dishwasher before pouncing.

The light *oof* sound made me smile as we impacted with my hug attack. It'd been a while since I'd done this, feeling certain she'd push me away or be frustrated. But tonight, she hugged back, and we rocked side to side like the weirdos we were before releasing each other. Her smile looked loose and happy.

"You look great, by the way. He's going to be blown away."

My heart did a double thump. One for how sweet this kid was, and one when I realized it must be about time. "Thanks. I'm not sure a man who's been linked with super-models and actresses and fellow billionaires is ever really blown away, but hopefully, he'll be happy enough."

Even as I said it, it rang hollow. Julian had never seemed like a man about town to me—certainly never mentioned any past conquests, and for that matter, I knew for certain he wouldn't think of or refer to a previous relationship as a *conquest*. I did hope we could talk about our pasts. I wanted to understand what he wanted with me. As much as he said our differences complimented each other, I wasn't certain.

"Whatever. He doesn't seem sketchy like that. Plus, you're a hottie, Mom. I've heard more than one of the seniors call you a *MILF*."

I cringed. "Oh, no. No no no. That's just not right."

The doorbell rang and I nearly jumped out of my skin.

"Okay, okay, don't freak out. Deep breath."

Cara's chants brought me back to the moment, and I laughed loudly at her small show of nerves, which thankfully helped dispel some of my own.

"I'll get the door. Are you going upstairs to make a grand entrance?" She shuffled forward and unlocked the deadbolt, then threw open the door.

So much for grand entrance, not that I had planned to waltz down the stairs. I wore jeans and a black turtleneck tank shirt tucked in. It flattered me. Over it, I had a jacket, and on my feet, black heeled short boots. Nothing particularly mind-blowing, but I did feel good. He'd seen me in all levels of fance thus far—black-tie weeks after the great coffee half-shirt debacle, so I didn't worry too much about impressing him.

But of course I want to impress him. Yeah. Of course I did.

"Hello, Cara. How are you?" Julian focused on Cara, though he did sneak a glance at me, and meeting his eyes made a thrill shoot through me.

"I'm good. Glad you're here. This one was pacing like a caged lion."

Well. We'd had a good run. But now, I'd have to lock her in the basement or maybe just off her altogether.

"Interesting," he said, that barely there smile curving his lips.

"Not that interesting. Just anxious to get going. So! I'll see you later. Text me when Grandma comes to get you, and I'll—"

"I got it. We're good. Just *go* already," she said and shoved me toward the man waiting just inside the door.

I stumbled forward but shot her a glare over my shoulder before sending her a, "Bye Cara, love you even if you are a punk."

She cackled as I pulled the door closed and faced a smiling Julian.

Oh. Yeah. I'd somehow forgotten how devastating his smile was, and here he stood hitting me with it so soon in the evening? I thought I'd have to work for it a while before he showed me this absolute vision.

"What?" One brow rose.

"I just—you don't smile all that often," I said, smooth as peanut butter. *Ugh.*

He chuckled low and held out his hand. I took it. Our palms met and fingers laced together, sending butterflies on wings in my chest.

"I'm happy to see you. And I like seeing you and Cara together. Your dynamic is so unlike what I experienced as a child." He opened the side door of his car, which I realized was in fact *his* car. Scott wasn't driving for him tonight.

Somehow, this made me more nervous. This was a real date. Not some fancy, overblown billionaire thing for press or whatever. This was exactly up my alley. Especially him in those jeans and a wool jacket with something undetermined underneath, no suit. Only the second time I'd seen him out of a suit.

Call me crazy, but my nerves quadrupled. Some part of me had known this wouldn't be wining and dining—that it'd be both more and less of a big deal. But now that we were here, inching down my driveway in his luxury sedan clad in jeans and jackets to ward against the late-fall chill, it clicked.

I wanted this. So freaking much. And everything about the last five minutes told me he did too.

Crap.

CHAPTER TWENTY-NINE

Julian

I'd never regretted driving my own car more.

If I'd had Scott drive us, I'd be sitting in the back seat holding her hand. Maybe with her arm pressed against mine. But like an idiot, I'd decided to drive, and now I was stuck wishing I could touch her and look at her and knowing I had to keep my attention on the road or we'd literally perish.

"Is this your car?" Then she chuckled under her breath. "I mean, obviously it's your car. But is it the one you prefer driving?"

"I'm a mood driver, so I like to have a selection. And while it's a stereotypical thing for a man like me to have multiple vehicles, I accept that I'm a cliché." I glanced over to see her grinning.

"Such a cliché. Handsome, kind of odd, cutthroat businessman with a dozen cars."

Now I could hear the smile and cursed the need to watch the road yet again. "*Kind of odd* isn't all that stereotypical, is it?"

She hummed, thinking to herself, but the warm sound sent heat through me. Every sound she made had a musical, luscious quality somehow.

"I guess eccentric is more the thing. You're not exactly eccentric. Just... *odd*."

I knew this but was curious to know what aspects of my life she saw as such. "In what way?"

She flicked out a finger. "You own a private jet—that's just weird. You are a workaholic. And you collect famous friends like prized pennies."

I eyed her, then shifted gears as we merged onto the canyon road. "None of that sounds all that unique to me. Maybe the famous friends bit, but that's not something I do as, well, it's—"

She laughed full out and grabbed my hand with both of hers. She slipped her fingers between mine and covered the back of my hand with the other. Sensation traveled up my arm in dizzying waves, the contact so purely pleasurable despite it being relatively unexpected. At this point in our relationship, a part of me was always hoping she'd touch me, so I never recoiled. I wanted her touch more than I'd wanted almost anything. Almost as much as I wanted all the rest of her.

"You don't have to explain your fancy friends list to me. Plus, realistically, I'm just as bad. Jamie's my best friend, I'm newly in friend love with Miss Mayhem, and now I'm dating peculiar billionaire genius Julian Grenier."

She beamed at me from where she sat with her head resting against the seat, facing me. She'd curled her legs and tilted them toward me too, and her knees rested inches from the gear shift. The urge to slip my hand from hers and feel her leg hit me hard—hard enough my gut clenched.

"That's true. If anything, I should be concerned about your intentions for me."

No answering laugh or retort arrived after a moment, so I glanced at her to find a thoughtful look on her face.

"What?" I asked, wondering if she'd taken the comment I'd made in jest some other way.

"You don't need to be concerned about me." Her tone was sober and earnest.

I nodded, then extracted my hand as I shifted gears and accelerated. I needed to park this car and look her in the eye for more than a few seconds at a time. If she'd give me a few minutes to get us to our destination, then I could do just that.

"You know that, right? I'm not... *after* you. And I'm definitely not after your money."

After a steadying breath, I replied. "I know that, Quinn. I imagine that if anything, it's a detraction. I can't blame you for your feelings because in some ways, even for me, it is. But I hope you'll come to see it as a positive, or maybe better, a neutral element between us." Or preferably, *not* between us.

"I don't mean to think of it as negative, but our... relationship hasn't exactly developed in a typical way."

"What's typical? Honestly, it's not something I have much experience with." Finally, I pulled into the gravel parking lot on the side of the canyon road.

She eyed me for a moment. "Let's get inside, and then we're going to just... do this. Okay?"

I nodded, though I didn't know what she meant. But there was little I wouldn't agree to with Quinn, and I'd accepted that recently. Whatever *this* was that she wanted to do, I'd be glad to do it.

Inside the log cabin-style structure, a harried waitress nodded to a table in the back of the room. I waved a hand and then settled the same one on Quinn's lower back as we proceeded through the crammed spot to sit.

"I love this place. I'm surprised you—*Wait*." Her eyes narrowed as she scooted in her chair.

I'd had to forbid myself from tucking her in, somehow sensing that the hand on her back was enough and any further polite gestures would become grating for her. "Yes?"

"Did you ask Jamie about this? Did he tell you I love this place?"

"If I did?"

"Seems like cheating."

A quiet laugh escaped. "Should I have asked you?"

She made a face. "No. Or yes. I don't even know."

Bewildered but not unamused, I took the menu in hand and reviewed it, though I knew it well at this point. "I chose this place because I love it. I like that it feels like a secret, and I like being next to the river. And their rolls with honey butter are almost as good as something Sadie Miller makes."

She beamed. My heart twisted to the point of being painful at the sight. She had many burdens, but she didn't carry them in a way that weighed her down. Maybe that wasn't quite right, but I admired the way she smiled generously.

"Well then, I approve. And honestly, I don't know what protocol is for this—if asking a friend for recommendations to take someone out is weird or not. I've only gone on a few dates, usually with people I meet through gigs in the city or online. I tend not to date people from Silverton." Shutting her menu, she folded her hands atop the plastic-covered front.

"And has that been successful for you?" I asked, hating the twinge of inappropriate jealousy I felt for every person she'd ever dated.

She huffed a small laugh. "Obviously, it's gone gang-busters."

I chuckled and shook my head. I loved that sarcastic edge she had. It wasn't ever mean, just droll as anything I'd encountered. No wonder she and Jenna Halter had hit it off.

"But seriously, it's been..." Her gaze swept around the room and landed back on me before she sighed. "To be honest?"

I nodded, sensing she needed assurance that her honesty wouldn't scare me away. If only she knew how *not-scared* I was.

"It's been lonely. Really lonely."

Tectonic plates shifted in my chest, new mountains and valleys springing up in the wake of her confession and how familiar it felt. Her vulnerability unlocked my own. "I understand. I'm not sure I remember a time I wasn't lonely."

Her lashes fluttered and she swallowed hard. With eyes on me, her hand reached out to cover mine. A simple gesture, but the moment held power. I sensed it almost like I'd sensed other things in my life—the night I broke through the mental block before finalizing the structure of one of my more complex patented designs. The night I'd met Jamie, and the day before he'd dragged me to Silverton to consider a little side project partnership with him.

And this. Tunneling toward me came the reality I couldn't quite grasp but knew in my gut—in my soul—had significance.

CHAPTER THIRTY

Quinn

Our waitress plunked down waters and a basket of steaming rolls with a little bowl of honey butter already glossy from melting a bit on our table, took our orders, and said something as she turned to her next task.

"It's a wonder they don't hire more waiters. I don't think I've ever been here when it wasn't packed at every table and the two mainstays just scrambling from place to place." I craned my neck to see our waitress loading a huge tray with countless dishes.

"It'd dilute their income considerably, I'd guess. Aren't they all family?" He glanced up and gave a chin nod to someone and it clicked. He'd said he loved it, but he genuinely did.

Why I'd suspect he was saying that just to charm me, I wasn't sure, but of course he wasn't. He meant it. He loved it here and he came often—or at least often enough to know the waitresses and have a table he preferred.

"That's a good point. How many times have you been?" I let my eyes wander down over his close-trimmed beard and the curve of his jaw. I'd touched his face for a few fleeting moments, and I could almost feel the crisp bristles of his beard against the pads of my fingers.

"I used to come whenever I was in town when they were open. Once I started staying in Silverton for longer stretches and using it more as a home base than I did LA, I ended up easing off because I didn't often have time to make the trip up." His brow furrowed and he focused on buttering the roll he held gently pinched between two fingers. "Actually, I've missed a lot with that excuse."

I tilted my head in question while chewing a bite of the glorious honey-buttery delight.

"I've always found time as a measure a dually useful and plaguing thing. I'm motivated by time—I move through my days endlessly cognizant of how long things take and what they require. Sometimes, I even use it as a game. But I've started to wonder if I haven't always just been counting down to something."

"What?"

His eyes were piercing in their depth as our gazes locked and I felt it. I knew what he'd say before his alluring lips shaped the words and my heart bottomed out.

But then his attention cut away and he said, "I'm not sure yet."

I'd been certain he'd say something like, "meeting you." But how arrogant was that? Thinking a man like Julian would've felt his *whole life* had been barreling toward someone like *me?*

"Did I say something wrong?" he asked, interrupting my thoughts.

"No, not at all."

I cleared my throat, the thready sound of my voice reflecting that sad little strain I'd been thinking. No need to stay there. We were here now, and I needed to enjoy this. He did like me, and I did like him. What it meant and where it could go, I genuinely didn't know. But that was part of why we were here tonight, right?

"Good. I hope you know I don't feel that way with you. I don't count the minutes until I leave you. Time slows down with you and I—I like that."

I smiled and saw it reflected in his gaze and that gentle upturn at the corner of his mouth. "I'm glad. I hope it stays that way. I guess we'll know if you get to the place where you're counting and playing time games with yourself, we've got a problem."

"That won't be an issue. I can promise you that."

I raised my brows at him. "You can't know that."

He held my gaze, seeming to debate something, but then did that chin dip thing he did that I'd started to find completely adorable. "Fair enough. But I have a strong feeling."

I waved that away along with the nerves that'd cropped up with the realization that now was the time to bring up... everything.

"So, can I ask you about your dating history? Obviously, no one that stuck around, and same for me. But I guess I'm trying to figure out what you want." I adjusted in my seat, discomfort with putting it out there so bluntly racing through me.

"Can you possibly not know that by now?" he asked, completely serious.

A breathy laugh escaped. It wasn't exactly funny, but something about his almost confused question made me feel slightly hysterical. Instead of breaking out in a deranged cackle, a breathy laugh was miles better. "Uh, yeah. No. You're not exactly upfront about things, as you know."

His lips pressed into a line, clearly remembering the whole sham of a gig situation. "I want to date you."

I nodded and did *not* roll my eyes, thank you. "Well, that is clear enough. But... to what end? Forgive me for asking that, but I have a kid. I have a life. You are—*you*—so I don't think it's wise for us to continue if we're not both sort of on the same page."

His lips twitched. "Please tell me what page you're on, then, and I'll reciprocate."

I laughed at that. "Yeah, right! I'm not about to start."

He grinned at that, and my heart flopped around like a little fish out of water. No one had gotten this visceral reaction from me in... ever.

Morgan, the waitress I'd had most often, swung by the table and dropped our food with a quick, "Lemmeknowify-ouneedanythingkguys" and off she went. They were nice, just slammed.

We chatted about how good each of our dishes looked—his a beef stew with a puff pastry crust and mine a shepherd's pie I'd had around this time last year and had been craving ever since. The place was tiny and had a diner-like feel in terms of service, but their food was seasonal, simple, and delicious.

After we'd each enjoyed a few bites and my food had fortified me enough to circle back, I prompted, "So you were about to tell me."

He finished chewing and gulped down some water before answering. Anticipation burned through me, but I suspected that Julian wasn't a man to be pushed. He was accustomed to doing the pushing. If I wanted to know the truth, I'd need to wait. Which I could totally do.

Completely fine.

Just as I was about to beg him to say something, he spoke.

"I want to date you indefinitely."

Elation shot through me, chased quickly with doubt. "*Date?* Is—do you plan to be monogamous? Do you ever plan to marry?"

His eyes crinkled at the edges like this was a hilarious question and not a very obvious one. Based on my experience, clarifying a man's interest in monogamy, if I wanted it from him, was an important step.

"I have only ever been monogamous and have no desire to date anyone else, even though we're only halfway through our first date. We've been circling each other a while now, and we've had plenty of interactions to tell me I like you enough to want to continue and to have no interest in anyone else. And yes. If my given partner and I decide we want to marry, I'll be all for it. I think for people who want it, marriage can be wonderful. Life-giving, even."

He'd surprised me again. He was unconventional enough that I'd thought he'd eschew marriage in terms of life partnership or something more modern-sounding.

"And you? Would you marry, if it were with the right person?"

I exhaled slowly, formulating the words. "I liked your caveat—that for people who want it, marriage can be great. My grandparents have a beautiful marriage. Jamie and Bel. The Morrisons. But my dad left my mom early on. And while Chuck and I were never close to marriage, being tied to someone like that feels huge. So I guess I'm saying I could be open to it, but it's not some childhood dream I'm waiting to fulfill. My dream has always been simpler."

His eyes sparked with interest then. "And what's that?"

"To just... be loved. And love. I've got that with family and friends, but..." Heat bloomed in the apples of my cheeks. "The idea that you're with someone and they get you. And you do things for them because you love them. You take care of them without their having to ask, and it's not a burden, but a joy. And those times when it is a burden, it's still a privilege to be there for them in that way."

Why had my throat tightened? Maybe I'd veered off into thinking more of my family members than what I wanted out of romance. In truth, caring for my grandparents, my mom, and even Cara was a load that sometimes felt like a burden. But only because it was so important to me, and them, and my mom. It wasn't something that caused resentment, and I never begrudged them for needing help. Because truly, it was my privilege.

What I'd realized the last few weeks as the bills kept piling up and emotions heightened was that the feeling of the burden didn't mean I didn't love my family. It didn't mean I was failing them, though I felt like a failure for plenty other reasons. And it didn't mean *they* were the burden. *They* were the joy.

Julian studied my face. "You carry a lot, Quinn. I'm guessing you always have."

I nodded, my emotions ever so close to the surface. Crying on a first date was probably not how he'd anticipated this night going, but Julian always surprised me so I could do the same for him. I swiped under one eyelid.

"The people in your life are lucky to have you. You're a wonderful daughter, granddaughter, and certainly, mother."

Growing desperate for a subject change, I scrambled for

something and grabbed onto the nearest obvious question. "Do you want kids?"

His steady gaze never wavered. "Do you want more?"

This was happening too fast. Wasn't it? We were here asking each other these questions like we'd been together for... some amount of time. And we hadn't. And yet, we'd gotten close. Our interactions had braided into a cord that could reasonably be called a relationship. A romantic one? Maybe not entirely, at least not in the beginning, though I didn't make out with any of my other friends. But still.

In the last few weeks, Julian had become the first person I thought of in the morning. He'd quickly turned into the person I couldn't wait to see instead of the person I dreaded encountering. Could I imagine a life with him? Kids?

I swallowed hard. "I don't know. It's hard to think of going back to those early years, but I know it'd be so different at this age than it was at twenty. I'm just not sure..."

"You don't have to be. I—I don't mean to put pressure on you. That said, I'm relieved we're discussing this. At my age, I don't want to invest in someone who isn't as interested in me as I am in them."

"Makes sense."

He leaned over the table, that handsome face zeroing in on me with intensity and purpose. "To be clear, I want everything with you, Quinn. Pending that we do actually get along as well as it feels like we do already, and assuming you end up feeling the same way, there's not a limit. There's no obvious end point for me."

CHAPTER THIRTY-ONE

Quinn

It'd been, by far, the best date I'd been on.

I hadn't expected that. Yet again, I'd sold Julian short in my mind before I gave him a chance to prove himself, and then he came in and knocked it out. Where I'd expected pomp and show of resources, he'd gone for quaint, homey, and familiar. After dinner at Riverside, we chatted on the drive home. He mentioned his disappointment that Scoop, the ice cream shop in town, wasn't open full-time just yet and that he'd originally chosen it for dessert. The shop would expand its hours once the town flooded with tourists for ski season, but in the fall and spring shoulder seasons, they kept weekend hours only.

Smart move, really, though I wouldn't have minded watching buttoned-up Julian lick an ice cream cone. I must've smirked to myself at that thought because he raised his brows expectantly.

"I was just thinking I would've liked to watch you eat ice cream."

An amused *ha* shot out of him, and the muscles in his jaw flexed. Desire and expectation spiraled through me when he parked the car in my driveway and gave me a look so heated that I finally understood the idea of someone's toes curling in response.

"I'll make sure we have a weekend date next time so they're open," he said, then exited the car and walked around the vehicle with that trademark steady gait and opened the door wide for me.

I took his hand, though we both knew I didn't need it. Same for the courtesy of opening the car door. I hadn't waited for him to come around, but I saw he was making the move, and I liked it. He was a man who constantly had people doing things for him—opening doors, driving, even handing him things he needed before he entered a meeting, or so I'd heard. But with me, he did the work. It was a sign of respect and care, and if he wanted to make it, I'd accept it.

Plus, taking his hand gave me an excuse to then hang on once I stood up and we very slowly inched our way up the sidewalk to my front porch.

"We're not going to see each other until the weekend? You know Friday and Saturday nights are tough." For some reason, the thought of going another three full days before I saw him again, maybe more, sounded awful.

"I have to fly back to LA first thing tomorrow, but I'll be back Friday morning. Could you come to my office for lunch?" His thumb grazed over the skin of my hand as we mounted the stairs.

"I think so. I can confirm after I get in tomorrow, but

that should be fine. Want me to bring something?" We stopped under the soft glow of the porch lamp.

"I'll take care of it."

His low, quiet voice sent a thrill through me. Or maybe that was his words. How often had someone said *I'll take care of it* to me? I was the one who took care of things in my life, and though I loved that about myself, I had to admit that it felt luxurious and awesome to have him say it.

"Okay, bossy," I joked, covering the mental jig I was doing at having him take charge.

A smile flashed. My heart kicked and the butterflies took flight in my chest.

"Thanks for coming out with me tonight," he murmured as one of his hands cupped the back of my neck and his thumb slid along the side under my ear.

"It was fun," I rasped, my pulse pounding under the drag of his finger.

Our gazes locked and I met him halfway, all pretense gone. We both knew what we wanted, and that was this. Our lips met in a gentle press, then firmer, then slipped into a teasing rhythm that stoked every smoking little fire in my body. I arched into him, and his hand slipped down over my body while mine slid into his open jacket and mapped his firm waist.

The kiss deepened into searching, near-frantic contact. The only thing in the universe I could think of was Julian—wanting him and wanting *more* of him. Some distant part of my brain signaled there was something else, and I should consider it *right* now, but I batted that niggling thought away and pressed even closer. He groaned softly and held me tighter, as though he could hear my thoughts and felt the same.

It would've kept going like that—probably would've

spun out into something a little dangerous and a lot inappropriate for the front doorstep, if we're being honest. But that thing I'd not quite remembered?

Cara. My daughter. Who pulled open the door with a forceful yank and said, "Hi guys! How was your date?" in the fakest, most irritatingly pleased-with-herself tone I'd ever heard.

I jumped back, though Julian held me firmly enough I didn't actually stumble backward and fall like I would've otherwise.

I kept my head ducked as I knew the light streaming in from the now-opened door would show swollen lips and flushed faces, letting me break this down.

I'd just been caught making out with Julian on my front porch *by my teenage daughter*. Shouldn't this be the other way around?

Well, no. No, it should not because she was only fourteen and had no business doing this. So there.

"Hello, Cara. How was your time with your grandmother and great-grandparents?" Julian recovered long before I had, his voice smooth and devoid of embarrassment.

I admired that. I also hated that I was embarrassed. Why should I be? I was a fully grown woman! But... this was painfully awkward.

"Oh, it was just peachy. How was the date? Obviously ending pretty well."

I gave her a hard look. Was she upset? Or just being a little jerk because she could?

"I think so. What do you think, Quinn?" Julian squeezed at my waist where his hands held me, then released me fully and gave me a small smile.

"It was great, yes. If you'll give us a minute, I'll be right in, Car." I didn't hold back the annoyed expression or tone. She knew what she'd done.

"Sure thing. Just—uh, Julian. I have a concert in Salt Lake on Friday. I know you're busy, but my mom and everyone is going, so you're welcome to come too. If you want. But no pressure. Like, really, you don't even need to—"

"I'd love to. I'll be there. Thank you for inviting me."

Cara beamed. "Okay, cool. Well, I'll just be inside." She stepped back and gently closed the door behind her.

The frost I'd felt for her interruption melted away completely with her invitation. "That was..."

"Unexpected. But very welcome," he finished, looking pleased and serious.

"Yes. And you're free?" I rested my hands on either side of his chest over the thick, fine wool of his coat.

"I am. I could find a car big enough for all of us so your family doesn't have to drive, if you like."

My heart warmed even more. "That's so nice. But actually, my mom loves driving, and since she rarely gets out of Silverton, it's kind of a treat for her to shuttle my grandparents around. I'm off that night, and I wouldn't mind not driving. I could ride with you, if you want."

One side of his mouth slid up into that half-smile that made me fluttery and desperate to kiss him again. "I do want."

I did kiss him then but kept it short and sweet. And very regretfully, I moved away, still connected to him by one hand and very much not wanting to let go.

"Wait."

I stopped, one foot up on the threshold of the door.

"Come here."

He tugged gently on the hand he still held, so I stepped

back. He wrapped his arms around me and tucked his face into my neck. He was hugging me, firm and sweet, with all of himself.

I returned the hug and had the strangest urge to laugh and cry all at once. Emotion sprang to my eyes and scratched at my throat, and I held him tighter.

It might've been a first date, but it didn't feel that way. It felt so much less like the beginning of something and more exactly like the middle. Like things had been decided and we were already on a path heading somewhere. Together.

CHAPTER THIRTY-TWO

Julian

Kelly escorted Quinn into my office at exactly noon on Friday. I had approximately six hours of work to do before we left for Cara's concert and only four and a half hours to do it in, but I'd make it work. I'd need Scott to drive so I could work on the way, and I'd have to let Quinn know.

But for now, I savored the way my heart lurched in my chest at her arrival.

"I'll have lunch right in," Kelly said with a smile, then closed the door behind her.

Good woman. I wouldn't have closed it myself, but since she'd taken the liberty, now I had one less reason to stay away. Like a starving man inexorably drawn to a feast, I moved toward Quinn, who stood just inside the door.

She swallowed and shifted on her feet, almost like she was nervous. But that didn't make sense since I didn't think anything made Quinn Darling nervous.

"Hello. I hope I'm not late. I—"

She let out a little breath when I reached her and leaned in to press a kiss to her cheek. I wanted to pull her close and take her mouth and drown in her a minute, but she held herself a little stiff in my arms.

"You're exactly on time. Thanks for coming to me today." I hoped to make it clear in every possible way that I wanted more lunch dates, more all kinds of dates, more of her any way I could get her.

"Sure, of course." She'd clasped her hands in front of her and gazed around the office like she'd never been there before. I supposed she hadn't for any personal reason—or at least, not any personal reason she realized. The last time she'd been here was when I'd lied about there being a gig at Jack's party.

Did I regret that? All things considered? Not a whit.

Once her eyes landed back on mine, I held them, urging her to keep her focus on me. I touched her elbow, then slid two fingers down her arm, unclasped her hands, and she took mine just as it reached hers.

"You're nervous?"

She shook her head but said, "Yes."

"Why?"

She blinked a few times. "I—it's been a while. Since I've actually cared what happens with someone."

My heart blazed in my chest, but I gestured to the small table and chairs near the wall of windows to cover the sensation. As though this woman didn't already set me afire, she said something like this? She gave me too much hope. Too much hope wasn't good for a man, especially one with so much overblown expectation already. This confession was better than any gift someone could give me.

"That means you care what happens with me?" I asked, my voice still low and calm.

After a big breath, she nodded. "Unfortunately, yes. I really do."

I cracked a smile and pulled her along to the seating area. "I'm not convinced this is a bad thing."

She huffed but grinned. "You wouldn't be. Jury's still out for me."

I sat in the seat next to the one she'd taken, and Kelly knocked, then entered, bearing a tray with steel-domed dishes and paper-capped glasses of water.

"You could've had service bring it," I said, wondering if she'd retrieved this from the kitchen.

"They delivered it to my desk. I told them I'd bring it in so they could get back. Enjoy, and just buzz if you need anything."

"Thanks, Kelly. This is great," Quinn said, cheeks deliciously pink as Kelly was leaving.

"Are you embarrassed to be seen with me?" I asked, mostly joking.

"No. Why would you ask that?"

"You're blushing. I thought maybe I was the cause."

Rather than watching her face for a reaction, I focused on removing the food covers and appreciating the plating. We had a new chef, and she was working out beautifully. We'd be able to open the new restaurant by the holidays, just as I'd hoped.

"I'm just... off-kilter. I don't know. Tired and wired at the same time. A little anxious for Cara's performance tonight and—" She cleared her throat and folded her napkin in her lap before meeting my eyes again. "I enjoyed our date. And I've been looking forward to this, but also just nervous to see if I'd made it up."

"Made up our date?"

"No. Made up our chemistry. My reaction to you. The way you..." She reached for her water and drank half of it down like she'd never had water before.

"This is all very unlike you," I said inanely, not sure what to do to help her. Quinn was a woman who knew herself and her mind. Today, she seemed positively unmoored around me. "I don't like the idea that I've made you so uncertain."

I stood and held out my hand to her. She immediately took it, though looked obviously confused, and rose from her seat.

"I'm going to kiss you now. It's the least I can do to remind you that no, you have definitely not made up what's between us."

So I did. I slipped a hand around her waist and pulled her into my body. At this range, I could see every beautiful sunburst of color in her eyes and the light blush across her cheekbones. My pulse raced through me at her touch, her nearness, her scent. And then, her taste.

The kiss moved from a sweet start to a ravenous discourse between lips and tongues, hands and bodies. I'd never wanted someone so thoroughly and in every way, and I'd certainly never experienced the surety that she wanted me—*Me*—in the same way.

I broke the kiss, hoping we'd return to the subject later, after we'd eaten and gotten her over her nerves. She didn't realize she had no cause for nervousness with me. I might be a bulldog in business, but she owned me. Already.

"Okay. So, yeah. Didn't dream that up," she said in her silken voice, grasping the lapels of my suit jacket.

"No, indeed."

She smiled and bit her bottom lip, then shoved me away

as she released me. "Don't look so proud of yourself, Grenier."

She took her seat and picked up her fork and knife, her entire demeanor seeming more relaxed and less tentative. Relief and a sense of triumph pumped through me at the knowledge that I'd done that for her. I'd calmed her, reassured her, and pleased her.

I didn't often worry about such things—reassuring and pleasing others. I hadn't found it necessary, and in many circumstances, saw such cognizance in others to be a true weakness, both in business and in engineering. Worrying about another person could hamper one's efforts to focus, to create dynamically, and to win.

Perhaps it was why I maintained the friendships I'd managed to develop rather doggedly. I didn't want to have to explain my love for work, my need for solitude at times, and my aversion to touch. But here, with Quinn, all of that felt entirely peripheral to being with her.

I wanted to please her—*good God, how I wanted to.*

"Shouldn't I? You seemed to have enjoyed it," I said, managing to sound casual and unimpressed despite the leaping sensation in my chest.

She chewed a bite with her lips pressed into a smile but shook her head.

And while I enjoyed her playful approach, I wanted her to know. Suddenly, I needed her to understand the depth of what I felt. Not everything, of course.

"I hope you realize that bringing you pleasure is a duty I hope to take very seriously, and I would like to demonstrate my devotion to the cause at your earliest convenience. After that, I will endeavor to ensure you are pleased in every possible way, every desire met, indefinitely."

She swallowed hard and her fork lowered to the table

like she'd lost function in her limb. She started to speak, cheeks brighter than I'd ever seen them, then stopped. Finally, she did. "Julian, you can't just... say stuff like that."

"Can I not?"

"No!"

"Why?"

She gave me a look I couldn't read but then gestured wildly. "You can't talk about bringing me pleasure while we're sitting here having lunch."

"No?"

She laughed, a disbelieving and yet maybe charmed sound. "No! You can't. I'll end up choking and then all your plans for pleasuring me will be out the window anyway."

I chuckled, delighted by that response. She wasn't suggesting she didn't want my efforts, only that being so overt about it might be unusual for her. I wouldn't regret the flaming blush at her cheeks or the falsified outrage.

"Fair enough. I concede your untimely demise would absolutely ruin my plans."

She laughed quietly as she shook her head and speared more salad on her fork. "It's going to be like this with you, isn't it? All the time. You're going to push me in one way or another."

I grinned. "Yes. And then, you'll push right back."

CHAPTER THIRTY-THREE

Quinn

We'd both finished our lunches and sat chatting as snowflakes floated down in the easy November afternoon. From the time I'd entered the hotel, my nerves had been pinging around my belly, making me tongue-tied and blushy.

Then he'd kissed me, and that had loosened me up. The time apart had made me unsure, though I hated admitting it even to myself. But with a kiss to lubricate the moment and delicious food between us, I relaxed. And when he went ahead and said the thing about wanting to please me and... whoa. I now knew for certain that I could liquefy and still sit upright—quite a feat.

The man's direct approach to everything naturally translated to romantic interactions. He'd demonstrated that with his "I'm going to kiss you now" and he'd done the same with that comment. But did he understand how restless that'd made me?

Especially when his alarm sounded and he stared at it like a foreign object had landed in his coat pocket instead of a reminder to wrap up our lunch.

"I'll get going and leave you to your work. Can we pack up these dishes for Kelly?"

He rose from his seat and somehow rounded the small table and my chair to help me scoot it out. I shot him an amused look, and he gave me one of his smoldery *I do what I want and what I want is to pull out your chair* looks that sent both a thrill through my body and a little chuckle out my lips.

"No. I'll call service to get it."

He took my hand in his, guided me toward him, and curved our hands gently behind my back so I arched into him. An odd, controlling move, except he released my hand and pressed me close. Both hands now free, I rose to my toes and wrapped my arms around his neck as our lips met.

The kiss never had a prayer of being gentle—not after all that talk and him in his suit and just *everything*. It exploded into a dizzying whirl of kissing until he finally broke free and carefully set me away.

"If I keep touching you, I won't stop. You need to go, and I'll see you later. I'll pick you up right at five." He buttoned the suit jacket's top button with deft fingers while his eyes raked over me hungrily.

"Okay. Yeah. See you at five," I said, my voice a little shaky as I breathed through the desire flooding every inch of me. But the image of Julian on the edge of losing that carefully guarded control proved too alluring. "Scott's driving, right? So you'll be, uh... you'll have your hands free?"

He scowled even as his eyes heated. "Regrettably, I have to work."

I beamed at him, pleased at the disappointment written on every line of him. "I'm joking. And I knew you'd need to work since you took the lunch break and just got back to town."

Emboldened by his blatant staring, I snuck a kiss to his jaw. He leaned his head into the kiss, increasing the pressure of what would've been a light peck, but his hands stayed in his pockets where he'd slipped them. I kissed his cheek for good measure, then grabbed my jacket from the coat rack and slipped out the door.

I practically floated through the rest of the day. The snow had stayed relatively mild so roads wouldn't be terrible, and I got to go with Julian. He'd finally see Cara play, and we'd be at an event for her together. Normally, missing a Friday night at the lounge would ratchet up my stress since the pay was essential these days, but I couldn't feel that way over tonight. I'd requested the night off weeks ago, and Chase and Angel would handle it beautifully by themselves. I'd see my girl perform and be with my... Julian.

I should've been disgusted with how quickly he'd wrapped me around his finger, but it felt great. After so long on my own and without anyone who even remotely interested me, free-falling into Julian sounded like the ultimate way to treat myself. On that note, maybe I'd have some ice cream tonight after the concert. Something about ice cream on a snowy night made me so happy.

Though ice cream with Julian sounded good too. Or ice cream *on* Julian... I snorted at my own messy little fantasy and focused on finishing my makeup for the concert. Cara had taken a bus with her fellow school orchestra students so I'd have an hour or so to listen to music I loved and think about the evening ahead. One beautiful feature of owning a super-small business? I could close early on slow Friday afternoons and not feel bad about it.

I'd spent no less than a combined full hour of the day dreaming about the way Julian kissed me. Guh, it was appealing. He had this incredibly tender side I never would've seen coming, and any time he touched me, he did it with such purpose. That whole hand behind my back thing had been smooth and a little possessive, but somehow also sweet.

Determined to focus on sending a few e-mails and other tasks on the ride to the concert since Julian would be working too, I grabbed my phone and a small list I'd made to tuck into my purse. It wasn't a formal concert, but I'd still dressed up in a black knee-length dress, leather booties, and I'd need a wool coat. The November evening would be cold now that the sun was on the way down, and by the time we left the concert hall, it'd be in the teens according to the forecast. So far, the snow wasn't sticking, and they'd had plenty of time to prep the roads, so hopefully, we'd make it back before the heavier snow set in tonight.

With ten minutes until Julian arrived, I reviewed the protocols for finding our students after the concert. The evening would be held at Abravanel Hall in Salt Lake and there would be two other high schools participating, all of whom had won the opportunity to perform in a competition in October. Considering how recently the groups had started playing together, it had been a lot to ask, but Silverton High had pulled it off.

I tucked away Cara's dress for her winter formal, knowing I wouldn't have time to work on it for the next few days, until Monday at least. Maybe by her senior prom, I'd be able to buy her a really nice dress instead of needing her to settle for my slightly better than decent work.

Fine, I was good. I could sew almost anything, and I'd learned to do that years ago. But I suspected that part of the fun of dress shopping was just that—going and trying something on with girlfriends and reveling in the flouncy, crazy, awful before finding the exact right dress.

That had never really been me, but I wanted it for Cara if she wanted it. It felt imperative that she have opportunities I hadn't and that she make choices better than I had. On one hand, I hated that line of thinking because the choices I'd made had led me to having her. Plus, I loved my life here. I loved my shop, my friends, singing at the lounge on weekends—truly, I had no complaints.

If I went to Jamie, or even Calla, and told them I wanted to make a go of things in the music industry, either one of them would do whatever they could to help me get started. I'd known that to be true with Jamie all along because he said it every time we talked for years. But it wasn't an exaggeration to say that Cara changed me. She tore open the threads of my heart and stitched them back together in a new weave that made me different.

I hadn't lost my love of music or performing, but I'd found a different vision for my life. Of course, at twenty-one I didn't know what anything else looked like, but I knew I had my baby and I wanted to be with her every second. Maybe it came from being abandoned by my dad or the desire to stay in a community that knew and loved me already, but leaving Silverton had instantly become an impossibility. And rather than the possible missed opportunity feeling like a heartbreaking loss, it seemed only like a distant road not taken.

My phone vibrated in my hand, drawing my focus. A

flurry of emojis wishing Cara good luck and me safe travels and lots of fun from Sarah, Dahlia, Sadie, and Calla came through in our group chat. My heart warmed at their messages, then I chuckled and refused to blush when they took a turn toward suggestions that I make the most of the ride to Salt Lake.

I'd told them how well the first official date had gone, and I'd mentioned today's lunch too. Though we were newer friends, they all understood that my liking someone enough to tell them about it held significance. Paired with where we started, which they also knew, Julian and I were progressing fast. They seemed nothing but supportive, and I took as much solace in that as I could.

With two minutes to five, I knew Julian would be pulling in any second, no doubt extremely punctual as always. I took one last glance at myself in the mirror of the small hallway bathroom, then I grabbed my water bottle, purse, and slipped on my wool coat. I'd unbutton it once I sat down, but I didn't want to catch a chill between the house and the car.

A buzz came from my pocket and I fumbled to reach it, wondering if Julian would call to ask me to meet him outside instead of coming to the door. But my mom's name flashed across the screen.

"Hey, are you guys heading out? Julian should be here any—"

"Quinn. I'm at the hospital in Ogden. There's been an accident."

CHAPTER THIRTY-FOUR

Julian

I'd never been the kind of man who looked forward to things.

Well, no. That's not quite true. There were a great many pleasures a person could find to anticipate, and of course I had a handful of them. Namely, Friday and Saturday evenings watching Quinn sing.

Lately, there were precious few *anythings* that did much for me unless they had something to do with Quinn.

So tonight's concert—a children's orchestral concert an hour's drive away—brought me no end of anticipation. I couldn't wait to sit next to Quinn in the car. She wouldn't interrupt me, and I'd do my best to focus. But on the way back, her daughter would ride on the bus, and we'd have the car to ourselves. I would hold her hand, and maybe convince her to sit close to me. Maybe I could hold her a while.

I hadn't held someone. Ever. I'd never wanted that kind of closeness and intimacy—never craved it to the point of *need*. Until Quinn.

But a great many things could be filed away in the category of *until Quinn*.

Namely, genuinely looking forward to this concert. I eagerly awaited seeing and hearing Cara perform. Apparently, she had a featured solo amongst the group efforts. The concert would be close to three hours long and I'd be exhausted in the end, but something about this night felt pivotal. From Cara's invitation to Quinn's willingness to go with me, it all felt weighty in a very good way.

Scott parked in Quinn's driveway, and I jumped out before he'd fully stopped. The path to her door was wet but not frozen. The just-above-freezing temperature meant the snow fell in wet flakes that melted almost before they touched the ground.

At her door, I rang the bell and waited one minute, then another. An anxious twinge in my chest had me shifting on my feet to resist ringing again. Not everyone was ready at exactly the time planned and I'd had to learn that again and again. Quinn had been punctual for every meeting after our first, but she was a busy woman with many demands on her time.

After another moment of waiting, she swung the door open and waved me in with her phone to her ear. She didn't even spare me a smile, which made my heart sink in my chest until I noticed her pallor and the tension in her face.

"I'll be there as soon as I can. Please pay attention to your phone so I can call you on the way if I need to."

Alarm spiked at her tone—shaken, tight, enervated. I wanted to go to her, but she paced away—not moving away from me as much as it was an action she didn't realize she was taking.

"Okay. Yes. I love you too. See you soon." She tapped her phone and her hand fell to her side, still holding the device.

Her shoulders rose in a long, slow pull of an inhale.

I didn't speak. She'd let me in and she'd tell me what was going on when she gathered her thoughts, but I had to admit I hated the wait.

After another beat or two, she turned to me. "So, my grandma had a stroke, I guess?"

It wasn't a question, but her voice made it sound that way. Less questioning the occurrence and more a reflection of her disbelief and upset.

"What can I do?" I approached, arms out and ready to offer comfort.

She bit her lip and struggled to compose a sharp flood of emotion that brought tears to her eyes, but she held up a hand.

"Um, no, can't do that. I need to get to Ogden and make sure my mom and grandpa are okay. They took Grandpa in the ambulance and my mom followed in her car. I guess she got the paramedics there quickly and they—I don't even know what they did, but she said it's looking pretty good but—" She crushed her eyes shut and sucked in a sharp breath.

My throat tightened around words of reassurance. I hated false promises that everything would be okay, and I'd never understood offering them to placate someone or lessen someone's pain at the expense of honesty. *Until Quinn.*

Her eyes opened, and the pain in them struck at me like a fist to my heart.

"I don't know what to do about Cara. She'll be devastated."

Cara. Of course. That was something I could manage. "I'll go. I'll watch the concert, and then I'll find her and bring her to you at the hospital."

"I don't know. I—I don't want her to be more upset by my not being there."

"I understand that, but you're needed at the hospital. I can't do much for you there, but I can do this. Let her do the concert without this concern, and then I'll find her. You can talk with her in the car, and I'll make sure she's comfortable. We'll keep the privacy screen down so she's not alone with me, if that's something that would be awkward, and—"

"She'll be fine with that, I think. I just..." The last word shook with emotion.

She didn't want a hug, so I wouldn't force one on her, but I gripped her shoulders. "Let me help you. Please. Then you can do what you need to do. In fact, we could drive you —drop you at the hospital and—"

"No. We need another car there so we can take shifts or whatever needs to be done. I have to drive."

"Will you be safe? You're understandably upset and I hate the thought of you driving all that way alone while you're thinking about all this."

She straightened her back. "Yes. I'm going to change really quick and get on the road. Please keep in touch and I'll let you know when I get to the hospital, if you want."

Her eyes darted around the living room like she was already making a list of items she needed to take with her.

"Yes, please do. I'll do the same." And because I needed it, I kissed her cheek and put my hand under her chin to draw her face to mine. "You're going to be okay. Get there. We'll deal with this."

She nodded and swung around to strip off her coat as she moved in the other direction. I slipped out the front door and jogged to the car.

"Slight change of plans, friend. We're going to have a long night, if you're up for it."

Hours later, I'd enjoyed the concert as much as I could with less than half my mind on the matter at hand and I'd retrieved Cara. She'd taken the news as well or better than I imagined anyone could in her circumstances, and she'd come with me without any display of discomfort. Her focus was on getting to her family, and we were only a few minutes from the hospital in Ogden when she finally spoke for the first time since we'd entered the car.

"Do you think she'll be okay?" she asked, her voice sounding so painfully young.

"I wish I could tell you of course she will, but I don't know. I do know the hospital is a capable one, and from what I understand, she's in very good hands. I also know that if your great-grandmother needs someone to fight for her, she has no better advocate than your mother."

Cara chuckled lightly at that. "I pity the fool who tries to do anything less than perfectly for her while she's there."

I smiled, glad she could see the humor and knew her mother's doggedness would come in handy in this situation if needed.

Quiet settled between us before I said, "You were magnificent tonight, Cara. I don't know if I told you that amidst speaking to your teacher and getting to the car. I am honored I got to hear you perform."

Her chin dipped down. "Thank you. It felt good to play a concert grand on a stage like that."

I made the mental note to ascertain whether the high school had a concert grand and if it didn't, donate one immediately. It struck me as something Jamie might've already done, but the child should have access to a large instrument like that.

"Can I ask you something?" she asked quietly. Not shy—tentative.

"Of course. Anything."

A pause filled the space between us like she was weighing her words. "You're dating my mom, right? Like not just one date, but *dating*."

"Yes."

"So you're her boyfriend?"

I would've laughed if I didn't think it would strike her as insulting. Was I Quinn's boyfriend? I absolutely wanted to be, and she'd made clear there was no one else. Would she want me telling her daughter I was when she and I hadn't even discussed it? Likely no.

"I would like to be, but that's probably a better question for your mother."

She smirked. "Are you scared of her?"

"No. Not scared. But I respect that she has opinions and knows her own mind. She wants to determine how things go between us, and I'm more than willing to allow it to unfold however she wants."

As long as she did still want something between us, she could set the pace. So far, she hadn't minded my tendency to push a bit—at least, not in the end. But if she wanted to slow down, we would.

"Do you love her?"

I inhaled a silent breath, my mind blank and my body rigid. "That's probably something I should tell her first, don't you think?"

CHAPTER THIRTY-FIVE

Julian

Cara studied me from her seat, though I could only see the glitter of her eyes pointed in my direction when we passed streetlights. The sun had set long ago, and the pitch-black sky was dotted with stars and a bright, bold moon. We wouldn't see the pinprick stars until we got back to Silverton, but even here in Ogden, they were visible in a way they never were in LA.

"You know that's not really an answer, right?" Her voice came stronger now.

She'd gained confidence during our discussion, which I hoped meant she'd grown comfortable, at least a little more so, with me. "It's all the answer you're going to get."

"Oh, I see how it is," she said, the words irritated but with enough humor in her voice to signal she wasn't upset.

I thanked God she gave me hints, because I didn't spend much time interacting with teens. Jamie's kids, even some of the other Morrison children, I delighted in. Cara was the oldest child I'd interacted with and this conversation, like every other we'd had, however short, had shown me yet again how close to being an adult she was.

"Good. Because I'm certain you have more than enough of your mother in you to attempt to badger more information out of me, but you should know that if your mother is stubborn, I am steel. I won't bend to your wily teen ways."

She burst out laughing. "Oh my gosh, I'm embarrassed for you."

I chuckled low, glad she'd had the desired response.

"We'll be there in two minutes, Julian," Scott said from the front seat.

Cara sucked in a breath and let it out slowly.

"You'll be okay."

"You don't know that," she said, tension laced through her voice.

"I don't know if your great-grandmother will recover fully, no. But I know for a fact you will be okay. You are surrounded by people who love and care for you. You will have support and whatever you need."

Her hard swallow became visible as we pulled into the front circle of the hospital. "Thanks."

She reached for the door, but I stopped her. "Cara. If there's ever anything I can do, say the word, and it's done."

She nodded, mumbled a thanks, and exited the car. I followed soon after, hoping Quinn wouldn't be too hard to find. The minute we stepped in the door, she pulled Cara into her arms and held her tight. I couldn't see her face or anything but her black sweater-wrapped arms at Cara's neck.

When they pulled apart, her eyes found mine.

"Thank you."

"Of course," I said, and meant it.

"Can you come up? Not to the room, but just, let me take Cara up and then have a minute?"

She had no idea. No idea what I'd do for her.

"Of course."

Quinn tucked an arm around Cara and guided her ahead to a bank of elevators. I followed a few steps behind, hoping to provide them space to talk or whatever they needed to do. A few floors up, the elevator dinged and we exited into a long hallway full of doors that ended in a nurse's station.

"Let me just get her through and I'll be back. There's a little spot to wait right there. Is that okay?"

I stepped into the empty alcove with chairs lining the walls. "Yes. I'll be right here."

While waiting, I turned my focus to work, allowing the least demanding of my tasks to take over since I couldn't be relied upon to execute anything complex at this point in a long day. A few minutes later, Quinn approached and stopped a few feet from me.

"Hi," she said, her voice small.

I saw her crack just as I waved her forward and rose to my feet to catch her in an embrace. The hitching sound was my only clue that she was crying, but I *felt* it. The tension in her as she broke open in my arms. I held her to me, one arm across her shoulder blades, the other cradling the back of her head. Her face was tucked into my neck and her shoulders rose and strained when she pulled in more air.

She cried almost silently, and the effect of her soundless sobs slayed me. This woman made so much beauty and she was so strong, but here, she stifled her emotions. I held her tighter to me, willing her to feel any sense of comfort I could give.

"You're all right, love. You're okay." I petted her hair and rubbed a hand up and down her spine.

For long minutes, we stayed like that. I would've stood there all night if she'd wanted to, but eventually, she eased back and pulled a tissue from her pocket and wiped her nose before looking at me with puffy red eyes smeared with mascara. I leaned against the wall, enjoying the way she swiped under her eyes. Such a simple, small thing, but the shared moment, her sharing her grief and emotion, made knowing how she wipes her eyes after crying something precious.

"I'm beautiful, I know," she joked with a roll of her eyes.

"You are. But you're also exhausted and stressed. Tell me how to help."

She smiled, but it looked pained. "You already have. Bringing Cara made a huge difference. Everyone's so relieved she's here, including me. I don't know how to thank you."

I twined our fingers together. "You don't need to. Just tell me what else to do. Give me a job."

She dropped her head to my shoulder in a familiar move, but this time, she slipped a hand around my waist and flattened herself against me, turning her head so it rested fully against me. I inhaled, savoring her scent against the sterile hospital and the feel of her pressed into me amidst the frenetic atmosphere of the last few hours.

"You can go. I'm leaving soon anyway, and—"

"Let me drive you."

"No, I have my car, remember? I'll need to get back down here again tomorrow."

"I'll be at the office all day. Leave your car and let me take you home. Scott can bring you back whenever you like tomorrow."

She stepped all the way out of my reach. "I can't do that. I just... I don't feel right about it."

Knowing now was not the time to pick this battle though I knew I could lean hard on her being tired, I tried a different tack. "Okay. Then why don't I physically drive you and Cara home? Scott can pick me up from your house, but that way, you're not driving back this late after an exhausting day."

I could tell she wanted to say no by the little purse of her lips, but she sighed instead. "I hate to say it, but that might be smart. I can tell my vision is impaired after all that crying, and I didn't think to bring my glasses."

Curiosity spiked through me. "You wear glasses?"

"Yeah. Only at home, though, like right before bed."

As though I needed another reason to want to spend the night with her, here was one. I wanted to see her completely undone.

"What's that face?" she asked, tilting her head as though to get a better look.

"I'd like to see you in your glasses."

She tucked her lips between her teeth to hide a smile, but it broke free. "All right, I cannot talk to you about that kind of thing right now and you know it."

"I know nothing."

She shoved me. "Are you up for meeting my mom? Probably not my grandparents, but I know she'd like the distraction."

No. I didn't want to meet her mom. I didn't want a handshake, and I didn't want to delay getting home. But for this woman, of course I would. "Lead the way."

Down the hallway, around the corner, and past a few more doors, Quinn gave my hand a gentle squeeze before releasing it to peek into a room. I stayed well away from the door, recognizing that a stranger in one's hospital room wouldn't be welcome.

Quinn returned with an older, slightly more petite version of herself with caramel hair instead of her blond. She ushered her mother close to me with a small smile on her perfect lips.

"Mom, this is Julian Grenier. Julian, this is my mom, Dana."

My stomach clenched when Dana extended her hand to me. I hadn't taken my usual approach, but it would be fine. I'd handle it, and I'd shake it off eventually. The day was almost over, so it wasn't like it'd stick with me for all that long.

"Nice to meet you, Dana."

Our hands clasped in a shake, and she pressed her free one over mine so she sandwiched my hand. Her skin was warm and dry and she shook firmly, then released me. Relief and honestly, a bit of wonder flooded in. I glanced to Quinn to see a soft look on her face, and then she gave me a wink.

"Likewise, Julian. Thank you for helping tonight. Cara enjoyed riding back with you."

I nodded. "I'm glad it worked out."

"And thank you for being such a good friend to Quinn. I know she appreciates you so much."

Dana's voice held an edge I couldn't decipher, but it was enough to gain an elbow to the ribs from Quinn. *Hmm.* What could that mean? A thought wriggled around in my chest—a not-unwelcome idea that perhaps Dana knew about some of my loathsome help and thought Quinn should more willingly accept it.

Maybe Dana would be an ally in this next phase. I'd need at least one, if things went my way, and tonight's events—every one of them—had only solidified my plans. So I'd do whatever I could do to pull Dana to my side and make sure that when the time came, she'd be an ally.

To do what, exactly, I still didn't know. But it was just a matter of time.

"It's my pleasure to do whatever I can for your daughter. She's an amazing woman. And from everything she's told me about you, she learned from the best."

Dana beamed, but Quinn raised a brow in mock-disbelief. Only that little quirk to her mouth said she didn't mind me charming her mom. She couldn't know how much I loved when she gave me a little grief because only the people closest to me did that. Really only Jack and Jamie, and occasionally Scott.

And Quinn. Who was quickly becoming the most important person in my life.

CHAPTER THIRTY-SIX

Quinn

Jamie wrapped me in a tight hug before releasing me and shaking my shoulders. "We would've come sooner."

"You couldn't have, and you know it."

He scowled. "Would've."

I rolled my eyes. "Whatever. You're here now, and we'll do Thanksgiving tomorrow. I had my fill of cafeteria-style saltless turkey and gravy at the rehab facility to tide me over for today."

Jamie made an irritable sound. I'd told him my grandma had been moved to a rehab facility but hadn't mentioned we'd changed our usual Thanksgiving day feast to one where she was being treated. It'd been nice to be together, but the food had been depressing, and even the space had been. It was all their insurance would pay for, and while I had forbidden myself from thinking about how much the ambulance ride had cost, of the many tests they'd done, or the three nights' stay in the hospital she'd had, the anxiety crept in.

When I'd offered to bring Cara by today, Jamie'd latched right onto our availability and railed at me for not telling him we didn't have Thanksgiving plans. We *did*—they'd just happened to be the day before. And he and Bel almost always flew in Thanksgiving day and the whole Morrison family did an obnoxiously huge dinner that they insisted on looping me and Cara into, so we'd get our fill of celebrating.

"Daddy, can Cara stay the night?" Ally's sweet little voice popped up between us and Jamie's grumpy face instantly dissolved.

"It's fine with me, tiny, but you'll have to ask Cara's mom, and probably also Cara herself." He glanced at me as he tacked that last part on, suddenly realizing he probably shouldn't commit my daughter.

He didn't have to worry. Cara loved his kids, and it'd be good for her to enjoy the distraction. On top of Grandma, her dad had missed seeing her today. He was supposed to come take her to breakfast since we didn't have plans. Supposedly, his plane got delayed, but we'd heard nothing from him until well after noon, as though the two-hour flight from LA could've occupied so much of his phone time that he couldn't shoot off a text to let her know he was running late.

By the time he bothered to check in, she'd moved from sad to that beautiful teen zone I liked to call *over it*. I hated when the *over it* attitude was aimed at me, but I had to admit I didn't mind Cara moving into that phase with Chuck. It made me slightly less murderous to see her dead-eyed *I don't even care* look than to see her jaw clenching and eyes filling with tears as the minutes ticked past when he was supposed to arrive.

Ally scampered away after I told her that of course Cara could stay if she was up for it.

"And what'll you do all by your lonesome?" Jamie asked, moving to the fridge and holding up a bottle of beer.

I waved it away and checked my phone for the time. Forty minutes until I needed to get to Julian's. "Actually, I have plans."

His Cheshire grin told me he already knew.

"You're an idiot."

He chuckled. "No. I'm happy for you."

I couldn't criticize that, and my smile grew into something genuine and a little too large. "Thanks."

Jamie's eyes brightened. "Oh, and now you have overnight childcare. You're welcome." He winked.

My stomach and heart and lungs and *everything* swooped low. *Oh.*

I'd been looking forward to our date night in since Julian had mentioned it a few days ago. He'd promised me we'd stay in and eat at his place so I wouldn't get bombarded with people checking on my grandma and everything else. You'd think people wouldn't interrupt a date, but in a small town like this, they absolutely would.

They had already. Julian and I had met for lunch on Sunday before he flew to LA. We'd sat in a corner booth at Diner and no less than five people had interrupted our meal to ask me how my family was. They acknowledged him, if warily at times, and we'd still had a nice time. We laughed about it, and Julian seemed slightly less curt when talking to people than I remembered him being, which had surprised me a bit.

I'd always thought of him as more of an introvert, and I

knew for a fact he was extremely private. His welcoming the interruptions had surprised me. Not that he was chatty —he always got right to the point in that direct, business-like way of his. But it felt less rushed than I'd seen him before. It felt like he wanted people to talk to him.

But I *hadn't* seen him since then, and it felt like way too long. I'd taken Friday night off from the bar for Cara's concert, and thankfully, that'd simplified life since I'd ended up at the hospital until well after midnight. Then Saturday, I'd gone in for two short sets that I would've loved to skip. Julian had been there, but he'd sat at the bar instead of his usual spot, setting a hand on my back whenever I took a break, and telling me I could go home if I needed.

He'd been painfully sweet and concerned. He'd insisted on driving me there and home again, and he'd walked me to my door and given me a soft, far too quick kiss.

Sunday had been the same because Cara had been there waiting. She'd chatted Julian's ear off about all manner of things, including some article they'd both read about Lincoln Center's piano. Cara was clearly half in love with the man, which warmed my heart.

But also terrified me. Because that moment after his tenderness with me all night, his helpful contributions during the crisis the night before, and his clear focus on assuring he was doing whatever he could... all of it had added up to me realizing that I wasn't just halfway in love with him.

I was all the way there.

So tonight was a big deal. I didn't think I'd tell him just yet... not yet. I didn't really want to tell him at all since once I did, I'd be wide open to the eventualities that came from love. And in my romantic life, that meant only pain and regret.

Julian was different, though. I knew that like I knew my name. And whether I told him or not, I couldn't even pretend not to be completely pleased that Cara was staying at Jamie's and that most likely? I'd be staying at Julian's.

Dinner was amazing. Julian's house was ridiculous, but also amazing. And the man himself?

Mouthwatering.

I couldn't remember the last time I reacted to someone the way I did to him. I'd noticed him years ago when he'd first showed up in Silverton all brusque and business and not-quite-socially-capable, and yes. I'd thought he was good-looking then. When I'd found out he was an actual billionaire, that had put me off. Wayyyy off.

I didn't want to equate wealth with evil, but in my gut, people with that much money just probably were corrupt by the mere proximity to that much money. When you could buy a small country just for funsies, you were probably kind of messed up in the head.

Obviously, I'd been wrong. That's not to say Julian was what I'd call *normal*, but neither was I. I'd been kind of odd all my life, but I covered it with charisma, talent, and honestly? A pretty face. I owned the weird—my pushiness, my short temper, and my refusal to be impressed by anyone if I thought there was even a chance they were impressed with themselves.

That was something I saw in Julian. He had his quirks, and I still hadn't decided if he was actually an introvert or not, but he didn't apologize for his down-to-business way of doing things. And he didn't apologize for the way he took control of the handshake in any situation and then moved away.

Except with me, when he'd flinched away from my touch and he'd explained a little about his sensitivity to unexpected touch. I had yet to see him appear surprised or upset or anything but entirely welcoming of contact with me, but I still wondered if it might be an issue. And as the evening drew to a close, I wondered if he'd want me to stay.

I hadn't said I could. I didn't want things to stall out and figured I'd mention it when he brought up taking me home. He'd sent Scott to get me so he could receive the food from the chef at Silver Ridge Resort who'd catered our fantastic meal tonight, and I was more than willing to take the ride solo and not drive over. He'd promised to take me home at whatever time I felt comfortable, and I couldn't wait to tell him that sometime before noon tomorrow would be just fine. But I needed to be sure he'd want that.

All his talk sure seemed like he would. But I also hadn't been in a relationship with someone as enigmatic as Julian. I'd made so many assumptions about him before I really knew him and still found myself doing it, so I'd vowed to stop and just ask him or see how things went instead of assuming I knew how he'd handle something.

"Wine?" he asked, holding a bottle out in offer.

I nodded, very happy to feel free to drink another glass and know I wouldn't have to drive home. He'd had a glass at dinner and poured himself another half before standing and holding out a hand for me to take. Apparently, we were moving.

Nerves lit me up as I followed him from the dining room into the gorgeous, high-ceilinged living room. This was it. I felt the confession of my feelings on my tongue but didn't want that to be what I said first. I may have accepted that I'd opened myself to Julian in many ways I hadn't with anyone else and I recognized with that came vulnerability, but I didn't need to be the first to hang everything out and *ask* for rejection by sharing that level of emotion.

But I did want to tell him I could stay. I wanted to see his reaction—craved it. *Him.*

We sat on a gorgeous couch placed perpendicular to a roaring fireplace. We set our glasses on the coffee table and then he reached for me, urging me to rest back in the cradle of his chest and arms.

"I'm glad you're here," he said in a quiet, low tone next to my ear.

He nuzzled into my hair, and tingles shot down my spine. "Me too."

After a quiet moment filled with only the distant sound of music he'd been playing and the crackle of the fire, he asked, "What time do you need to be back?"

I turned enough so I could see his face. His handsome features were all the more stunning tonight, softened by being in his own space, maybe a little by the wine, and if I wasn't fooling myself too much, by his feeling comfortable with me.

Our gazes hooked into each other when I responded. "Cara's spending the night with Ally at Jamie's. So... I don't."

CHAPTER THIRTY-SEVEN

Julian

I hadn't allowed myself to imagine this eventuality, but I was more than glad to see it play out. I could feel Quinn's nerves between us, as though she thought I might be anything less than elated at these words or what I thought they meant.

"No curfew?" I asked, wanting to confirm I'd understood.

She shook her head slowly side to side, those eyes the best invitation I'd ever received. I leaned down and took her mouth in a soft, lazy kiss. As much as I wanted everything I saw in those eyes, I did not want to rush this. "Good. Then we've got some time."

She flattened her lips to stay a smile. "Yes, we do."

My heart did stupid things in my chest and I tried to ignore the way every part of me connected to hers felt better —better than it did without her touch. Better than I ever had. Anticipation for more closeness surged through me, but I leaned forward to retrieve our glasses and handed off hers. "Tell me something."

One brow tilted up, and she scooted away just enough that we were no longer nested together and she could face me. "Okay. What?"

I held the glass by the slope of hard, cool glass at the base vessel where the stem joined to the upper portion. Something about these glasses was so pleasing in my hand. I didn't often drink wine, but when I did, this juncture made me oddly pleased. Whether the night behind and in front of us, or the glass in my hand, I decided not to delay approaching something I'd been planning to talk to her about the night of Cara's concert last week but had never gotten a chance.

"As you know, I haven't been in a relationship. I want to make sure I meet your expectations."

She bit her lip and frowned, but just slightly. Like my question confused her. "I don't feel like I have all that many expectations. I don't think I've had many *relationships* either, as we've discussed, and I think we get to make that up as we go. I think we're doing well."

"No. That leads to disappointment and I—" I cleared my throat, shifting to fold my fingers with hers. "I don't want to disappoint you. I want to know what you want so I can give it to you."

A small chuckle snuck out before her beautiful mouth pressed into a smile. "That's not how it works."

"No?"

Her expression seemed endeared, not irritated, but of course she still firmly disagreed. "No. You don't just give me whatever I want. We're going to disagree. And I mean, I'd say that normally, but you and me? We're probably going to disagree all the time."

I scowled, and she laughed and reached up to smooth a hand from my brow back through my hair. The gesture was so... so purely *loving*, I had to clear my throat again. "I have no illusions we'll agree all the time. But I want to ensure that we can agree on whatever possible ahead of time to avoid any friction."

She grinned. "Friction's not always bad."

A reluctant laugh escaped me. "True enough. But let's say, I don't want any disagreements between us we can avoid."

She shook her head. "I don't think *that's* a reasonable expectation."

I studied her, hoping to decipher her meaning. "We will disagree. I know that. But I want—"

She squeezed my hand. "Julian, you have to know that if you're with me, we're going to fight. We're both bull-headed and we frustrate each other. You exasperate me and I—I'm sure I drive you insane sometimes. But that's not all we have. Getting along isn't all there is in a relationship—and for what it's worth, I do think we get along really well."

"I do too," I said quickly, wanting to make sure she knew I agreed.

"I think you've been doing a lot of what I think of as relationshippy stuff already, honestly," she said, her eyes ducking to her glass.

"For example?"

"You show up when you say you will. You give me your full attention when you're with me. You check in and ask how my day has been when we don't see each other. You help when I need you."

A slow burn of fizzy ecstasy filled my veins at her saying

when I need you like it'd happened more than once. "I hope so."

"You have. Last weekend, I don't know what I would've done. I'm sure Cara would've come home on the bus and I would've—I don't even know. But I didn't have to worry because I trusted you'd take care of her. And for some reason, she's obsessed with you, so she was glad for you to be the one picking her up, even in those circumstances. She told me that via text like ten times on the drive from Salt Lake."

"I'm glad."

She gave me another smile, a satisfying reward for a simple response.

"See? You care about what happens to me and my family. You show up when I need you, and you try to make my life better, whether it's giving my daughter a ride or holding me when I cry. You don't have to anticipate my every desire to be a good partner. That's not what I need."

"It's too simple. It's not ever this easy with someone," I argued.

"Maybe that's because you haven't—" She paused, apparently gathering herself. When she continued, her gaze held mine in an intense lock. "Maybe you haven't been with the right person."

I'd had the thought and believed it. Her saying it—her suggesting that she might be the right person made three words press into my heart—into my soul—and spring to my lips. But it was too soon, wasn't it? Sure, I'd been admiring her for years now, obviously wanting her for weeks, but she'd only just begun to soften to me.

Yes, she was here now, but I wasn't fool enough to believe she loved me. She's just proved how little I had to offer her, and her refusal to accept things she wanted, not just that she needed, threw everything out of balance. As usual.

I didn't know how to know what she needed. The fact that I'd helped in the last few instances had been coincidental. I couldn't have been happier I'd met the need, but how could I do that going forward without knowing what they were?

Still, she needed to know she was right. I'd never been close, because no one in my past had been even remotely like Quinn. No one would ever be like her, either. And she should know I agreed with her.

"You're right."

"I am?"

I nodded.

"Guess I better savor you saying those words, huh?"

Tempting though it was, I didn't bite the bait. "I have even better words for you."

Her expression cleared and she blinked. "Oh?"

I nodded and reached for her glass, setting it down before closing the space between us, a hand on either side of her face. "I shouldn't say them now, but I can't keep this from you. I love you, Quinn. I know it's too soon, but I want you to know it. Count me among your most ardent admirers and fans, but please also know I love you."

She looked stricken for a moment, or shocked, but then she reached for me and crushed her lips to mine. Every song and note I'd heard her sing paled in comparison to the fiery passion in this kiss, an expression of greed and longing and hope so intense, she must've set me ablaze.

Soon, she was crawling over me and her weight above me was far more glorious than any weighted blanket or calming sensation. My heart thundered in my chest, reaching out to hers and begging it to be mine, mine, mine.

A desperate, hungry beat that mingled with the rhythm of our breaths and the slow, deep slide of lips and kisses and sighs.

Nothing had ever felt so good. No one would ever own me this thoroughly.

When we finally made it to my room, I smiled at the realization that she'd packed a small overnight kit in her little bag I hadn't paid much attention to. Standing next to Quinn as we brushed our teeth and she took out her contacts made me feel strangely light. Like it'd happened before, or would again. Like all of the mess I'd made in starting things with her had been for a purpose, and here it was, a beginning.

Watching her crawl into my bed, folding back the heavy comforter and smooth sheets and sliding beneath them in almost non-existent clothing masquerading as pajamas made my heart clutch and my body forget the late hour and how early I'd awoken that morning.

She stared back at me through her thick-framed glasses, her eyes sleepy but alert.

"Come here." She patted the middle of the king-sized bed.

I obeyed immediately, climbing in and moving toward her with purpose. But instead of sating that ravenous look in her eye, she kissed me tenderly. "I didn't say it earlier because I didn't want you to think it was forced or only because you said it, but I want you to know. I love you."

We spent the rest of the night in each other's arms. I

pushed away every thought threatening to steal me from the moment, every voice whispering this was all too good to be true, every impulse telling me she was far too close, far too dear to me, and it couldn't possibly last. I would do anything to keep her, and for once, I wouldn't allow myself to cave to those fears before I'd even taken the chance.

Something had clicked inside me when she'd said those three words back, and that's what I would focus on.

CHAPTER THIRTY-EIGHT

Quinn

I left Julian's house on a high like I hadn't felt in... ever. Truly. That odd, sweet, maddening man loved me, and I loved him, and I had no idea what to do about it except revel in the good feelings.

Seriously, I had no idea how to process everything that'd happened last night, let alone the last week. I was in love. I'd told the man I loved that I loved him. *Who the crap was I?*

He kissed me goodbye at the doorstep—thankfully, Cara didn't feel the need to interrupt us this time—and I walked inside to find her clicking through channels on the TV.

"Looks like *someone* had an eventful date," she said with a glint in her eye.

"You were at Jamie's, so I thought it was better I stay than have him drive me home."

She nodded, and wisely didn't offer more commentary. I'd hoped to be home before she got back so this wouldn't be on her radar, but she was almost fifteen and she deserved to understand this was something significant.

"It's serious between us."

She gave me a classically teenage look. "Uh, *yeah*. Pretty sure I figured that out like a month ago."

"Oh, did you? Funny, we just figured that out last night." And oh, wow, did we.

She rolled her eyes. "Well then, you're both slow. I knew you guys were a big deal the second I saw you with him at Uncle Jamie's. I've literally never seen you like that around someone."

I'd been nervous and weird, so that made sense. I didn't get like that with people—she was right.

"Plus, then you went on that trip to Jack McKean's house? Hello clue number thirty-five."

"Okay, now you're just bragging. Plus that was a work thing, and you know it."

"*Mmmhmmm.*"

The amount of sass in the sound should've made me want to scream, but I couldn't summon anything but amusement.

"Fine. You knew it all along. Round of applause for you, oh wise one."

She preened. "Thanks. And I'm happy for you."

Oh, my heart. As often as she gave me grief, she also turned around and said the sweetest thing. "Thank you. I am too. And I'm glad you like him."

"I do. He's a weirdo but in a good way. It'll be a little strange if he ends up being my stepdad since more than one of my friends has commented on how hot he is, but I'm used to that with Uncle Jamie, so I guess it'll be fine."

With that, she launched off the couch and stomped upstairs, hollering she was taking a shower and to be ready by one as though her dropping something about me marrying Julian like it was no big deal wouldn't shock the response right out of me.

But what could I say? Plus, we had Thanksgiving with the Morrisons this afternoon and she did need a shower. This evening, we'd go by the rehab center and visit Grandma and then stop by my mom's to see her and Pops, all before dropping Cara at home and hauling it to the lounge for my Friday night shift.

All I wanted to do was curl up by the fire and remember every little detail of the last twelve hours, but as was my reality, I had no time. I also knew if I did that, I'd have to face up to what all this meant. We loved each other, but hadn't actually talked about how our lives would fit together. And more than a little bit of me worried they simply wouldn't.

The raucous energy of a Morrison family meal had intensified over the years. Jamie had often invited me, and when Cara had been younger and the only kid, I'd declined. But once Danny married Mia and she toted along her adorable son, Kai, the atmosphere proved irresistible to my kid-loving daughter.

She would be such a good big sister. I'd had the thought so many times, and it circled back around yet again. She was a sweet adoptive cousin as it was—with Jamie's two kids, with Danny's *four*, and with Liam and Wells's kid, as well.

Leo was apparently pregnant now too, and that was after quite a bit of heartache, so I was thrilled for her and Jonas. That said, something about being around these people meant pregnancy was catching, and now that it was technically possible for me to be in the maternal way again, I supposed I needed to be aware.

It wouldn't be a bad thing.

The thought echoed through me, and my heart somersaulted around in my chest. I couldn't give that my full attention because two people were talking to me at once—Bel on one side and Ally on the other. I'd already promised Alice and William, Jamie's mom and dad, that I'd see them again sooner than next Thanksgiving, and was slowly making my way to the door. Jamie would take Cara home later, once she'd worn out all the kids by being the de facto babysitter.

But I had to get to work. And as stupid as it was considering I'd seen him this morning, knowing Julian would be there made every second I lagged here, despite being surrounded by people I truly cared about, fill me with an anxious restlessness.

Just when I almost broke free, Will Morrison, the senior member of the Morrison family and a truly excellent human, reached out his weathered hand to take mine. "Tell your mom hello for me, Quinn. And tell your grandparents I'm excited to have them as neighbors soon."

I smiled. "Of course, but... neighbors?"

He nodded, his wrinkled face still handsome and his Morrison blue eyes just as bright as his grandson's. "I saw them hanging the plaque outside one of the suites on my hall. Marietta Wilcox moved in with her daughter, so the place freed up, and sure enough, this afternoon I saw Sidney, one of our best people, sliding in a nameplate that said *Josiah and Cara Darling*. I'm delighted we'll be closer. Give them my regards, will you? And I'll be looking forward to helping them settle in."

He patted my shoulder with a fond smile, then ducked his head to listen to Kai, who'd come bounding up to escort him to wherever he was needed next. He must've been nearing a hundred, but he was sturdy and spry, and entirely unaware he'd just dropped a bomb.

I'd wanted to get my grandparents into Silverton Springs Retirement Community for years. But even if I'd had the money, there hadn't been space. Now there was evidently space, but I still didn't have the money.

A sick dread swirled in my gut, but I promised myself I wouldn't jump to conclusions. I said the rest of my farewells with a slightly less genuine smile on my face and beelined for my car. Within the safety of the cab, I dialed my mom and put it on speaker while I drove to the resort.

"How was the Morrison family feast?" she asked, sounding weary but cheerful.

"Are you moving the grandparents into Silverton Springs?" So much for keeping my cool—my tone emerged as sharp and accusatory as my thoughts felt.

She was quiet for a moment. "They are moving in next week. Well, Grandpa will move, and whenever Grandma is done with the rehab facility, she'll join him."

"With what money? How did you get into the line? Why didn't you tell me about this, and seriously, again, *with what money*? Have you thought about the expense of the ambulance ride alone? Have you even thought—"

"I've had them on the list for years. I've had to turn down spots before, but refused to do it this time. When I saw the chance, I—I took it."

Something was off, and my heart quaked in my chest

because I already knew. I wished with every bit of me I didn't, but I knew. "Did Julian have anything to do with this?"

A beat of silence filled the space, and I slammed my hand against the steering wheel. "Tell me!"

"He was involved, but I'm not saying anything else. He made me promise to have you speak to—"

"*He made you promise?* You're loyal to Julian Grenier over your own daughter?"

A sigh filled the other end of the line until she'd exhaled all her air, and then she responded. "You are my daughter and I care about you. This has nothing to do with loyalty. That's what you need to know. Anything else, speak to him."

And because I couldn't possibly say anything to that, I hung up.

I didn't know exactly what he'd done to make this happen, but I hoped it was just pulling some strings to get them in. I knew right down to my toes it wasn't that simple and that I would feel far worse than I did now once I spoke to him, but as I pulled into park, I shot Brandon a text telling him I'd be ten minutes late and I'd owe him a favor next time.

I had to talk to Julian, and it had to be now. I couldn't go sing for hours and feel his eyes on me mixing with the memories of the last twenty-four hours and not know the truth. So right now? Julian was going to give me the truth.

CHAPTER THIRTY-NINE

Julian

I'd forbidden myself to count the hours until I saw Quinn again and had failed miserably. I hated to think I was that desperate to be near her, but I couldn't deny how wrong everything felt after she'd left this morning.

Having her in my life—my bed, my morning, my every hour, waking or not—it had all clicked into place. Suddenly, I'd known what to do.

And I'd done it. Now for bringing Quinn around slowly to that idea. Being away from her didn't help, but fortunately, she'd be singing tonight.

Jamie had invited me to join the Morrison family, but I'd worried it might seem like I was encroaching on her life too much—just showing up and insinuating myself into every part of her holiday traditions might've been overkill. Jamie had invited me before, but I'd historically spent this holiday in LA and then settled into my Silverton house for

Christmas. I'd already committed to spending the holiday with my mother, so even if I'd wanted to change plans, I didn't. I flew back late Thursday night after the obligatory post-dinner socializing, and relished knowing I wouldn't have to be in LA again anytime soon.

By Christmas, the snow would be better, and though crowded around the actual holiday, I wasn't ashamed to admit I found the town and atmosphere more than a little charming at Christmas.

I wouldn't get to take Quinn home with me or fall asleep next to her tonight, but I'd spend the evening wrapped in her voice after missing her far too much. An acceptable consolation prize if I couldn't have her all the time. Yet. If my mind had strayed to what it would be like to have her come home with me every night, I couldn't be blamed. Our proclamations of feelings last night had advanced our relationship in the best way, and I was eager for whatever came next. I just hoped she'd be on board—give it time enough to settle in as a way forward.

A sharp knock on my door had me standing and shutting my computer. Maybe I'd wander down to the bar early and have some dinner now to eat up the rest of the time before Quinn's first set began.

Whoever was in the hallway knocked again, this time louder. When I pulled open the giant wooden door, I wasn't entirely shocked to see Quinn.

"Quinn, hello. It's so good to—"

"Did you do it?"

Her expression, posture, and the angry knocking clicked. The Quinn Darling standing here exhaling smoke from an internal fire was a different version of the woman I'd spent the night with. As warm and lovely as our time together last night and this morning had been, this was perhaps an even more familiar version of the woman I'd fallen for.

I could easily guess what'd brought her here, though I wasn't entirely certain how she'd found out so quickly as her mother wouldn't have told her. But I couldn't pretend I hadn't anticipated her ire to some degree. I just hadn't imagined it coming right this moment.

"Did I do what?" Obviously, she didn't know the whole story—I'd sworn Dana to secrecy, after all.

Her jaw clenched. "Did you get my grandparents into Silverton Springs?"

"A room opened up for them. Your mother had placed them on the list some time ago."

She gritted her teeth and swallowed. "You paid. To get them in. You paid for them."

I breathed through the disconcerting jump of nerves that rose from her tone. "I assisted in securing their room, yes."

Her eyes shut slowly, like this was terrible news. "Why?"

It came out in a whisper.

My pulse shot into my throat in response. This wasn't purely argumentative or frustrated. This was anger and worse, *hurt.* I jumped into my response.

"They need the help. Your mother shouldn't have to manage all of this on her own, nor should you feel obligated to help her. The retirement community offers nursing care as needed and they can assist your grandmother far more adeptly than can your mother alone."

And her mother, when I'd explained that I planned to spend my life with Quinn, as a part of their family—and yes, I'd been that bold—she'd agreed. Dana Darling had accepted my offer because she saw how serious I was—how permanent it was for me.

Quinn straightened and gave me a look full of fury. "She's not alone. Of course they can provide better medical care, but how are we going to manage this going forward? How can I possibly pay for Grandma's regular medical care outside of insurance, her room and board there, and the added expense of the nursing-level care? Don't you think I know exactly how much that is? I've calculated everything with their Medicare, their social security and retirement, and it's not possible with what I can do yet. Not yet. Do you realize how long I've wanted this for them?"

I approached, hoping to offer comfort with my touch, but she stepped back. "I do know. That's part of the reason, though only part, of why I did this."

She needed the help. She wouldn't take my money, so this had been the next logical step. It had also made sense emotionally. After last night, what else could there have been for us?

"And the other part?"

"Because it's best for them. And you care about them, so I want the best for them too."

Her eyes flicked back and forth between mine. "How am I supposed to respond to this? What did you think I'd say?"

I studied her, fully aware that what I'd hoped for would not be happening. "Thank you? I'm so happy they're living in a place they've wanted to for years?"

Her mouth opened slowly, like my words were more unbelievable than anything else that'd happened. "You want me to thank you for being the most high-handed, controlling—"

"I'm not controlling anything. I wanted to help. I did. This isn't some *move* I'm making."

She scoffed. "So if we hadn't slept together last night, you would've done the same? It's not a way to make sure I'm beholden to you and therefore *yours*?"

Damn, the woman didn't mince words. Could she really think that of me? Yes, I'd done a little something like that in the past with her, but it hadn't been all bad. My own hurt and disappointment swirled in my gut.

"After we said we loved each other? Yes. I did it once I knew you felt for me even a fraction of what I feel for you. And after we discussed what being together means. You said yourself it means meeting needs, showing up for the other person. And this is me doing that, because I know you would never ask this of me."

And I could so easily give it. Wanted to. *Needed* to, because what else did I have to offer her?

Her arms were crossed over her chest and pressed into her so hard, she was nearly shaking. If her hands weren't tucked under her arms, I would've bet her knuckles were white from being balled into fists. The tension and tremors were a sure sign of the anger coursing through her.

"I would beg, borrow, or steal for them. But not like this."

"Then you would not, in fact, do any of those things. I know Jamie's offered to help you with this in the past. You wouldn't accept him, and now you're infuriated with me for moving ahead. Your refusal to simply accept this shows you wouldn't."

The red at her cheeks and neck grew to a burning bright crimson. "You can't possibly gauge that based on this. You don't know what I've done for them or how much I—" She cleared her throat. "This is backwards. It's messed up, Julian, and I think you know that."

My pulse hammered in my chest and at my temple. I kept my arms locked at my sides to keep from reaching for her and shaking the nonsense out of her. "I don't know that. And I've already done it. It's case closed."

She threw her hands up. "Are you kidding me? Is this really how you live your life? You can't declare something *case closed* as though there aren't other people involved—other humans whose lives are affected by your actions."

Frustration spiraled through me. "Yes, Quinn. People whose lives are now better because they'll be living in a facility that can care for them surrounded by their friends and community members."

She sucked in a breath. "You can't expect me to agree to this."

I saw it in her eyes and knew. I couldn't keep pushing this because she needed time and she refused to take it herself. So I'd give it to her. "It's not your choice—it's theirs and mine. I've already made my choice, as have they. They are under no illusions about how this occurred or who is involved. Agree, or don't. But your grandparents are moving to Silverton Springs on Monday."

Her chest heaved and she must've been grinding her teeth to dust, her jaw was clenched so hard.

Maybe if I appealed to the part of her that cared for me, that did trust me... though clearly she felt I was some sort of villain in disguise if she was still so suspicious of this.

"Quinn," I said in a low, calm voice, hoping to draw her gaze from the floor where she stared.

She shook her head and spun, then flung the door open and stomped out. Quinn leaving without a parting shot was no victory. It signaled that she was so mad, she couldn't speak.

I'd known she wouldn't be *happy* about this at first. I thought there'd be a little fight of some sort, especially since I did it without mentioning it ahead of time. But I didn't think it'd be like this. Though was it that much of a surprise? Probably not.

I'd jumped at the chance to do this. I'd thought of doing it long before now, but knew it would go down about as well as it did just now. I'd hoped she knew me enough by now that she'd understand. I wasn't trying to buy her affection or tether her to me. I was doing something I could do. This was easy for me in the same way it would be impossible for her —completely.

It hadn't occurred to me that she might not adjust to this. That she may in fact be too stubborn for her own good, and she might never be able to forgive me. I'd assumed we'd get past this, and next up, a proposal. Promising our futures to each other. It was the natural next step for me, but her reaction tonight had me doubting something I'd been certain of. If she couldn't forgive me, I didn't know how to move forward.

I didn't know how to be in a relationship, but she'd told me it was about giving. What I had to give? All of me, and that meant everything to my name, money included.

If she couldn't forgive me for doing the one thing I absolutely could for her, then we definitely had no future.

CHAPTER FORTY

Quinn

Because he had at least one semi-intelligent bone in his body, Julian didn't show up to the lounge Friday or Saturday night. I sang angry girl songs from Alanis and Avril on Friday, and I sang a completely charming repertoire of Frank Sinatra classics Saturday just to prove to myself I was capable of more than functioning at emotional rage level ten thousand.

And I'd needed that proof.

I didn't sleep Friday night. I rode the angry wave all the way until Saturday around noon when my energy flagged and I got weepy. Thankfully, I was working, so I couldn't very well break down in a poor me sob fest as middle schoolers browsed sheet music and the high school band teacher placed an order for new cymbals.

Shoving a brownie I grabbed from Sadie's on the way home into my face was the best I could do before hauling back to the lounge. It was later that night I started getting messages in the group chat. Sadie must've mentioned I looked bad when she'd seen me that afternoon because Sarah, Dahlia, Calla, and she were all peppering me for updates, wondering if something had happened with my grandparents.

Had something happened? Yes. But not with their health. In fact, my grandma was recovering well, and my grandfather had been practically walking on air when I chatted with him on the way to work. I hadn't spoken to my mom, but she'd messaged to say she thought I should be grateful and leave it at that.

I didn't want a chorus of women I cared about telling me I was being too prideful and should just accept Julian's generosity. I didn't need that, because frankly, part of me got that I was blowing this up. That for him, the amount of money they'd owe every month was pocket change. But the rest of me knew it to be a sign that he wouldn't give me himself. He'd give me money, and he sure as heck wanted to keep me for himself by creating a debt I could never pay.

I'd been there before with Chuck. I wouldn't do it again. And yet, I'd played a role here too. I'd kept the stupid dryer after he'd replaced it. I'd never paid him back for the work Chip did. All of that must've seemed like a message for Julian—a big blaring sign that said something like, *"Actually, Can Be Bought!"*

I hated myself for it. Because I should've rejected that, and every other little push he'd given me toward letting him wield his money like a lure—*crap*. Just thinking about all that made my insides lurch.

By Sunday afternoon, he'd texted me a handful of times and I'd responded. I didn't need to freeze him out, and I wasn't twenty. I was an adult, and yes, I was pissed, but as angry as I was, most of that anger fell on my own shoulders. Julian had done what Julian does. The last twenty-four hours had been less about raging against his choice to fund my grandparents' move to Silverton Springs and more about disappointment in myself and in him.

Sunday night, I got the message from my friends: Meet them for lunch at Guac at noon the next day, or risk them hunting me down and making a scene. As dramatic and ridiculous as that would be, I had no desire to draw attention to the fact that I was an idiot and had gotten myself into this situation. It'd be bad enough discussing Julian in Guac, but most of the patrons would likely be tourists now that the ski season had officially started, so it shouldn't matter.

I dropped Cara at school that morning, both of us as quiet as we tended to be when things were strained between us. Hating the quiet that'd been the signature of my weekend except the shifts at the lounge, I stopped her before she hauled out of the car once I pulled up to the school.

"Are you upset with me?" I hated asking that—*hated* it. I didn't want to push her about anything, not while I knew my ability to cope with whatever she came back at me with would be low.

"No, Mom. I'm not upset with you."

We just stared. She had more to say and we both knew it.

She sighed. "I just think you're being kind of dumb."

I searched around for the calm I knew I possessed somewhere—that magical *be the mom in the moment* skill I'd developed over the last nearly fifteen years.

"Why do you say that?" I finally asked in a deceptively level voice.

Her lips flattened into a small frown, and a pang shot

through me. She looked exactly like my mom when she did that. I hadn't spoken to her since Friday when she'd all but said she was Team Julian.

"I'm pretty sure you're mad that Julian paid for Great-grandma and Great-grandpa to move, right?"

I nodded.

"It's just... why? You're with him, and he wants to do that for you. You've talked about getting them moved to Silverton Springs the first minute you could, so I don't get why you'd reject it."

I exhaled through my nose, searching for calm. "I can't maintain it. When Julian's gone, I don't know—"

"He's leaving?"

"No. Well, not that I know of."

"He's leaving you?"

Ice shot through me at her words and I had to answer honestly. Even through all the upset about the current issue, the thought of him walking away made my heart freeze over. "I—I don't know now."

She blinked back, absorbing that. "Well, whatever. I just think you should consider thinking about someone other than yourself. I know you've done that your whole life and everything, but..." She frowned. "I don't know. I guess it just seems like you need to do it now too."

She pushed open the door and shot me a look full of regret, like she knew her words had hurt me, but like she hoped I'd listen. I'd seen the expression before, on her face, and on my own. I wanted another minute, watching her walk toward a friend and then hustle inside, before I left.

Her words haunted me every step of my morning at the shop. *Consider thinking about someone other than yourself.*

Crap, that was brutal. Out of the mouths of babes and all that, right? But was this me only thinking of myself?

I crushed my eyes shut against the resounding *yes* in my head and had to steady myself on the display case. The truth was there, plain as the chill in the air today. If I was thinking about my grandparents, this was a good thing. If I was thinking about my mom, same thing. But when I thought about me?

This was where I got stuck. Because if I thought about me, I felt only fear. If I didn't push back against Julian doing this, what did that make me? Some kind of prostitute willing to be paid via grandparent care? How sick was that?

Julian had been so sharp about all of it, claiming it was done and it didn't matter what I said. But what did that mean? I didn't understand what he wanted from all of this. He'd said it was to take care of the people I cared about, but how could I trust that? How could I trust him?

I heaved a sigh and flipped the sign on the front door to *Closed.* I wouldn't make myself feel any better by moping around the shop and ignoring my friends. This lunch had the potential to be brutal, but I felt battered enough, and yet strangely numb to much other than an overwhelming sense of loss.

Maybe they could tell me how to feel and what to do.

CHAPTER FORTY-ONE

Quinn

Sarah arrived at the same time I did, and she pulled me into a hug.

"We're going to need you to tell us where you are with all this today, okay?" She dipped her chin and gave me a soft, kind smile that made emotion bubble to the surface.

I cleared me throat. "Not much new."

I'd told them the gist of things in the chat, and eventually explained how messed up I felt. How it felt like Julian was trying to buy me, and yet how that didn't make sense. How he'd reached out to me and checked on me but hadn't apologized.

Sarah's arm came around my shoulders in a protective gesture I had to love her for and we walked together to a booth to find Dahlia and Sadie already seated. I still got a kick out of seeing Sadie out in public. It'd been months since her first time joining us for a quick hello, and we'd had countless lunches and girls' nights by now, but I still loved having her with us.

"I'm just going to say I need some guacamole and chips, stat," Dahlia said, eyes wide. "Maybe a margarita too, though that might make going back to work a little tricky."

"Isn't that part of the beauty of owning your own business? You can have yourself a little post-lunch nap when you need one?" Sarah joked.

"If only," I said, wishing I could sleep the rest of the day and somehow into tomorrow. Though if I did that, then I'd miss helping my grandparents move. And here we were, back at the crux of the issue.

Brodie swung by, delivering salsas, chips, and a large bowl of guacamole with a wink. Good man, he knew without our asking.

"So... how are you?" Sadie's soft question punched through the raptures over the guac.

"I don't know." I released a breath. "Isn't that stupid? How do I not know?"

They all studied me, similarly empathetic expressions on their faces. Gratitude swelled in my chest, filling me up. They weren't judging or demanding I listen to their opinions. They were simply here for me.

"I guess I just want someone to tell me what to do. Cara said I need to think of someone besides myself this morning and that hurt, of course. I see the point—it's good for everyone. Except me."

Sarah dipped her head and spoke in a low, soothing voice. "What makes it bad for you?"

"It puts me in a vulnerable situation. I'll owe him. Forever. And it makes me feel cheap, even though somewhere inside me, I feel myself fighting against that. Like I shouldn't, but I just do."

"Because of Julian? Or because of Chuck?" Dahlia asked.

She'd posed the question gently, but it struck deep enough that it took me a minute before I could answer. When I did, my voice shook a little. "Mostly Chuck, I guess. Which is probably why I keep trying to talk myself into being fine with this. But what does it mean? Like, if he's really doing this out of the goodness of his heart or whatever, what happens when he decides to leave? To take that away, pack up all his favors and go?"

And if I hadn't been so certain that each of them knew, in her own way, what it meant to be left, I would've felt humiliated by the utterly clear fear ringing through my words, but I wasn't. Not with these women I knew cared about me, who'd become essential to me in such a short time.

"What if he doesn't, though? Has he given you the sense he has plans to leave? That this is a short-term relationship for him?" Sarah asked.

I ran through every conversation we'd had lately—or ever. And no. None of it had seemed transitory or fleeting. Not to him, and in my heart of hearts, not to me, either. I'd sensed that from the beginning, hadn't I? That Julian would change things for me?

And he had.

"I don't think so, no. If anything, it seems like he has long-term plans. I mean, we talked about marriage and kids —not specifically about *us* and those things, but it was getting a feel for each other in that way. And I know he hasn't had many relationships at all. I just..." My throat locked up so I took a drink to wash away the tightness. "I wish I knew what would happen, you know?"

Sarah took my hand and Sadie set hers on my back next

to me. Dahlia was farthest away but she reached out as though to console me too.

Sarah spoke for all of them. "There's no way to know what'll happen. You know that just as well as any of us. But you know exactly what'll happen if you shut him out—you lose him. We haven't been friends that long, but even we can see he makes you really happy, and it might be worth the risk to let him love you."

And that was it. The heart of it. It wasn't really the money or anything else, but the reality that this meant I was trusting him to stick around. I was saying I believed what he said—that he'd done this for me, but also for the people I cared about because he cared about them too, simply because they were a part of me.

Trusting him with that—with me and my family—I'd never planned to let anyone in this way again. But I already had, and maybe it was time to stop fighting it.

After a delicious lunch that eventually shifted from the heaviness of my emotional mess to lighter conversation about a destination wedding Dahlia was doing the flowers for and the nightmare mother of the bride she'd been dealing with, Sadie gave an update on things with Warrick and her Loaf Monthly subscription.

We chatted about what we'd each heard from Calla lately and all agreed they'd do better at messaging her while she was out of town. Dahlia mentioned she'd heard a rumor a bookstore was coming into the space next to Wallace and Sons, and we all got excited about that prospect since Silverton had a great library, but nowhere to buy anything other than mass-market paperbacks. Eventually, we exited the restaurant and exchanged hugs on the chilly sidewalk.

Sadie crossed to her store, and Sarah, Dahlia, and I wandered in the direction of Silver Street. We rounded the corner to Elk and I froze at the sight of Julian in a sharp black wool jacket, leather gloves, and sunglasses standing next to another man outside of the Wallace and Sons law firm.

"Quinn," he said, surprise, and if I wasn't totally bonkers, pleasure at seeing me in his voice.

"Julian, hi," I barely eked out. Nerves bubbled up and zipped through me on strings. I was pretty sure I knew what I wanted and how I felt, and I knew for certain I didn't want to talk about it here in front of my friends and whoever this guy he was meeting with.

This guy who—*oh*. My eyes shot to Sarah, and I reached for her.

"Do you know Wilder Saint? I'm never certain who knows who in this town." He gestured to the three of us. "Wilder, this is Quinn Darling, Dahlia Price, and Sarah James."

The man he introduced us to was so vastly different from the kid I remembered as Wilder Saint, and yet somehow, I'd known him on sight. A swarthier version of his brothers, he had a long, dark beard and unruly hair crushed down under a ball cap.

Wasn't he in the Army? I'd never seen a military man like this, but I didn't really keep track, truth be told.

"Yeah, I think we knew of each other way back when," I said, offering my hand for a shake, which he took in a swift move.

Dahlia waved but had her hand in Sarah's. "Nice to meet you."

He nodded. "Likewise."

And Sarah? Sarah had gone sickly pale. Her eyes had grown larger and her mouth had shrunk up to a tight little dash.

My gaze swung back to Wilder's in time to see his meet Sarah's and hold, unblinking. Good grief, the force of the man's focus was a visible thing, like energy radiating around him in waves of intensity. And with all of that bearing down on sweet, frozen Sarah, my instincts made me step in front of her and push her behind my back.

"Okay, well—" Dahlia had the same impulse because she'd pulled Sarah with her across the street before anyone could do anything else, and I stepped to the curb. Wilder's focus had moved past me, that serious, almost brutal face looking no different than it had when we'd walked up.

Julian skirted Wilder and grabbed for my hand. The leather of his glove against my palm made heat crawl up my neck.

"I need to go check on her," I said dumbly, my thoughts a jumble and my heart pounding.

"Of course. Can I see you later? Can we talk?"

"Yes. Come to my house at three, if you can. I'm helping them move at three-thirty, but we can talk before I leave."

He nodded, clearly knowing *they* were my grandparents. I didn't ask if he could come then—he'd clear his schedule. As the reality that I did trust him and I did want him always sank in, I knew he'd be there.

I hustled across the street after one last look that sent hope fizzing through me and arrived in front of Dahlia's shop door just as Sarah was begging off.

"I swear, I'm fine, I just—I didn't expect to see him. I

figured I'd hear he was in town—that Sadie would know he was coming or something." Her smile was forced.

"What did he do to you? I want to tear into him for even looking you in the eye, but I need more information." Just standing near her, I could feel her nervous and upset energy, almost as intense as Wilder's stare had been.

She shook her head though, staring at nothing for a moment.

"It's not what he did to me. It's—" Her eyes filled as she looked from me to Dahlia. The tears spilled over, but she wiped them away and shook her head with a bitter smile on her face. "It's what I did to him."

And then she took off, not quite running, but clearly not ready to say any more than that. Dahlia and I shared a concerned look, and she slipped into Bloom and I made my way back to Pluck. I couldn't fix things for Sarah, especially since I didn't understand what was happening there. But I would work as hard as I could for the next two hours before I ran home to meet Julian and hope... hope we could get through and move on to whatever came next.

Together.

CHAPTER FORTY-TWO

Julian

Rejoining Wilder Saint after that unusual encounter, I eyed him. He didn't betray that he'd noticed, but by now, I knew well enough that the man noticed everything.

"I gather you and Ms. James have a history?" I asked, not exactly wanting to pry, but definitely interested in the details of what could shake a man like Wilder Saint.

"We do."

"Is it something you anticipate causing a change in your plans?" If whatever lay between them delayed or changed his course, it would drastically alter my plans related to him.

"No."

I waited for elaboration, though I didn't know why I'd expect that. Wilder Saint was, among many things, a man of few words. What he did say, I listened to. What he planned to do, he did. So if he said this wouldn't change things, I trusted that.

I'd heard light gossip about Sarah's history with Wilder—that they were high school sweethearts gone wrong in some way, but beyond that, I knew little. It would be odd for a man like him to be deterred at all, but having witnessed them seeing each other for what I gathered might be the first time in well over a decade, I could attest to powerful feelings on both ends. And I wasn't even very good at reading emotions like that.

Not long after, we shook hands in a brief farewell with a plan to communicate his needs to Kelly and to see him in a few months when he returned to Silverton for good upon his retirement from the Army. We had time to get his business going since there hadn't been many security incidents in Silverton to date, but with the increasing number of affluent residents, and particularly an influx of famously wealthy ski-lovers, he'd have a booming business as soon as he could get things rolling. I was all too happy to facilitate since I'd learned a fair amount from my friends in LA when dealing with Jamie's security issues years ago.

Now I just had to burn through a little less than two hours of time before I could meet Quinn and figure out where she stood. She'd mentioned moving her grandparents in so she hadn't canceled that plan altogether—she was stubborn enough I wouldn't have been shocked if she had, though I was glad she hadn't.

After the way she'd left, I'd been tempted to shut it all down. To step away and never look back. But my life now consisted of everything before, and then after. All of it *Until Quinn...* I didn't think I could cross back over that line. So here I stood, looking ahead, hoping there could be some chance we'd cross another line that led to *After Quinn.*

At three exactly, I rolled into her driveway in the car Scott usually drove, and knocked on her door. Cara answered, a little smile on her face. "Glad you're here. She's inside, and I'm going to wait in Mom's car."

"Thank you," I said, a surge of affection for her rising in me. We'd only begun a fledgling relationship, but I hoped I'd have time to develop something more. To help her and cheer her on and see what she did with all that talent and determination.

The door shut behind her, and I waited until I heard Quinn bustling around in the kitchen.

"Are you ready for me?"

Quinn startled but nodded. She wore jeans and a T-shirt and looked a bit harried, though when I stepped fully into the kitchen, she halted loading the dishwasher and pressed both hands onto the counter in front of her.

"You wanted to talk?"

I did. Had I hoped she'd get things going by giving me a temperature check for where she stood? Of course. But this wasn't the first time I'd had to open negotiations with a potentially less-than-warm audience.

"You haven't canceled your grandparents' move to Silverton Springs. I assume this means you're letting that plan proceed without interference."

"I am."

She was not going to give me anything. Fine then. "And us? Have you decided I was trying to buy your affection, or that I truly care for you?"

She swallowed then huffed. "I'm sorry for reacting the way I did. I wish you'd told me what you were doing. It wouldn't have felt so underhanded if you'd said, 'Hey, Quinn, I'm going to do this thing whether you like it or not, but I hope you'll like it.'"

"But I did say that."

She raised a brow. "Yes, you did, after the fact. After I found out from someone else—Mr. Morrison, of all people—and had to come track you down to confront you."

"Yes, I remember that part rather well."

She rolled her eyes. "I'm sure you do. At some point, we'll get past me storming into your office to deal with things."

I took the chance and stepped into her space, setting a hand on the counter next to hers. "Do you think?"

Her eyes flickered back and forth between mine, genuinely considering the question. "I think so."

"Good."

"I need to know that if something happens between us, it's not all going to go away. I don't think I can move ahead if it feels like this is leverage, or something you were hoping would cement our relationship—even if that came from a good, but messed-up, place."

Her cheeks were reddened with a flush and her brow furrowed, the concern in her voice clear as anything I'd ever heard.

Dipping my head, I spoke softer now. "I didn't do it to buy you, Quinn. If ever a woman couldn't be bought, it's you. But this is something I could do for you, and I wish you'd believe that there is nothing I'd rather do than care for you—make your life easier and better in any way I can. I don't have other means to do it, but I do have money. If everything between us goes up in flame, this will not change. I'll draw up a contract or whatever you need to feel confident."

Her hand covered mine, and I almost shuddered in relief at the contact of her palm against my skin and her fingers slipping between mine, effectively spooning my larger hand.

"I don't need paperwork. And logically, I get that you arranged this because, like we talked about, you saw the need and could meet it. I told you loving me takes the form of caring for those I love, and you took that to heart. But my past makes it hard to swallow, especially when I'm in a reactive place. And I'm sorry you got that part of me but not the part that knows you care about me and therefore, by extension, my family. I haven't been—" She cleared her throat and gazed at me. "I haven't loved someone like I do you. Ever. And after Chuck, I swore it off. I didn't see you coming, I didn't *want* you, but here you are, in way too deep, and it's a little terrifying."

My chest felt tight in that too-full way it did so often when I was near her. My fingers sifted into her hair at her nape under her ponytail and I brought her lips to mine.

"I've seen you coming since the day I stepped foot in Silverton, but I didn't think I had anything to give you. Especially since you don't *want* me to give you anything." I'd stripped everything away with that—admitted the thing I didn't want her to realize about me.

And in response, her face softened and she placed her palm over my heart. "I don't need anything from you, Julian, but *you*. I'm realizing that I can accept your ridiculously over-the-top generosity if I have you."

"You have me," I said, my voice raw and more earnest than it'd probably ever been.

"I think I finally know that," she said, a smile dawning on her face.

I gripped her upper arms. "Do I have you?"

She laughed and held onto my shirt under her hands.

"Yes. As much as I never imagined saying it, you have me completely."

"I love you, Quinn. I'll mess up again—do something without telling you that'll piss you off again, no doubt. But I love you."

"I love you, too. I'm sure I'll lose my temper or accuse you of being insane again, probably regularly, but we can come back to this." She cupped her hands around mine between us, like inside our nested palms, we held something precious and worth protecting. "We'll come back to each other."

"Always."

The front door rattled when it cracked opened. "Okay, I'm not looking or listening, but we're going to be late. Can you two move along with whatever is going on and let's get going, please?"

Cara's voice sliced through our promises with the sardonic tone only a teenager could affect while being polite and respectful.

"Be right there!" Quinn hollered, grinning at me.

"I guess we better go," I said, taking her hand and leading her to the door.

"Yeah. Are you coming with us?"

"I figured I better officially meet your grandparents and assure them my intentions are good."

She made a face. "Oh, they're going to love you."

"I certainly hope so. If not, I'll offer to upgrade their room."

3.5 years later

"Cara Darling," the announcer called.

A roaring cheer went up—all the Morrisons, their kids, my grandparents, my mom, Julian. Cara beamed out at the crowd, then shook the principal's hand and walked on. The tiniest cheerleader, Josie, didn't stop when she left the stage despite quite possibly being the loudest. "Sissy! Sissssyyyyyy!"

Josie's little two-year-old voice made my heart ache in the moment. My eighteen-year-old daughter was graduating high school, and my tiny little surprise was her biggest fan. Cara must've heard her sister's cheering because she laughed and waved right at her, which made Josie squeal with delight at seeing her number one sister acknowledge her. She adored Cara like no one else.

With the possible exception of her stepfather. And yes, her biological father had stepped up in ways I hadn't ever imagined him capable of, including showing up today just like he said he would. Chuck was seated in a different section, but I'd caught his eye and smiled. I was generous and calm like that now—all kinds of magnanimous for a man I used to loathe.

The feelings of rage had calmed a bit when he started following through. The one lunch date he'd missed was the only one—he'd learned quickly how fragile his standing with Cara was and he'd made sure he never missed another *anything*. I gave him kudos for that. They'd developed a nice dynamic—friendly, warm, and healing, I thought.

But Julian had fallen almost as hard for Cara as he had for me in the last few years and, with the possible exception of her toddler sister, he held the spot of Cara's biggest fan. I used to think that was me, but when he took Cara's side on nearly everything, I knew.

After our initial discussions on our feelings and every-thing with my grandparents, I hadn't doubted. Julian had been a steady, stubborn, fairly pushy force in our lives, and I pushed right back. We'd married six months later, a quick elopement to Vegas that we'd surprised my family and a few close friends with when we loaded them on Julian's jet and told them where we were going. We avoided the publicity a big wedding would've cost, and it was everything I'd never dreamed of.

And not long after that, we got the surprise of a lifetime when morning sickness hit and we found out about Josie. I'd never had any doubt that Julian was the right person for me between his love for me, my family, and my daughter, and his general persistence and generosity, but seeing him hold his daughter for the first time destroyed me. I actually cried harder at that image than I had in years because it knit something together in me.

I'd been with my mom when Cara came. She'd supported and loved me so much, I never felt abandoned in the way I probably should've. And when Julian came into our lives, he accepted and loved Cara in ways I couldn't have hoped for. He was her encouragement, her sounding board, and her friend. He was also her safe place when she and I butted heads, but thankfully, he was mine in those same moments too, poor man.

But seeing him hold Josie and talk with her, whispering things I'd never hear and pressing kisses to the dark, downy hair on her head, all the jagged edges of my heart that remained—though they were few—smoothed out. Julian was a man who would stay, and love, and wasn't scared of tenderness and devotion.

"You did an amazing job, love," he said into my ear so I could hear him over the cheers for the next student.

He didn't mean with organizing the post-graduation party or with the dress Cara wore underneath—something she'd begged me to make for her even though she'd long-since had the pick of anything she wanted thanks to her stepfather's propensity for spoiling her.

He meant with the girl. The young woman who leaned over to chat with her friend as they watched their fellow seniors make their ceremonial graduation walk across the stage. And even with all the doubts that cropped up and would continue to do so, I knew he was right. I did. She was an amazing kid, of course, but I'd gotten her here. Not by myself, but thanks to the people surrounding us and so many more in Silverton. And thanks to Julian, who'd been my rock in some truly challenging teen years.

"Thank you," I whispered back, hoping he knew I meant it for far more than just his compliment.

He looked at me then, tearing his eyes from the place where Cara sat to focus on me. "No, Quinn. Thank *you*."

Thank you for reading Julian and Quinn's story. I loved discovering their relationship and I hope you enjoyed the read! Don't miss Wilder and Sarah in Almost Home!

Back to Silver Ridge Series

Almost Perfect, Book 1

Almost Real, Book 2

Almost Sure, Book 3

Almost Home, Book 4

The Silver Ridge Resort Series

Unexpected Love at Silver Ridge, Book 1

Second Chance at Silver Ridge, Book 2

Patrolling for Love at Silver Ridge, Book 3

Fire and Ice at Silver Ridge, Book 4

The OCONUS Bonus Series

The Problem with Planning Love, Book 1

Finding Happiness in a Hoax, Book 2

Learning to Fight after Flight, Book 3

The Bright Side of Brooding, Book 4

Holding On to Hope, Book 5

The Rambler Battalion Series

Where You Go: The Rambler Battalion, Book 1

As You Are: The Rambler Battalion, Book 2

Don't Stop Now: The Rambler Battalion, Book 3

Home With You: The Rambler Battalion, Book 4

All of You: The Rambler Battalion, Book 5

ACKNOWLEDGMENTS

Thanks to everyone who has eagerly awaited Julian's book. I hope you loved seeing his squishy insides. (Ok, that sounded gross, but you get me.)

Thank you to my editor, Zee Monodee, for your relentless pursuit of Julian's narrative. This book wouldn't be nearly as strong without you, and I'm thankful for your input!

To my beloved Beta readers Amanda, Ashley, and Genny. THANK YOU for your time and attention! I feel so much more confident in the book once you've read it.

Thank you, as always, to Emma Robinson for the beautiful cover!

Thank you Amanda Cuff for the encouragement and for catching the preponderance of stomachs :)

Thanks to Jamie McGillen, Julie Dobbins, and Laura Ziesel for being choo choo Charlies. You each inspire me and I'm so happy to call you friends.

Thanks to my husband for being an increasingly silvery fox and loving me.

Thanks to all the bookstagrammers, book bloggers, and readers who've supported this new series by reading, reviewing, and sharing! Reviews and word of mouth really do make a difference to indie authors, so thank you!

ABOUT THE AUTHOR

Claire Cain lives to eat and drink her way around the globe with her traveling soldier and three kids, but is perhaps even happier hunkered down at home in a pair of sweatpants and slippers using any free moment she has to read and cook. Or talk—she really likes to talk. She has become an expert at packing too many dishes in too few cabinets and making houses into homes from Utah to Germany and many places in between. She's a proud Army wife and is frankly just really happy to be here.

You can also join Claire's facebook reader group for exclusive content and fun: https://www.facebook.com/groups/clairecain/

Website: http://www.clairecainwriter.com

E-mail: Claire@ClaireCainWriter.com

Newsletter sign-up for new releases, exclusives, and freebies, including a free book:

http://www.clairecainwriter.com/newsletter

amazon.com/author/clairecain

bookbub.com/authors/claire-cain

instagram.com/clairecainwriter

facebook.com/clairecainwriter

goodreads.com/clairecainwriter

pinterest.com/clairecainwriter

twitter.com/writeclairecain